Burying
Bad News
A Much Winchmoor Mystery

Paula Williams

Read **Murder Served Cold** and **Rough and Deadly**, the first and second in the series.

www.darkstroke.com

Discover us online:
www.darkstroke.com

Find us on instagram:
www.instagram.com/darkstrokebooks

Include **#darkstroke** in a photo of yourself
holding this book on Instagram and
something nice will happen.

To you, my lovely readers.
Without you, I would spend my days
sitting at my laptop talking away to myself.
My love and thanks to you all.

Acknowledgements

My sincere thanks to Laurence and Steph at darkstroke for taking yet another chance on me thus enabling my Much Winchmoor Mysteries to continue. Thanks, too, to Laurence for making the editing such an enjoyable process.

Thanks are due, as always, to my friends and neighbours who are by now frightened to tell me anything in case it ends up in one of my books. But even though the setting is mostly based on the small Somerset village in which I live, the characters bear no resemblance whatsoever to any real persons, alive or dead but are a total figment of my over-active imagination. Apart, that is, from David Tennant and Judge Jeffries.

Special thanks to my friend and neighbour, Gilli, for allowing me to pick her brains about the ins and outs of hairdressing. Any hairdressing mistakes are entirely mine and will teach me to listen more carefully another time.

A big thank you, too, to Rachel Gilbey and her wonderful team of bloggers who do such a fantastic job of spreading the word about my books and leaving such lovely reviews. You are all totally awesome. And if you're ever in the Winchmoor Arms, Kat says she'll treat you to a pint of Headbender cider.

About the Author

Paula Williams is living her dream. She's written all her life – her earliest efforts involved blackmailing her unfortunate younger brothers into appearing in her various plays and pageants. But it's only in recent years, when she turned her attention to writing short stories and serials for women's magazines that she discovered, to her surprise, that people with better judgement than her brothers actually liked what she wrote and were prepared to pay her for it and she has sold over 400 short stories and serials both in the UK and overseas.

Now, she writes every day in a lovely, book-lined study in her home in Somerset, where she lives with her husband and a handsome but not always obedient rescue dog, a Dalmatian called Duke. She still writes for magazines but now writes novels as well. She is currently writing the Much Winchmoor series of murder mysteries, set in a village not unlike the one she lives in - although as far as she knows, none of her friends and neighbours have murderous tendencies.

A member of both the Romantic Novelists' Association and the Crime Writers' Association, her novels often feature a murder or two, and are always spiked with humour and sprinkled with a touch of romance.

She also writes a monthly column, Ideas Store, for the writers' magazine, Writers' Forum. And she blogs about her books, other people's books and, quite often, Dalmatians at paulawilliamswriter.wordpress.com. She can also be found on her author page at **facebook.com/paulawilliams.author** and on **Twitter @paulawilliams44**

She gives talks on writing at writing festivals and to organised groups and has appeared several times on local radio. In fact, she'll talk about writing to anyone who'll stand still long enough to listen.

But, as with all dreams, she worries that one day she's going to wake up and find she still has to bully her brothers into reading 'the play what she wrote'.

Burying Bad News

A Much Winchmoor Mystery

Chapter One

The Dintscombe Chronicle, July 15th

Heads Roll in Murder Village
By Kath Latcham, local correspondent.

A gruesome discovery was made in in the sleepy Somerset village of Much Winchmoor recently when Gerald Crabshaw, aged 52, owner of the Winchmoor Mill Guest House found a severed head in his garden.

"I was sickened and heart-broken," said the shocked villager. "I called the police immediately, of course, but they were worse than useless. They haven't a clue. And even when I told them who'd done it, they didn't do anything about it."

Much Winchmoor has become known as the murder capital of the south west as there have been no less than four murders in this not-so-sleepy village in the last couple of years.

But thankfully residents can sleep easily in their beds this time. This latest outrage is not Murder Number 5 - and the perpetrator is not facing life imprisonment if caught. Unless, of course, there's a little known, obscure law making the over-enthusiastic pruning of a privet bush a capital offence.

The severed head does, in fact, belong to a peacock. Or rather, it did. One that had been lovingly and patiently fashioned over many years from an old hedge.

Heartbroken Crabshaw was close to tears as he explained. "Topiary is my passion. I've spent years working on that peacock. It was my pride and joy. Now it has come to nothing, because of the callous action of a single maniac."

And he hasn't had to look far for the villain. Just over the hedge, in fact. Or, rather, what's left of his hedge. He knows 'who done it' and isn't afraid to point the finger. And name names.

"Paul McAllister is the neighbour from hell," he told our reporter. "Since he moved in next door, he's made our lives a misery. I've tried to extend the hand of friendship, but he has spurned it every time. And now this. But he's gone too far this time. There will be consequences," he added darkly, but refused to be drawn when asked what sort of consequences.

An unrepentant Paul McAllister, a 45-year-old estate agent, declined to be interviewed, although he denied having decapitated the peacock and said all he had done was to prune a neglected and dangerous hedge. It was, he declared, ' a fuss about nothing'

"He's not getting away with it," Crabshaw says. "I've got evidence linking him to the crime."

We've all heard of a storm in a teacup. But here in the West's murder capital, where warring neighbours are nothing unusual, they do things differently.

Watch this space. It could be that in Much Winchmoor even more heads will roll.

***

The folk of Much Winchmoor don't much care for change. They didn't like it when the government brought in decimalisation back in 1971.They didn't like it when Dintscombe District Council changed from weekly to fortnightly rubbish collections because of the economic situation.

They didn't like the new traffic lights on the by-pass. And they certainly didn't like the new look and content of their local paper, The Dintscombe Chronicle.

They didn't like the pages and pages of crossword puzzles, word searches and other nonsense. They didn't like the grabby headlines and the gossipy style of reporting that was better suited to the trashiest tabloids.

No, they didn't like anything about the new look Chronicle. Particularly this latest article that made them look and sound like a bickering bunch of carrot-crunching yokels.

They didn't like that one little bit.

Except, that is, for one person.

That person loved the story of the decapitated peacock. For it had handed them the solution to a problem that was making them break out in a cold sweat just thinking about it. How to prevent everything they'd planned and worked towards from crashing down around their ears.

In short, it had just given them an idea of how to commit the perfect murder - and to get away with it too.

Chapter Two

Three days earlier. Monday, July 15th

There's nothing like a severed head to brighten a journalist's day on a rain-spattered Monday morning. Especially this journalist who spends most of her working life writing about malfunctioning streetlamps, un-emptied dustbins and the overcrowding crisis in the village burial ground (although not necessarily in the same story).

I shook the rain out of my hair and knocked on the door of Mill Cottage. As I waited for it to open, I couldn't help running a few headlines through my mind.

"*Headless horror haunts Much Winchmoor.*" Or how about, "*Heads roll as warring neighbours' feud hots up.*"?

But of course I wouldn't write anything that sensationalistic. I have to live in this village (more the pity) and put up with the hard stares and grumbles when I write something they don't like - which is most of the time.

But when your editor suggests you follow up on a story about a dispute between neighbours which had escalated to such an extent that one of them had (allegedly) taken a pair of garden shears to a topiary peacock and cut off its head, it wasn't the sort of story (or the chance for some great punning headlines) to pass up on. Particularly when that same editor was leaving and this was, in his words 'a chance to impress the new boss', although he had been very vague about who that was.

"I'm not really sure myself," he'd said. "All I know is that the paper's been bought by some big media company and they'll be bringing in their own editors. So that's me out of a job."

"I'm sorry to hear that, Mike," I said with genuine regret. He'd been a good guy to work for, if a bit over-zealous when it came to cutting my copy down, something that could be very painful for a freelance like me who got paid by the line.

"Don't be," he'd said cheerfully. "The wife's been nagging me for ages about retiring and this has given me the push I needed."

Paul McAllister was taking forever to answer the door and, as I waited, I rehearsed what I was going to say to him. He was a relative newcomer to the village and, according to Elsie Flintlock, Much Winchmoor's gossipmonger-in-chief and the source of much of my local knowledge, he was a 45-year-old estate agent who kept himself to himself as he recovered from a traumatic and expensive divorce.

Although I'd not spoken to him before we'd exchanged nods when we passed each other most mornings, he on his early morning bike ride and me on my daily run.

As I waited for him to answer the door, I caught a scent that was achingly familiar. Sweet peas had been my Gran Latcham's favourite flowers and their scent used to fill her house and garden every summer. I bent down to smell them and, as I did so, the cottage door was opened by a man carrying a pair of garden shears and wearing a bramble bush.

"I'm so sorry," he said as he attempted to disentangle himself from one particular strand that had wrapped itself across his back. It snaked around his waist in what must have been a pretty uncomfortable embrace. "I was in the middle of cutting back some overgrown bushes. Took me some time to extricate myself."

"Not to worry. I was enjoying your lovely sweet peas. You've got quite a show there."

He smiled. "I can't take the credit for them, I'm afraid. My father planted them. I've been trying my best to look after them as well as he did, but they're a bit overgrown by his standards. So, what can I do for you?"

"It's Mr McAllister, isn't it?" I said with my best reporter smile. "I'm -"

"No, don't tell me. I'm usually good with faces," he said, as

7

he wrestled with the ultra-clingy bramble, then pointed at me with a triumphant smile. "I've got you. You're the girl I see out running most mornings, aren't you? I didn't recognise you for a moment. You look different with -"

"With my clothes on, you mean?" I said with a grin.

It was meant to put him at his ease. But as a tactic, it was an epic fail. His eyes widened with alarm and he took a step back, his hand on the door as if he was about to shut it in my face.

"I'm sorry-" he stammered. "I meant, with - without your running gear, of course. I didn't mean -"

"And I didn't mean to embarrass you," I said quickly before he could close the door in my face. "Look, shall I start again? I'm Kat Latcham and I work for the Dintscombe Chronicle. I've just interviewed your neighbour, Gerald Crabshaw, about the incident with the –"

"Not that damn peacock again." He gave a sigh of exasperation. "What's the wretched man been saying now?"

I got my notebook out and leafed through the reams of notes Gerald Crabshaw had insisted I take.

"He claims that you…" I flicked through the pages of utter nonsense to find the relevant quote. "That you deliberately cut the head off his pride and joy, a topiary peacock that he'd spent the last five years lovingly sculpting into shape. That you did it in an act of unprovoked vandalism."

His weary sigh was the sound of a man who'd not only reached the end of his tether but had left it way behind. "Of course I didn't. And if I did, it was an accident."

"You're admitting you cut the peacock's head off?"

He gave a weary sigh and pushed his hand through his thinning hair. As he did so, he dislodged yet another length of bramble which he flicked away. "Did he show you this - this so-called peacock?"

"He said there was nothing left to show. Just a flattened hedge where his peacock used to be."

"Ok, then I will. Follow me. But be careful as you go, won't you? That broken fence is lethal. I've tried telling Crabshaw about it, but I might as well be talking to a brick wall."

I've known Gerald Crabshaw most of my life and knew that

Paul McAllister would probably have a more interesting conversation with the brick wall. I followed him along the narrow path that ran between the two properties. It was bounded by Paul's cottage on one side and a straggly hedge on the other.

"You see what I mean?" He pointed to the hedge that was so overgrown it had pushed out the iron uprights of an old post and wire fence that had once contained it. Now they leaned, like a row of Saturday night drunks, across the path. He pulled on one whose angle was more pronounced than the others, and shook it vigorously.

"Look at this! I keep my bike in that shed down the bottom of the garden and when I came out for my ride - you know how dark it was this morning - this one was right across the path. If I hadn't been looking out for it, I could have ridden straight into it."

I shivered as I looked at the vicious looking metal post that was jutting out from the hedge.

"That's really dangerous. Can't you pull it out?" I asked.

He shook his head. "I tried, but the whole thing toppled over and came down across the path. I had to cut it back to clear a way through. That's what I was doing when you arrived."

I stared at the tangle of brambles and overgrown bushes that loomed over the path like a storm cloud and was only held back by the overstretched post and wire fence.

"So where's this headless peacock?" I asked. Gerald had been evasive when I'd asked him the same question and reluctant to let me see it - particularly when I asked if he had any before and after pictures. Said they were 'too upsetting' to share.

"You're looking at it," Paul said.

If the hedge was meant to resemble a peacock, then it was unlike any I'd ever seen. Even giving it the benefit of the doubt by assuming it was squatting, it looked more like a badly stuffed cushion than a bird.

"It doesn't look anything like one," I said, then added, "At least, not now."

He shrugged. "If it ever did. I'm no gardener, but that doesn't look like topiary to me. Nor, I'll bet you, has it ever done. Does it to you?"

"I suppose not."

My heart sank. This was turning into yet another non-story. After all, neighbours exchanging insults over an out of control hedge was hardly newsworthy, was it? Even by The Chronicle's standards.

I took my phone out. "Could I just take a picture of you standing by it?" I asked.

He shook his head. "I'd prefer you didn't. It's all a fuss over nothing. Besides which -" He broke off to pick another bit of bramble out of his hair, then gave me a searching look, like he was trying to make up his mind about something.

"Go on," I prompted.

"Ok. Well, to be honest, it wouldn't do my reputation, my career, or the value of my property any good to have it bandied about that I'm involved in a dispute with my neighbours. I'm an estate agent and I see only too often the detrimental effects disputes between neighbours can have on property values."

I frowned. This was a new one on me. "How do you mean?"

"When you're selling a property, you're obliged to complete what's called a Seller's Property Information Form," he explained. "That requires you to highlight any previous or current disputes with people from neighbouring properties. A vendor could find himself on very dodgy ground if he was found to have kept quiet about something he should have declared."

"What? Even when the dispute wasn't his fault? That doesn't sound very fair to me."

He shrugged. "That's the law. By failing to declare something like that, you're technically committing a fraud. And as it's possible I'll be selling this property in the near future, the last thing I want is a very public airing of a silly fuss over nothing splashed all across the front page of the local paper."

"Yes, I can see that."

"I even began to wonder if Gerald Crabshaw deliberately engineered this so-called dispute to make the cottage more difficult to sell, apart, that is, to him. I know he was bitterly disappointed when I had to tell him I'd decided to live in the place myself, after Dad died. Gerald had been hoping to buy it and extend his guest house. It's a sizeable cottage and has four good bedrooms so it would make good commercial sense. But maybe I'm just being paranoid. I wouldn't have thought he was capable of such deviousness."

"You wouldn't?" He obviously didn't know Gerald very well. He'd be a dead cert for a gold medal if deviousness ever became an Olympic sport.

"Well, whatever," he went on. "But I really think it's one of those cases of least said, soonest mended, don't you?"

Well, actually, no. I didn't. I mean, I could see where he was coming from, of course. But all I could focus on was what a rubbish week this was turning out to be, linage-wise. (I did mention I got paid by the line, didn't I?) The first performance of the village's new choir had been cancelled after an outbreak of laryngitis among the sopranos, while the visit of our local county councillor to see for himself the shocking state of the potholes in the village's High Street had been postponed due to 'other commitments' - that's politician speak for 'There aren't enough votes in that back of beyond place to make it worth my while dragging all the way out there'.

As far as I could see, my chances to impress the new editor with my work were getting slimmer by the day.

I felt sorry for the guy and totally understood his problem. Of course I did. But my problem was, covering this story wasn't my idea. It had come from the editor, after he'd had his ear bent by Gerald Crabshaw. And whilst I didn't mind telling Gerald that his headless peacock had as much news value as the village's erratic recycling collection since there'd been a change of operatives, I didn't fancy telling the new editor that.

"The problem is, Mr McAllister, I already have Gerald Crabshaw's statement," I said. "Which is quite lengthy seeing as he was the one who contacted The Chronicle in the first place. It would be a shame not to be able to put your side of

11

the story."

But he wouldn't be persuaded. "There's no 'other side' to put," he said firmly. "It's all a fuss about nothing. As you can see."

"Can I quote you on that?"

He shook his head. "Do what you want," he said wearily. "You probably will anyway."

I gave him an apologetic smile, thanked him and made my way back down the path. I turned back and saw he was still watching me.

"You should pick them," I said, pointing to the sweet peas. "That's what my gran always used to say. It prolongs the flowering season if you cut them before they grow their seed pods."

He smiled. "A friend of mine has persuaded me to enter them in the Flower and Vegetable Show at Little Mearefield next weekend. They probably don't stand a hope in hell's chance. But she's the sort of woman it's hard to say no to."

His face softened as he spoke. I remembered Elsie saying how he was recovering from a traumatic divorce. From the twinkle in his eyes and the way his face softened as he spoke about this 'friend', I'd say the recovery process was well under way.

"And, of course," he went on. "It would be a nice tribute to my father if they won."

"Indeed it would," I said. "I'll be covering that show for The Chronicle and look forward to seeing your name among the prize-winners."

But I didn't have the heart to tell him that the Sweet Pea class in the Little Mearefield Flower and Vegetable Show had been won by the wife of the show's chairman for the last eleven years.

And Little Mearefield, like Much Winchmoor, didn't go in much for change. Particularly in the Sweet Pea section of the annual Flower and Vegetable Show.

Chapter Three

Before we go any further, I'd like to make it clear that I didn't write that rubbish about the headless peacock which appeared in the paper the following Friday. Even though it was *almost* my name on the by-line.

My name is *Kat* Latcham. Not Katie, as everyone in Much Winchmoor insists on calling me, no matter how many times I ask them not to. Not Kathryn, which was what Grandma Kingham wanted me to be called as she thought Dad's choice of Katie was not posh enough for her only grandchild.

And I'm certainly not *Kath* Latcham, which is what whoever so-say 'edited' my very balanced and toned-down report on the dispute between Gerald Crabshaw and Paul McAllister called me. Not only did he (or she) change every almost every word I'd written, but had added a few cringe-making clichés that I certainly did not write.

But I'm getting ahead of myself because that Friday evening, which, now I look back on it, was where it all started. I hadn't even seen that week's paper. In fact, the only thing I was worried about as I set out for my evening shift at the pub was being late.

Which wasn't fair because it wasn't my fault I was running late. That was down to an annoying little hell hound called Prescott who'd disappeared down a rabbit hole when I was walking him that afternoon. By the time I'd coaxed him out (I promised him we'd go home the long way round so he could have a good yap at the ducks on the village pond), I scarcely had time to shower and change, least of all look at this week's Chronicle. I knew it wouldn't have much of my work in it, apart from a couple of paragraphs about the headless peacock, a mere fifteen lines.

Welcome to my life. I was forever rushing from one job to

the next and for precious little reward - or in the case of walking Prescott, no reward at all. But he did save my life once, even though he hadn't meant to. So I felt I owed him. Although, if he disappeared down any more rabbit-holes and made me late for jobs that actually paid me, that particular pool of goodwill would rapidly evaporate.

Back in the day I had a real job which paid me an adequate if not stellar salary, at an independent radio station where I worked as a research assistant (that's radio station speak for general dogsbody). But that was eighteen months ago in Bristol. Another life. Another me. A younger, more trusting - or, as my dad has told me several times since, a more naive - me.

That was before my Ratface boyfriend ran out on me with my now very much ex-best friend together with the contents of the joint bank account I'd so foolishly paid into, thinking Ratface and I were saving for a place of our own.

In that one nightmare day I lost my job, my boyfriend, and my savings, not to mention my treasured signed photo of Doctor Who (David Tennant, who else?!).

My pride was wounded, but for my finances, it was a death blow. So, after struggling to find another job and keep up the rent on the flat on my own and failing miserably at both, I was forced to return home to my parents, broke, broken-hearted and off men for the rest of my life. And, of course, jobless.

The broken-hearted bit didn't last. And as for being off men for the rest of my life - maybe I was a bit hasty on that one. But eighteen months on and the state of my finances was as grim as ever.

In this part of rural Somerset, which is buried so deep the middle of nowhere that it appears as nothing more than a vague blob on Google Maps, half decent jobs are harder to find than honest politicians.

According to Lexxi at Proper Job Recruitment, mine was a 'portfolio career.' No, I didn't know what that was either. But apparently it's when you don't have one decent full-time job but a variety of rubbish part-time ones that no-one else wants to do and for which you get paid peanuts. With, of course, zero staff benefits, such as holiday or sickness pay.

On that particular Friday, my 'portfolio career' consisted of three jobs, none of which was working out as well as I'd have liked. I was a community correspondent for the local paper where I was so valued they couldn't even get my name right. I had three weekend shifts at the village pub which were deadly dull and paid peanuts. And then, to complete my portfolio, there was my dog-walking business, *Paws for Walks*, which at least got me out in the fresh air.

But that hadn't taken off as well as I'd hoped, partly because Prescott was such an anti-social little horror that no other dog wanted to walk with him, except an elderly Labrador called Rosie who was so laid back she was in danger of toppling over.

The church clock struck the hour as I took a short-cut through the churchyard, hoping to avoid the vicar after the time Prescott had a very shrill exchange of insults with his Cockerpoo. I didn't want to stop and apologise to him on Prescott's behalf. I'd tried doing so at the time of the confrontation but both dogs were making such a row, there was no point.

My shift at the pub was supposed to start at six. With a bit of luck, Norina, the landlady, would be safely on her way to her regular Friday evening jaunt at the Cash and Carry, otherwise I'd be in dead trouble. She'd already had a go at me about my poor timekeeping. As I turned into the High Street, I broke into a jog but stopped when I heard someone calling my name.

I glanced back then hurried on. Gerald Crabshaw was the last person in the world I wanted to talk to at that moment - or at any moment, come to think of it because, believe me, that man could (and did) bore for England. Besides, I had a pretty good idea what he wanted to talk at me about.

"Katie. Katie. Hang on a moment," he puffed up behind me, his usually florid face an alarming shade of purple. "I want a word. About this."

My heart sank as he waved a copy of The Chronicle at me. I hadn't seen the paper yet, but could guess what he wanted a word about. Although knowing Gerald, it wouldn't stop at just the one.

"Sorry, I can't stop. I'm late as it is," I said, backing away. "And I realise the story's probably not what you were hoping for, but in the interests of balance and fairness -"

"Not what I was hoping for?" His little piggy eyes almost disappeared into his pudgy cheeks as he beamed at me. "It was everything I was hoping for. And then some. Front page too. I just wanted to thank you for a job well done."

I blinked hard. Had I just wandered into a parallel universe? The man who'd tried, on more than one occasion, to get me fired from my job on the paper was thanking me for a job well done?

I struggled to hide my surprise. "That's very kind of you to say so. I thought it best to keep things balanced and -"

"I must say, this new editor's really shaking things up. He's exactly what this more-dead-than-alive place needs."

"The new editor's started already?"

"Didn't you know?" His look of pretend surprise set my teeth on edge. "I'd have thought being as you're one of their ace reporters, you'd have been one of the first to be told."

Gerald could do a good line in sarcasm when the mood took him.

"I knew someone had bought The Chronicle and was bringing in their own editor," I said. "Nobody knew who, though."

"According to the editorial, there's a new fellow coming in as editor within the next few weeks, but in the meantime Mitch Muckleford himself is acting editor."

"Mitch Muckleford?"

"Muckleford Media. The owner of a very much going places company, one to watch according to the FT." He gave a patronising smile. "That's the Financial Times, in case you're wondering," he added.

"I wasn't -" I started to say but he ignored me.

"I'd have thought, given your - ahem, your journalistic ambitions, you'd have heard of Mitch Muckleford. Still, I can't stay here chatting," he said, like I was the one who was holding him up. "Just wanted to say well done, my dear. I believe in giving credit where it's due."

I felt a trickle of unease as he bustled off. Gerald Crabshaw being nice to me didn't feel right. As for the news that the paper had changed hands, it wasn't necessarily bad. I didn't know anything about Muckleford Media (although I wasn't going to tell Gerald that) but made a mental note to check it out when I got home after my shift. It could be good news for me. Maybe a chance to progress through a 'going places' company.

Going places would do me fine. I'd been going nowhere for way too long now.

But my little lift of spirits didn't last because when I reached the pub Norina's car was still in the car park. Just my luck that she was late leaving for the Cash and Carry that evening.

But when I got into the bar, neither she nor Gino, her husband, was anywhere to be seen. There was a party of six in the dining room, none of whom I recognised. They were probably tourists who'd found the place by accident when their Satnav tried to send them on a short cut to the M5.

There was only a handful of locals in. Rosie's owner, Shane, was propping up the bar along with the pair of losers I always think of as Neanderthals One and Two, who hung around with anyone in the hope of cadging a free pint. They'd hit pay dirt that evening with a relative newcomer to the village called Martin Naylor, who had yet to discover that the words 'It's my round, what are you having?' did not feature in the Neanderthals' limited vocabulary.

The only other customer was Ed Fuller who was married to my friend Jules. He was on his own at the table by the dart board, staring down at his phone.

Apart from that, the place was deserted. But this was nothing unusual. The pub had been horribly quiet since Gino and Norina took over.

Not that there was anything wrong with them, as such. They were a nice enough couple. She was Welsh, he was Italian with an Italian/Welsh accent, depending on his mood. They had bags of enthusiasm and were certainly a lot more sociable than the previous licensee, Mary, who'd regarded her customers as little more than nuisances.

But the people of Much Winchmoor don't like change. And they don't take kindly to newcomers. You have to live in the village for at least twenty-five years before you're considered otherwise.

But when newcomers move into the village and start making changes, that was an unforgivable double whammy.

And when those said changes involved the pub, which had not changed since the days when the infamous Judge Jeffries called in for a swift half on his way to round up a few rebels to hang, draw and quarter after the Monmouth Rebellion back in sixteen hundred and something, that was almost a hanging offence. Although maybe not a drawing and quartering one.

They didn't like the new decor. They hadn't liked the old decor either, but that didn't stop them moaning about the new one. Norina had removed the faded prints of Glastonbury Tor and Cheddar Gorge and replaced them with pictures of Cardiff Bay and the Leaning Tower of Pisa. The dusty old spider plant that had been there since Judge Jeffries' days had been consigned to the compost heap and a jug of plastic daffodils now stood in its place.

While above the fireplace, an old painting that was so darkened with hundreds of years of woodsmoke and nicotine that you couldn't tell what it was supposed to be, had been replaced by a blackboard, with an Italian flag in one top corner and a Welsh one in the other. Between the two flags, the words "Today's specials" had been written with a flourish, while at the bottom, "Genuine Italian cuisine at its best."

But their biggest mistake? The one that had caused a mass defection to the Black Swan at Little Sniddling?

They planned to convert the skittle alley into an extra dining room. The skittles team, along with the rest of the village, was outraged.

"You can't close the skittle alley," I advised Gino when he told me about it a few weeks ago. "Where will the skittles team go?"

Gino looked at me, his dark Italian eyes puzzled. "What is this .... how you say... skitters?"

"Skittles," I explained. "It's a bit like bowling, only you use nine pins. And you play it in an alley. Like that one, out there. The one with the sign on the door that says Skittle Alley."

His puzzled frown deepened. "But nobody plays. All the time we been here, no one has asked to play the skitters -"

"That's because the team are on their summer break. The skittles league matches don't start until September."

Gino was about to reply when a loud voice with a strong welsh accent boomed out, making him jump like a startled pony.

"Get on with it, Katie. I don't pay you to stand around gossiping," she said.

"I wasn't gossiping, Norina," I said. "I'm just trying to explain to Gino why I don't think it's a good idea to close the skittle alley."

"And I don't pay you to think either," she snapped. "But seeing as how you're interested, that alley is cold and draughty and smells of cats. I'm going to strip it all out and turn it into another dining room. Once the word gets around about my genuine Italian cuisine, we'll be packed out, you mark my words. It's just a matter of time."

"But the skittles team spend a lot of money on match nights and bring a lot of people to the pub."

"Not enough," she said dismissively. "I've been looking at the books and the alley doesn't bring in hardly any income. So converting it is a no brainer, particularly as Gino is a whiz when it comes to DIY. It's all settled."

Gino hadn't looked too enthusiastic about the prospect. But, as always when his wife was laying down the law, which was most of the time, he said nothing. Just shrugged in his Italian way.

"Gino, you're going to need to check the barrels in the cellar before we open," she went on. "And you, Katie, go and give those tables a good wipe down. Goodness knows what I pay that woman who's supposed to do the cleaning for. But she doesn't do a proper job, that's for sure."

It gave me no pleasure to be proved right when the skittles team defected to the Black Swan at Little Sniddling who were only too pleased to accommodate them. Friday nights in the Winchmoor Arms became quieter than the church graveyard, unless a minibus full of tourists took the wrong road on their way to the M5. As they had tonight.

I was about to go behind the bar and start checking the optics when I noticed someone had left a copy of The Chronicle on one of the tables.

I picked it up and that was when I saw what had made Gerald break the habit of a lifetime and say something nice to me.

My story had made the front page. I should have been pleased, except that it bore no resemblance whatsoever to what I'd actually sent in.

It was cheap, sensationalist rubbish with a deliberately misleading headline. No wonder Gerald had been so pleased about it. I wasn't looking forward to seeing Paul McAllister any time soon. He was going to be furious with me. I'd agreed with him when he'd said it was a non-story and had said I'd play it down, which I had done.

But now it had been blown out of all proportion. And it had my name on the by-line. At least, it would have been my name if it had been spelt properly. I was busily counting the lines (I did explain I get paid by the line, didn't I?) when a loud Welsh voice made me jump like Rosie does when I catch her with her head in a rubbish bin.

Chapter Four

"I don't pay you to stand around reading," Norina boomed as I pushed the paper out of sight behind the jug of plastic daffodils. "And what's more, you were thirteen minutes late. I don't pay you for that either."

"I'm so sorry, Norina, but -"

"And I thought we'd agreed on a 'smart, casual' dress code. Those ripped jeans are neither smart, nor casual," she said. "They look like a jumble sale reject."

I'd changed in such a rush, I didn't have time to hunt for the 'smart casual' black jeans I usually wore for my shifts at the pub, but it had would have made me even later. "I'm so sorry, but -"

She wasn't in a listening mood. Instead she held up her hand for silence and went on. "For some reason you seem to think you're irreplaceable. But let me tell you, young lady, I've just been on the phone to my sister in Pontypridd. She says that her Rhianna is looking to re-locate."

Relocate? It made this Rhianna sound like a branch of a High Street bank. "How do you mean, relocate?"

"She's done all her exams - tip-top student was Rhianna - and now wants to expand her experience in the hospitality industry so my sister thought of me. Bright as a button, she is, and full of ambition. A natural barmaid if ever I saw one."

"Your sister?"

"Of course not. Rhianna. She'll have the customers eating out of her hand, just you wait and see."

I thought of some of the customers who came into the pub. There was no way I'd want them eating out of my hand, thank you very much. Nor could I imagine someone who had ambitions in the hospitality industry wanting to come and work in the Winchmoor Arms. You've heard of the Last

Chance Saloon? This was the Somerset version. Especially since the mass defection of the skittles team to the Black Swan.

Nevertheless, I felt a twinge of unease. I couldn't afford to lose one third of my portfolio career. So I gave Norina my biggest smile and tried to look as if I too was 'a natural barmaid'.

"And I don't pay you to stand around talking either," she said. "Particularly when there are customers waiting."

I stopped myself from pointing out that she was the one who'd been doing the talking, not me, and went down the other end of the bar where Martin Naylor, Shane and the Neanderthals were waiting.

"At last," Martin said as I approached. "I thought I was going to have to phone ahead with my order."

"Phone ahead," chimed Neanderthal One. "That's a good one."

"Always the same when Katie's behind the bar," chirped Neanderthal Two. "A fellow could die of thirst waiting for her to stop nattering and get on with her job."

"A pint of Ferrets' Kneecaps for me," Martin said. "And whatever these three are having."

"Nothing for me, thanks," Shane said. "I'd better get back and feed the dog before she starts eating the furniture."

I didn't want to hurt his feelings by saying that if Rosie's over expanded waistline was anything to go by, it looked as if she'd already started on the first available sofa.

"I'm in no hurry," smirked Neanderthal One. "Mine's a pint of Headbender."

"Make that two," chimed his mate.

My heart sank. I quite liked the smell of beer, even Ferrets' Kneecaps, which seemed to be the bitter of choice at the moment. But cider, especially Abe Compton's Headbender, turned my stomach. I hadn't been able to bear the smell of it since the day Will and I had broken into Abe's cider barn (I was about fifteen at the time) and helped ourselves to a pint or two.

It didn't just upset my stomach. It turned it upside down and inside out. And ever since then even the smell made me queasy, which was a bit of a problem when you're working in a pub where cider is the drink of choice for the few locals who hadn't defected to the Black Swan.

"Here, Katie, what's this I hear about your mum opening a massage parlour?" Neanderthal One asked.

"A massage parlour? In Much Winchmoor?" Martin Naylor's eyebrows shot up in mock horror. "And here was me thinking this village was stuck in the dark ages. Certainly is if this pub's decor is anything to go by."

The Neanderthals started laughing like he'd just said something funny. As they did so, an angry Irish voice rang out across the bar.

Martin grinned and took out his phone. The Neanderthals laughed and a couple of tourists who'd recently wandered in looked across, bemused. If they'd been expecting a bit of genuine Somerset rusticity to entertain them, they were doomed to disappointment. Because what they got was a Welsh/Italian publican, a pub with an identity crisis and a mobile phone that screamed insults in a broad Irish accent.

If there was a competition for the owner of the most annoying ring tone, Martin Naylor would win hands down. He'd also sweep the board at 'the most annoying middle-aged man trying to look trendy' contest. Not to mention 'the most annoying newcomer to arrive in Much Winchmoor' since the aforementioned Judge Jeffries.

Martin moved down the other end of the bar, listened to the voice on the phone for a few seconds then said, "Sure. Why not? I'm in the pub. We could talk about it over a drink or two if it's that urgent."

As he finished speaking, he took out the copy of The Chronicle that I'd tucked behind the plastic daffodils and unfolded it. He held it up as he came back to us, grinning as he did so.

"What's all this? *Heads Roll in Murder Village*. Have I missed something?"

"You should ask our Katie here," Neanderthal One said. "She wrote it."

He raised an eyebrow and turned to me. "Did you now? You're obviously a woman of many talents."

"Many talents," echoed Neanderthal Two.

"And what's this about Much Winchmoor being the murder capital of the south west? The estate agent didn't mention that when my wife and I bought The Old Forge."

"It's all true. And Katie here is our very own Miss Marple," Neanderthal One went on. "She tracked down the murderers single handed."

"With the help of Elsie Flintlock's dog, they do say," Neanderthal Two reminded him. "Don't forget that."

"Is this true?" Martin asked me.

"Of course not," I said quickly. "They're winding you up. You can't believe a word those two say."

"Oh yes you can," they both chorused, and I was relieved to see one of the tourists approach the other end of the bar. I went down to serve him before the conversation descended into pure pantomime with choruses of "oh no you can't."

Martin took himself off to a table by the fire, leaving the two Neanderthals alone at the bar, looking hopefully across at the tourists who, very wisely, ignored them and went back to studying the specials board.

While they were still deliberating, I noticed that the mixers' shelf needed topping up. I'd just brought a new boxful into the bar and was starting to unpack them when I heard the door from the car park open and another customer come in. Maybe trade was picking up after all.

As I straightened up, my heart sank when I saw who it was. Paul McAllister was the last person I wanted to see that evening. I pushed The Chronicle out of sight, gave him my best barmaid smile and said good evening.

He'd obviously come straight from the office and his dark grey suit, white shirt and blue tie suited him a lot better than the bramble bush he'd been wearing the last time I saw him.

"Look, I'm really sorry about the piece in the paper," I went on. "It was nothing to do with me, honest."

He frowned at me for a moment like he was trying to work out who I was. "I don't have time to read newspapers," he said absently as he scanned the bar. "I'm looking for - oh, there he is."

To my surprise he crossed to the table where Martin Naylor was sitting.

"There you are," I heard him say as he sat down opposite Martin. "It's a bit dark in here coming in from outside. I couldn't see you for a moment."

I didn't realise Paul even knew Martin Naylor, least of all that they were drinking buddies. I'd certainly never seen them in here together before.

"I'm really glad to have caught you, Martin. This can't wait." There was something about the tone of Paul's voice, anxious, low, almost conspiratorial that piqued my curiosity. I strained my ears in their direction while pretending to focus on giving the copper topped bar counter an extra polish.

"There's something you should know," I heard Paul say as he sat down opposite Martin. "It seems -"

"It seems this may not be the best place for a private conversation," Martin said smoothly, "Especially when we're within earshot of a member of the Press. Even if it is only the local rag," he added and the look he gave me suggested he wasn't fooled for a minute by my sudden interest in polishing.

"Or the Comical. That's what we call it," Neanderthal One shouted across, obviously hoping that his razor-sharp wit would earn him an invitation to join them, or at least be included in the next round.

"The Comical," echoed his mate.

Martin very wisely ignored them and called across to me. "When you've finished earwigging, sweetheart, I'll have a scotch, seeing as you're looking for something to do. A large one and make sure it's the decent stuff, off the top shelf. Not that crap the landlady gets on special offer." He turned to Paul. "What will you have?"

Paul shook his head. "Nothing for me, thanks."

"Go on," Martin urged. "The world always looks that much better after a glass of good Scotch. Make that two, sweetheart and be quick about it."

I was about to tell him that, firstly, the pub didn't offer

waitress service and, secondly, that I was not his sweetheart. But before I could do so Ed Fuller shambled up to the bar, bouncing off a table and sending beer mats skittering off in all directions.

He had a couple of goes at setting his glass down on the counter in front of me.

"S- same again, p-please, Katie," he said. His voice was slurred, his eyes glazed.

"Don't you think you've had enough, Ed?" I kept my voice as low as I could so that the Neanderthals wouldn't hear. By the look of him he'd had more than enough and then some. He'd been sitting alone at the table under the dartboard, avoiding all eye contact, just staring into his phone ever since I arrived.

I've known Ed all my life. He'd been in the year above me and Jules at school, and in the same class as Will Manning, my on/off boyfriend.

It was unusual to see Ed in the pub on his own. He wasn't much of a drinker. He wasn't much of anything, come to think of it, although Jules assured me that he was a half decent builder, did a cracking impression of Clint Eastwood and was brilliant at getting their youngest, a hyperactive soon-to-be one year old, to sleep.

"Why don't you go on home, Ed?" I said gently, but he didn't appear to have heard me. Or, if he did, he chose to ignore me.

"I s-said, same again, p-please, Katie," he repeated, his thin, pale face even paler than usual. His hair was a mess. Not in that 'just got out bed' way, which can be quite cool, but in that 'hasn't seen a comb in over a month' way, which is *so* not a good look.

He seemed like he hadn't slept for a fortnight which, given that Jules had been moaning to me only the other day about how the baby still wasn't sleeping through the night, was probably the truth.

I sighed and poured him another pint. "Just this one, eh?" I said.

"What are you, my mother?" he growled with an

uncharacteristic show of spirit, and shambled back to his table under the dartboard, slopping loads of his drink as he did so.

He'd almost reached his table when he caught sight of Paul McAllister watching him. He stopped and peered at him the way Elsie peers at the TV Times when she can't find her glasses.

"Hah!" he exclaimed. "Where's my money? It's no good shaking your head. I'll get it. One way or another." He waved his finger at him, spilling yet more drink as he did so. "You two can sit here flashing the cash, but I know what I know. And I know what your game is."

Paul McAllister jumped up, his face scarlet. "I haven't the faintest idea what you're on about."

"Leave it." Martin laid a hand on his arm and gestured for him to sit back down. "He's just the village drunk. Ignore him."

Ed blinked owlishly at Martin, looked as if he was about to say something else then turned and staggered back to his seat. He sat down so heavily that yet more of his drink slopped out of the glass and splashed over his hand. He looked down at his now half-empty glass, a puzzled expression on his face. Then he shrugged and went back to staring at his phone.

I hadn't been going to take Martin's drinks across to him, but I was intrigued to know what it was he and Paul were talking about so earnestly. At least, Paul was talking earnestly. Martin was staring down at his empty glass, a deep frown creasing his forehead.

"So I just thought you both ought to know," I heard Paul say. "I really don't think we should -"

"Hang on a minute," Martin growled as I reached their table. There was silence as I put the drinks down.

"That will be -" I began to say, but Martin cut in with a brisk, "Put it on my tab. And if you don't mind, we're having a private conversation."

I was about to point out that a public bar wasn't exactly the ideal place for a private conversation, but he'd already turned away. He pushed a glass across to Paul then picked up his own and tossed it back.

"I did say not for me, thanks," Paul said as he stood up. "I'm afraid I've got to go. I'm expecting a call this evening which I don't want to miss. I just thought you'd want to know. Before you get in too deep."

"At least stay and have your drink," Martin said, but Paul shook his head.

"I'll pass, thank you," he said quietly.

"Fair enough," Martin said. "And thanks for telling me. I'll give it some thought."

Paul skirted around the edge of the bar to avoid passing Ed's table and had almost reached the door when it crashed open and Gerald Crabshaw came in. He was brandishing a copy of The Chronicle like it was Harry Potter's favourite broomstick.

"Hah! No wonder you weren't at home when I called just now. I take it you've seen this week's Chronicle?" he boomed at Paul.

"Comical," giggled the Neanderthals as they moved in around Gerald, effectively blocking Paul's path to the door.

Paul shook his head and went to step around them. "I don't read newspapers." He looked up at the Neanderthals. "If you'll excuse me..."

"Look. It's there in black and white." Gerald thrust the paper under Paul's nose. "On the front page. Your own admission. That makes you nothing more than a bloody vandal. You'll be hearing from my solicitor."

Paul looked down at the paper, then at me, his eyes darkened with barely controlled anger.

Chapter Five

I floundered around for something to say. My face was probably the colour of the dragon on Norina's beloved Welsh flag.

"I'm sorry. I didn't write -" I began. But I got no further. He pushed between the Neanderthals, paused at the door then turned back to face the room, his chest heaving.

"I don't know how many times I have to say this, Mr Crabshaw," his voice was firm. "But I'm telling you and ..." He looked around the bar, where everyone apart from Ed (he was still staring at his phone) was now watching with undisguised interest, "And anyone else who might be interested, that yes, I did cut something from that overgrown hedge of yours. But I did not realise it was supposed to be a peacock. In fact, from my side it just looked like one more bit of your out of control hedge. As I tried to explain to this young lady here," he gave me a withering glance. "But she was obviously too busy thinking up stupid headlines to listen properly. All I was trying to do was make that fence - your fence, by the way, not mine - safe. It's a potential death trap. I come down that path on my bike most mornings and the way those broken fence posts stick out - I don't know about your damned peacock being decapitated. I very nearly was the other morning. All I'm doing is trying to tie them in a bit. Where the hedge has been allowed to become overgrown, it's pushed the fence posts out so that they're sticking out at all angles along the path. And some of them are razor sharp."

"Your father never complained," Gerald grunted. "He was the perfect neighbour, never had any trouble from him."

"That's because my father never used that path," Paul said. "I, on the other hand, use it every single morning."

"It's up to you to look where you're going then," Gerald

29

said. "You damn cyclists are all the same. Think the whole world should be changed just to accommodate you."

"And while we're talking about employing solicitors," Paul, who'd obviously got the bit well between his teeth now, went on. "I'm telling you now, in front of all these witnesses, that if you don't make that damn fence safe, then I will. And I'll send you the bill."

He stormed off, leaving Gerald staring after him, his face almost as red as mine.

"Bleedin' newcomers," muttered Neanderthal One. "Not been in the village five minutes before they start laying down the law and wanting to change things. Good for you, Councillor Crabshaw. You told him, good and proper."

"Good and proper," came his mate's echo.

Now Gerald Crabshaw lost his right to call himself Councillor some time ago when he'd been 'invited to resign' his seat on Dintscombe District Council. It was discovered he'd been involved (as in not proven) in an iffy land deal and some extra-curricular goings on with a woman from the Planning Department.

But the Neanderthals' glasses were empty, so 'Councillor Crabshaw' it was. They'd have called him Sir Gerald of Winchmoor if they thought there was a chance of a free pint or two.

"A pint of Ferrets, please, Katie," Gerald said. "And whatever these two are having."

"That's ok, Gerald," Martin Naylor came up to the bar and took a well-filled leather wallet out of his pocket. He made sure that everyone saw the distinctive (and uber-expensive) Mulberry logo stamped on the front. "I'll get these. And I'll have another one in there, please, sweetheart. Bloody hell, Gerald, you told him where to get off. I wouldn't want to cross you, that's for sure."

"For sure," echoed the Neanderthals.

"You don't want to mess with Councillor Crabshaw," said Neanderthal One. "He was in the army, he was."

"In the army," echoed his mate, grinning at Martin and making a chopping motion with his hand. "Trained to kill, he was. Isn't that right, Councillor Crabshaw?"

"Well," Gerald preened and straightened his 'regimental' tie, which probably came from a charity shop in Dintscombe. "Let's just say, it doesn't pay to mess with me, as Paul McAllister is going to find to his cost, if he doesn't watch out."

I stifled a snort of laughter as Gerald strutted around the bar, like a little bantam cockerel who'd just seen off a rival. Martin then proceeded to buy a drink for everyone, including the two tourists who still couldn't decide whether to risk ordering something from the specials board. It was drinks all round, apart from for Ed.

It was one expensive round, but he didn't flinch when I told him the amount, except to say to put it on his tab and he'd settle it up at the end of the evening.

"Cheers," Gerald said and took a long pull at his beer. "I needed that."

"So what the hell was all that about just now?" Martin asked.

Before Gerald could explain, Neanderthal One snatched up the copy of The Chronicle and tapped the front page with a grubby forefinger. "He's the man responsible for the headless horror."

"*The neighbour from hell*, that's what you called him, Councillor Crabshaw, didn't you?" Neanderthal Two said.

"I certainly did. And for very good reason." Gerald took another long draught of his beer and settled down for one of his interminable stories. "His father lived in Mill Cottage for years, no trouble at all. But the old man died earlier this year and the cottage was going to be sold. In fact, Paul had promised me I could buy it as it's adjacent to my property and would have made a perfect extension of our very successful and upmarket Country Guest House." He fished in the pocket of his Harris tweed jacket and handed Martin a business card. "It's all the rage with the smart set from London, you know. Winchmoor Mill Guest House is putting Much Winchmoor well and truly on the map."

On the map? That would be the one entitled 'rubbish places to avoid' no doubt, I thought but kept it to myself.

"But then the blasted fellow changed his mind," Gerald droned on. "Just like that. After I'd gone to the trouble and expense of appointing a solicitor and everything. Said he was going to live there himself. He and that damn bike of his."

"He has a motor bike?" Martin sounded surprised. "He doesn't look the sort."

"He's not. This is a push bike. And the *mem sahib*, that's my lady wife, is a very light sleeper and he wakes her up every single morning, getting the bloody thing out. He bangs around on purpose to annoy us, I'm sure of it. He keeps it in a little lean to that backs on to our kitchen, you see. Old Mr McAllister used to keep his gardening tools in it, and we didn't mind that. But this damn bike. You wouldn't believe how the sound travels. Especially in the dead of night."

"He goes cycling at night?" Martin looked puzzled. "Why?"

"Not really at night. But very, very early. I'm talking six o'clock in the morning here. He says it keeps him fit and the roads are quieter then."

"I'm guessing you don't like him very much then?" Martin asked.

"Like him?" Gerald's mottled face went a shade darker and he took another long pull at his pint. "Let's put it this way. If he fell off that wretched bike of his and I found him dead in a ditch, I'd step over him. And his damned bike. I can't stand people who go back on their word."

"Tell me about it," Martin said with a sigh. "The world's full of people like that, these days, I'm afraid. Ready for a top-up?"

Gerald tossed back the rest of his pint like there was about to be a worldwide beer shortage. "Very kind of you, thanks."

"Here, Katie," Martin leaned across to me, his overpowering aftershave making my eyes water. "So when is this massage parlour of yours opening?"

Gerald leered. "Ah yes, the massage parlour. But sadly, that's not our Katie. She's too busy running around being our very own Miss Marple."

"So I've been hearing," Martin said and nodded towards the two Neanderthals.

Gerald was on a roll. "Did you know, this young lady here solves murders that leave the police baffled? You wouldn't credit it, would you? Neither do the local police, I can assure you. They weren't too pleased to find that plastered all over one of the tabloids a few months ago. I'm surprised you didn't read about it. Made quite a splash, it did. Especially around here."

I scowled at him but didn't rise to the bait. I'd taken enough grief over the article he was referring to. And, no, I didn't write it. And yes, I had tried to explain to people that some low life journo had taken what I'd said and twisted it. But nobody wanted to listen to that. They all preferred their version which got more exaggerated with every retelling.

"The massage parlour is down to her mother, Cheryl," Gerald went on, his little piggy eyes shining like he was having the time of his life. "Now if it had been Katie, I might have been her first customer. I could do with her magic fingers to take away the stress of the day."

"Magic fingers" came the inevitable echo from the Neanderthals.

I sighed. The massage parlour joke was wearing a bit thin and I couldn't be bothered to explain for what would probably be the twentieth time that Mum was thinking of extending Chez Cheryl, that's her hair salon, by adding a beauty parlour - or a 'spa experience' as she preferred to call the new extension that my dad was building in his every spare moment. The plan was to offer, among other things, a facial massage that was 'better than Botox' according to the advert for the very expensive course she'd just completed.

I looked up at the stupid grinning faces clustered around me - Martin, Gerald and the Neanderthals, who were ranged either side of Martin like a pair of hideous bookends - then down at the pint I'd just pulled while I debated whether or not it was worth losing my job over. I reckoned that, if I threw it hard enough, I could probably catch all four of them when someone put a hand on Martin's shoulder and yanked him out of my target range.

"You know what you are, Naylor, don't you?" a slurred

voice growled. "A genuine, f-f-four-star idiot."

I groaned. It was Ed Fuller.

Before I could remind Ed that I could take care of myself, he swung his fist at Martin's head. He missed, of course. Ed was always last to be picked at school sports, his hand/eye coordination pretty rubbish at the best of times. And after several pints of Headbender cider, this was so not the best of times.

Instead of connecting with Martin's jaw, Ed's fist thwacked into the upright beam on the corner of the bar, sending a shower of horse brasses and Norina's precious print of Cardiff Bay clattering to the floor.

As Martin stepped back to avoid Ed's windmilling fists, he cannoned into Neanderthal One, then ricocheted off into Neanderthal Two. The three of them went down like dominoes, ending up in an untidy heap against the kitchen door just as Norina came out with two steaming plates of spaghetti bolognese.

There were curses, followed by yelps of pain as hot bolognese sauce rained down on the three of them while Ed rubbed his sore knuckles, looking more Mickey Mouse than Mike Tyson.

"Wh-what was that for, Ed?" I spluttered, desperately trying not to laugh or to ask them if they wanted extra parmesan.

"I'll hit him harder next time." Ed clenched his fists again and swayed over the tangled heap of men and spaghetti that littered Gino's floor. "In fact, next time he'll stay down. Permanently."

The expression on his face was so completely un-Ed-like, I figured it best not to point out that he hadn't actually hit Martin in case he went back in for another go. The last time I'd seen him in this state had been at his and Jules' wedding when he'd tried break-dancing but ended up breaking his wrist instead.

But even that was preferable to skittling down three men and two plates of spag bol. – even if he had done it by accident.

Chapter Six

Martin was first to scrabble to his feet, plucking strands of spaghetti from his hair as he did so. He was incredibly vain about his thick, slightly too long dark hair and was forever tossing his head like he was auditioning for a shampoo advert.

He stepped towards Ed, fists clenched but before he could do anything, Gino hurried out of the dining room, alerted by the noise. He stood between them, a small stocky David between two hissing, spitting Goliaths.

"Let's all calm down now, boys, shall we?" he said quietly.

Ed rubbed his hand over his head, wincing at the pain from his already-swollen knuckles as he did so. "Sorry, Gino," he mumbled. "But he - "

"Go home and sleep it off, Ed," Gino said.

"Sleep it off?" Martin bellowed, giving his head an extra hard toss that dislodged a strand of spaghetti and sent it flying into the middle of the plastic daffodils. "Landlord, I insist you call the police. I'm pressing charges of assault."

"Assault," chimed the bookends.

"Come on, Martin," Gino said. "Is no call for that. Ed, he's willing to apologise, aren't you, Ed?"

"In his dreams," Ed snarled. "I got a load of grief from my boss for taking time off. I only did it as a favour to this - this moron. And now he's trying to weasel out of paying me. He can splash the cash, buying drinks all around but won't pay me what he owes me. If anyone's going to call the police, it'll be me."

"You threatening me, Fuller? Well, take a look at this." For the second time that evening Martin made a big show of taking out his fancy designer wallet, stuffed with notes. He waved it towards Ed. "I was going to pay you this evening if you hadn't whinged on at me. Now, you can whistle for it. Call it compensation for ruining a very expensive leather jacket."

"Leave it, Ed," I said softly as I put a hand on his arm. "Jules will be wondering where you are."

"Shouldn't think so," he mumbled. "I never told her I was doing this job for Naylor, see? Took a week's unpaid holiday and was going to surprise her with a nice wodge of cash to make up for it. When she found out, she went ballistic. Especially when I had to say I hadn't been paid a single penny for it."

"She'll have calmed down by now," I said, with more hope than conviction.

"S-said I was a waste of space -" Ed muttered as he zigzagged towards the door.

"She wasn't wrong there," Martin yelled after him as Ed smacked into a table on his way out.

I called him back. "Ed, you've left your hat. Your Kylie will never forgive you if you lose it"

I went across to the table and picked up the hat. It was a boring black beanie that his young daughter had given the mother of all makeovers to by making a huge bobble in her favourite purple and green sparkly wool and fixing it, slightly wonkily, to the top. Ed, to his credit, wore it everywhere.

He gave me a wry smile as I handed it to him, shoved it on his head then weaved his way out, bouncing off the door frame as he did so.

Martin watched him go, a sneer on his face, then turned to me. "I'll have another large scotch, please, darling."

"Sorry, Martin," Gino cut in. "We can't serve you anymore either. You've had enough."

Martin stared at Gino in open-mouthed astonishment. "Who the devil are you to tell me when I've had enough?" he snarled.

"I'm the landlord," Gino said with quiet dignity.

"Landlord? You're a flaming joke. Your so-called genuine Italian cuisine 'like Mama used to make' is cooked by your wife, Norina, or Nora as her real name is who's about as Italian as Cardiff's Millennium Stadium. And almost as big and loud."

"Big and loud," echoed the bookends, but with less conviction now, as even their pea-brains worked out that their newly found mate was going the right way to getting them all barred from the pub permanently.

Gino cast an anxious look at the tourists who'd taken a step back from the board as Martin pointed at it. "There's no need for that sort of talk. Why, only last week, your wife said Norina's *linguine marinara* was the best she'd ever tasted."

"Suzanne was just being polite. She told me she's not sure which is worse, your wife's cooking or –" Martin broke off, his face twisted in a cruel smile. "Fancy yourself as a bit of a singer, is that right?"

A bit of a singer? Gino warbled around the place like an Elvis loving, karaoke-mad canary.

"Well," he gave one of those shrugs that Italians, even when they're almost Welsh, are so good at. "I've been told I have a good tenor voice."

"See yourself as the next Pavarotti, do you?"

"I wouldn't say that –"

"Neither would my wife," Martin sneered. "Says she's heard better sounds from my dog when someone steps on his tail."

Everyone suddenly became engrossed in studying their hands, their drinks, the carpet. Looking anywhere but at Gino whose face had gone the colour of yesterday's porridge.

"That's it," Gino said stiffly. "Out. And don't come back. You're barred."

"Don't worry." Martin snarled. "I wouldn't set foot in this place if it was the last pub in the village."

Which, of course, it was, on account of the fact that it was the only pub in the village. Only no-one got the chance to point that out to him. As the door slammed behind him, his two 'mates' sloped off into a far corner while poor Gino looked like a little boy who'd just burst his lovely balloon.

"It's not true, Gino," I said, patting his arm. "What Martin said, about your voice. The customers love to hear you singing around the place."

"They do?" Hope flooded his face.

You'd think someone who's almost Welsh and mostly Italian, given both countries talent for music would be doubly blessed, wouldn't you? But, in Gino's case, this was sadly not so, something made even worse by the fact that he was totally unaware of it.

But I wanted to spare his feelings. So I lied.

He grasped my hand like he was drowning. "Is so kind of you, Katie, *bach*. So very –"

"Gino!" Norina's voice boomed out. "Take your hands off that girl this minute and clean up this mess!"

But before Gino could move, the door crashed open and Martin stood there, crackling with fury.

"Some moron's blocked me in," he roared.

"Ah now, that'll be me." Norina's cat-like eyes gleamed as she savoured her revenge for the Millennium Stadium jibe. "You parked where it clearly says No Parking, see? So when I got back from the Cash and Carry, where else could I go but in front of yours? But I'm not moving it now. Come back for it in the morning when you're sober. You can settle your bar bill at the same time."

"Unless," Gino chipped in, "you settle it now, seeing as you've got all that cash to wave about."

Martin stormed out, slamming the door so hard the horse-brasses clattered to the floor for the second time that night.

***

When I looked out of the window next morning, heavy grey clouds clung to the hills that surround the village. I couldn't even see the top of Pendle Knoll and Will's farmhouse was just a vague grey outline. Not the most inviting morning to take a run but I forced myself out of bed, put on my running gear and shoes and headed out.

Back in the day, when I had a real job with a real salary rather than my present 'portfolio' of rubbish jobs, I used to belong to a swanky gym and judo club. But that was in Bristol. These days I couldn't even afford the membership of the anything but swanky fitness centre in Dintscombe, so I relied on my daily run to keep my fitness levels up.

That morning, as I ran through the village and around the network of narrow lanes that surround it, I went over and over in my mind what I'd say if I saw Paul McAllister out on his morning bike ride, starting, of course with, "I'm sorry."

The way he'd looked at me after Gerald thrust that stupid piece in The Chronicle under his nose last night made me feel really bad and I hoped he'd give me the chance to explain.

But my well rehearsed apology was wasted as I didn't see him, in spite of the fact that I took my usual route. I could only assume that he, unlike me, had been put off by the threat of rain (the weather forecast had used the word 'torrential' several times) and had opted for a lie in instead. And who could blame him?

As I ran along what's known in the village as Back Lane, which links up, via a ford, to one of the roads across the moor, I passed the old stone barn that used to belong to Jules's grandfather.

Jules and I loved playing in there when we were younger. It was our magic castle to be defended against all comers and, later on, when we'd outgrown all that princess nonsense it was where we'd had our first cigarette. In my case, my first and last cigarette. It had burned my throat, caused my eyes to water and I nearly threw up. But Jules took to it and looked really cool. She teased me for ages about my pathetic attempts.

I grinned as I remembered the time her grandad came back and almost caught us. (Or rather, caught Jules. She was smoking. I was supposed to be lookout.) She'd quickly stubbed out the cigarette and tried to pretend we'd disturbed a tramp on our arrival, and he must have been the one smoking.

The look on her grandad's face told us he didn't believe that for one second and we braced ourselves for the inevitable telling off. Instead he merely said he hoped 'the tramp' had the good sense to make sure the cigarettes were put out properly, so as not to cause a fire. And then he added, with a twinkle in his eye, that he also hoped that 'the tramp' wouldn't be back for another smoke, otherwise he'd have to tell our mothers to stop us coming here in case we ran into him.

He was a lovely old man and I was really sorry when he died.

But that morning it wasn't Jules, or indeed, a tramp coming

out of the barn, but Ed. He stood by the door, scratching his head and blinking as if he'd just emerged into glaring sunlight instead of a grey, damp morning.

He looked as crushed and crumpled as if he'd slept in a hedge all night. Or, maybe, a barn.

"Ed?" I jogged across to him. "Did you sleep in there?"

He looked startled at the sound of my voice, as if he hadn't seen or heard my approach.

"Oh, h-hi, Katie," he mumbled, still rubbing his head. "What - what time is it?"

"Just coming up to seven o'clock. What are you doing here?"

"I - um, well, I just came down here to get some things." He scuffed at the ground with the toe of his trainer. "I keep a lot of my tools and stuff in here, you know."

I didn't believe him for a nano-second. "Yeah right. Course you did. So what happened last night? Wouldn't Jules let you in the house? Mind you, I can't say I blame her. You were totally trolleyed. You slept in there, didn't you?"

He looked as if he was about to deny it, then shrugged his skinny shoulders as he obviously realised there was no point.

"Yeah, something like that," he said. "Or at least, I think that's what happened. Vague memories of losing my keys. But I don't really remember much. It's all a bit of a fog this morning."

"You'd better go on home before Jules realises you didn't come in last night," I advised him. "Although I dare say she already knows."

He took a long, shuddering breath. "Yeah, you're probably right." Then he looked across at me. The expression on his face reminded me of the half hopeful, half resigned way Rosie looked when I had something to eat. It was like she knew she didn't stand a chance of getting any of it, but still she lived in hope.

"I don't suppose you'd like to come back with me, would you?" he asked. "Jules will have the coffee on by now."

I shook my head. "Sorry, Ed. You're on your own with this one, mate. Just tell her you're sorry. You'll be fine."

As I started running back up the lane towards the village, I knew without looking back that he'd be staring after me, still with that same hopeless expression.

But then, both he and I knew that when Jules caught sight of him, he'd be anything but fine.

***

When I got home, Mum was already up. She was sitting at the kitchen table, frowning as she flicked through the pages of her appointments book.

This was always a bad sign, because it usually meant she was overbooked and would 'volunteer' me into doing an unpaid shift in the salon. Or that her assistant, Sandra, (sixty going on ninety who was going through a better late than never mid-life crisis) had run off with her chiropodist again. Although as far as poor Sandra was concerned, that particular ship had sailed without her when Clint the fickle chiropodist found other toes to tickle. She was back with her long-suffering husband at the moment, but who knew for how long?

"Look, Mum, I'm really busy this morning," I said, going for a pre-emptive strike. "I've got to check out this media company that's taken over The Chronicle. And then -"

"It's all right. I won't be needing you," Mum said as she reached for a chocolate hobnob. Now I was seriously worried. She'd been on a new diet this week which was, according to her, the one that was going to change everything because it was so easy to keep to. But I'd yet to find a diet that included chocolate hobnobs for breakfast. Although if there was one, then I was up for it.

"Problems?" I asked, sitting down opposite her.

"Will you be seeing Elsie this morning?"

Elsie Flintlock was the owner of Mad Dog Prescott, the one responsible for making me late for my shift at the pub the evening before. Elsie was as feisty and with the same tendency to bite first, ask questions later as her dog. But I was fond of her, although I wouldn't dare tell her that. She'd be horrified. She didn't go for 'all that sentry-mental nonsense' (her words, not mine).

"I'm seeing her later on this morning," I said. "I'm picking Rosie up first then collecting Prescott. Why?"

"It's just that she and Olive should be due for their perms this week. And I've been looking through the appointments book and there's nothing in for them. And yet I was sure they booked the last time they were in. I distinctly remember Elsie making a fuss about wanting it done before the WI outing to Windsor Castle."

I laughed. "Expecting an invite to tea with the Queen, was she?"

Mum sighed. "Who knows with Elsie? But you know how she'll carry on if I've got it wrong, don't you?"

"So, has Sandra been fiddling the books again?" I asked. "She's been acting a bit weird ever since Clint dumped her."

"It's probably just a mistake. I'll ask her when she comes in on Tuesday. But in the meantime, could you mention it to Elsie? I've got several free spots coming up this week so I can fit her and Olive in quite easily. Too easily, in fact." She gave another sigh as she reached for a second biscuit and bit into it absently.

"Are you ok?" I asked.

"Yes. No. Well, I'm not sure." She frowned, her eyes clouded with worry as she put the biscuit down and picked up the appointment book. "It's just - well, I've been looking through here and there are quite a few of my regulars who are not there. I don't understand it. This isn't exactly a good time for my takings to start falling, not when your Dad's got on so well with the new extension and I paid out all that money to go on that beauty therapy course."

"I don't see Olive, Elsie and their cronies booking in for facials any time soon, Mum," I said as gently as I could, knowing how touchy she could be on the subject. "What you need is new customers."

"Of course," she said snippily. "I am well aware of that. But that doesn't mean I want to lose the old ones."

"I'm sure you won't." As I've said before, people in Much Winchmoor don't like change and some of Mum's customers had been coming to Chez Cheryl ever since Mum moved to the village thirty years ago when she married Dad. "But it's holiday time, and all that. People are all over the place."

What Mum needed was a good funeral in the village. That always led to a sharp increase in trade as all her customers, most of whom were elderly, would get dressed up to the nines in their Sunday best and have their hair done, especially for the occasion.

"Yes, you're probably right." She closed the book with a snap and looked a bit brighter. "You know what we need to give trade a boost? This village needs a good -"

"Funeral?" I couldn't believe that Mum and I were on the same wavelength for once.

She glared at me. "Certainly not. What this village needs is a good wedding. That will cheer everyone up. Speaking of which, how are things with you and Will?"

It was my turn to reach for the biscuits as I avoided her gimlet gaze. "Oh, you know," I said airily. "We're good."

"Katie?" She gave me one of her looks that, I swear, could see right into the far corner of my mind, including that little compartment labelled 'Things to be thought about later.'

"Well, you know," I muttered. "He's busy on the farm, with harvest and everything. And I -"

"You're not stringing him along, are you?" she asked. "Because that would be most unfair. Will deserves better than that."

Chapter Seven

She was right, of course. She always was. Will did indeed deserve better than that. He deserved better than me, to be honest. And I've told him that, on several occasions. And most of the time, he agreed with me.

But the thing is, you see, when I came back to Much Winchmoor, it was only supposed to be temporary. Just while I sorted myself out and paid off the bank loan, which would keep the bank's senior executives in Ferraris and second homes in the Maldives for the next decade or two.

But then I met Will. Of course, that's not strictly true. I met him on my first day at primary school when he tied my plaits to the back of my chair. Our mothers became best friends and, both only children, Will and I had grown up together. He was the brother I never had. And like all brothers was a pain in the neck most of the time.

Until the day he kissed me. I mean, properly kissed me. And I realised that somehow, when we weren't looking, our feelings for each other had become decidedly un-sibling-like.

And, like my mother, he too had been dropping hints about getting married recently.

And I'd been swiftly changing the subject every time he did.

Because if we did get married, that would be it. I'd be a farmer's wife. With 2.4 children, a Labrador or two, and (if my mother had anything to do with it) a wedding complete with meringue dress and hats the size of cartwheels. Although probably not in that order. Will was pretty old fashioned that way.

I did love him and couldn't imagine life without him. And I knew he loved me.

But I wanted - I needed - to get out of Much Winchmoor. It was never part of my plan to stay here. But how could I ask

Will to leave? He was as much a part of the village as the wonky-roofed houses that lined the High Street, or the river Winch that fed the pond and the mill stream. His family had farmed up at Pendle Knoll forever. I couldn't imagine him doing anything else. And I don't suppose he could either.

I wished we'd never had that first kiss, even though the memory of it still did things to my knees that beat anything Abe Compton's Headbender cider could do. In fact, now I think about it, the effect Will's kisses had on me was very much like the effect from Abe's cider. Except Will looked and tasted a whole lot nicer.

He made me forget who I was, what I was here for, where I was going as well, turning my insides upside down and inside out. Also, one of his kisses, like one glass of wine, was never enough, even though I knew I'd regret it in the morning.

"Katie?" Mum's voice brought me back with a bump. "You didn't answer my question. You're not stringing Will along, are you? Because, let me tell you, young lady-"

"Sorry, Mum. No, of course I'm not. But, look, I've got to go upstairs and check out the people who've bought The Chronicle."

I pushed my chair back and escaped upstairs to my room. Once Mum got on the subject of weddings - and my wedding in particular - there was no stopping her. I opened my laptop and my spirits lifted as I checked out Muckleford Media. If their website was anything to go by, it looked to have plenty going on, although some of their publications would have made the ladies of the Grumble and Gossip Group blush. Or reach for their magnifying glasses.

This, I reckoned, could be the breakthrough I was hoping for. Ok, I hadn't liked what they'd done with my peacock piece, but it had brought me a lot of extra linage and Gerald had seemed happy enough with it. Although I preferred not to think about the look in Paul McAllister's eyes when he'd seen the lurid headline.

But the thing that got me excited was that the company owned a couple of radio stations. And radio was, and always had been, my first love (after Will, of course). Could things be looking up for me and my portfolio career at last?

Since acquiring wheels in the form of a small scooter, (so underpowered Dad's lawnmower could leave it standing) my job at The Chronicle had received a bit of a boost when the now-departed editor, Mike, had extended my patch.

It now included several more villages, three additional parish councils and a disused railway line that a group of local enthusiasts (or 'totally deluded blokes with too much time on their hands' if you wanted Will's take on it) were hoping to turn into a cycle path.

At least this part of my 'portfolio' career was growing nicely, thanks to the enterprising and somewhat pushy leader of the Cycle Path Ninjas who was always after a bit of free publicity. And I was hoping that the quantity (and quality) of the work I'd been sending in recently would set me up nicely with the new regime.

Gerald had said it was a 'going places' company, which sounded just what I needed, considering Norina's dark hints last night about her niece. Wales' contender for Barmaid of the Year might well mean that one third of my portfolio career could be about to come to an abrupt end.

I was still checking out Muckleford Media's website when my inbox pinged. There among the usual offers of miracle things to improve my manhood and not to be missed bargain luxury world cruises was an email from Muckleford Media. It would have done more for staff relations if this had been sent before announcing it in the paper, but I told myself, emails often got delayed.

"Dear colleague. As from immediate effect, ownership of The Dintscombe Chronicle has been transferred to Muckleford Media PLC. A new editor has been appointed and will be taking up his post shortly. But in the meantime, our CEO, 'Mitch' Muckleford will be acting editor.

The company extends its thanks to the outgoing editor, Mike West, for his contribution to the paper over the years and wishes him every success in his new career.

Mitch will be in touch with you all to discuss on a one-to-one basis your place in the new set-up. Muckleford Media is committed to bringing The Dintscombe Chronicle into the twenty-first century and there are lots of exciting things planned. We hope you will be part of it."

Exciting things planned? I was up for that although I tried to ignore the niggling little doubts. It was bad enough getting my name wrong. But what sort of person does the same thing with the name of the outgoing editor? (It was Mike North, not Mike West.)

One thing I remembered from Lexxi's lecture on what she insisted on describing as the 'many advantages' of a portfolio career was that it gave a client control over 'career self-management'. In case you're wondering, that was Lexxi-speak for what my Gran Latcham used to call, "If you don't ask, you don't get."

So, in the spirit of career self-management, I started to compose a reply to the email. I was rewriting the opening line for the eighth time when my phone rang.

"Hi there, Kath." The gravelly voice sounded like it belonged to someone who'd smoked too many cigarettes. "Mitch here. You got my email?"

"Yes, hi," I said brightly, hoping he wouldn't hear the sound of my heart thumping against my ribcage. "Good to hear from you. But my name's Kat actually."

"Sorry, sweetheart. I'm not so hot with names."

Oh really? I hadn't noticed. I could have said. But, of course, I didn't.

"You and I need a little chat," he went on. "Now I've been looking at your area and -"

OK, Kat, time to make Lexxi proud. Time for a little bit of career self-management.

"Yes, I've been trying to speak to Mike about that," I said, my voice coming out a lot louder than I'd intended. "There's a new Craft Centre opening up just outside Glastonbury. I know it's a little bit outside my present area, but I think I could really do something with that. They've got some great things planned and -"

"A craft centre?" he cut in. "Boring snoring. Which leads me neatly to what I wanted to talk to you about. I've been looking at your copy and, for starters, you cover an awful lot of these parish council meetings, don't you?"

"Yes. But I can easily manage more," I said eagerly. "There are usually a few good follow-up stories to be found in those. Then there's the new action group that's campaigning to get the old railway line reopened as a cycle route. That would -"

"Stop you right there, Kath," he cut in. "Parish council meetings, cycle paths, mothers' meetings. Total yawn. People don't buy papers for that sort of rubbish. Right now, I'm looking at the last report you sent me. About the missing streetlights in Little Dreary -"

"It's Little Mearefield actually -" I began but he paid no attention.

"Whatever the place is called, no-one's interested in missing streetlights. You need to sex things up a bit. Like I did with that piece about the peacock. You completely missed a trick there, darlin'."

"Yes, I was going to talk to you about that. Actually -"

"Human interest, that's what I'm looking for," he cut in as I felt my tenuous hold on my attempt at career self-management slither through my fingers like wet seaweed. "News is about people. Not potholes and streetlights."

"I sent you something about the village choir. That was about people."

"Ah yes. The village choir. I've got that particular piece in front of me right now. A visit to an old folks' home. Have I missed something here? Did one of the old dears have a heart attack? Or was there a bit of hanky panky among the bedpans? Maybe there was some underage drinking among the choristers?"

I thought of Suzanne Naylor's recently formed Much Winchmoor choir, where the average age was probably sixty-five-plus. "Nothing like that," I laughed, assuming he'd been joking. "But from what I was told, the residents of the nursing home had a wonderful time, particularly those with dementia. Music is such a powerful -"

"But old folk having a wonderful time doesn't sell newspapers any more than missing streetlights do. And if there's one thing we can agree on, darlin', for all our sakes, is that we need to sell more newspapers, don't we?"

"Yes, Mr Muckleford. But -"

"It's Mitch. And but me no buts. I don't like buts. They make me edgy. Look, I'll spell it out to you straight up, darlin'. If we don't get the circulation up, then the paper closes and the site gets sold for housing. A simple question of economics, right? I've already got a property developer desperate to bite my hand off. So I'm giving the paper six months to turn in a decent profit or else -" He made a horrible swooshing noise that I assume was accompanied by him swiping a finger across his throat.

"So, come on, we can do better than old folks sing-alongs and missing streetlights, can't we?" he went on. "You can see the sort of thing I'm after. Your headless peacock was a perfect example. At least it was after I'd finished with it. You with me?"

"Yes - um, thanks. That's - um good to know," I lied as my heart sank.

"Now," he went on briskly, "I've been looking back over the last couple of years and see there have been a fair few murders in Much Whinge-More, or whatever you call the place."

I thought of all the moaning that went on in Mum's salon when the massed members of the Much Winchmoor Grumble and Gossip Group met up for their weekly 'shampoo and sets' and 'none of that fancy blow drying, Cheryl, thank you very much'.

I had to admit, the name Much Whinge-More suited the place a whole lot better.

"So, Kath. There you have it, sweetheart," Mitch was saying. "Either you sex your stories up a bit or..."

At that moment, the recycling lorry pulled up outside our house and the operatives, as ever, took massive pleasure in hurling Dad's empty beer bottles, one at a time, into their lorry with as much noise as possible. So I didn't get to hear what came after 'or'. Which was probably just as well.

By the time the recyclers had moved out of earshot, Mitch had ended the call, leaving me in a state of near panic. Sex up my stories? How do you sex up a report on the fruit and vegetable show I was supposed to be covering that afternoon?

As for more 'human interest' stories - I thought of the regulars of the Winchmoor Arms, some of whom were barely human and not remotely interesting.

It was my fault, I supposed, for daring to think that maybe, just maybe, things were starting to go my way, at least as far as the journalism side of my portfolio was concerned. You know how it goes. One minute you're bowling along in the cycle lane of life when wham! Something happens that sends you clean over the handlebars.

Mitch Muckleford had done just that to me.

Chapter Eight

Mitch's gravelly voice rang in my ears long after he ended the call.

He was totally wrong about people not buying local papers to read about potholes and parish council meetings. That was exactly what they bought them for. They wanted to see pictures of coffee mornings and jumble sales, and to exclaim over the asking price of the house that was for sale in the next road. They wanted to coo over pictures of little Josh's first day at school. Not to mention Elsie's favourite reading, the obituary pages which she always studied in minute detail.

All over Dintscombe and the surrounding area, factories, pubs and other places of work had been closing down and the buildings snapped up for housing. Even the town's one-time prison had been converted into a block of flats (after the inmates had all been transferred, of course) and a Prison Museum.

Imagine living there and the lift breaking down. It would give a whole new meaning to the phrase 'a prisoner in one's own home', wouldn't it?

The Chronicle's site was well away from the prison and in the middle of quite an upmarket residential area of Dintscombe. Mitch already had someone interested.

The paper looked doomed and with it my career in local journalism. Such as it was. Adding a new page to my portfolio suddenly became a matter of some urgency.

Unless, of course, there was an outbreak of murder in Much Whinge-More which would give the Chronicle's circulation a much-needed boost - and who wanted that? Not me, that was for sure. I still woke up in the middle of the night having flashbacks about the last one.

But there was no point sitting around moping. I wasn't out

of work yet. In fact, today being Saturday, I had a really busy day ahead.

There was my lunchtime shift in the pub then a quick dash out to Little Mearefield to cover the village flower show. (Or Little Drearyfield as I now couldn't help thinking of it.)

It was a pretty safe bet Mitch would print it - in spite of his preference for 'human interest stories' - seeing as the chairman of the flower show was also one of The Chronicle's biggest advertisers. The adverts for Bidwell Bespoke Conservatories had graced the front page of The Chronicle for as long as anyone could remember.

But, as far as the rest of the morning was concerned, that was taken up by my daily *Paws for Walks*.

I collected Rosie, the laid-back chocolate Labrador, for her daily amble from one litter bin to the next. The only time she got up a bit of speed was if, as we walked past the pub, Pitbull the pub cat was hanging about, waiting to pounce on any dog who came within hissing, spitting and clawing distance.

Of course his name wasn't really Pitbull. He didn't have one. But it was what the regulars called him, for obvious reasons. He was the feline equivalent of Prescott, which made them mortal enemies. He didn't really belong to the pub. He simply turned up there one day and decided to stay, the way cats do.

The litter bins must have been unusually enticing that morning because Rosie was even slower than usual. I was trying to persuade her to move on when a police car went past, blue light flashing.

In spite of what Mitch said about Much Winchmoor being the murder capital of the south west, it was in fact very unusual to see a police car around here, following the latest round of cutbacks in rural policing. So it was a pretty safe bet to assume this wasn't a normal patrol. The flashing blue light was a bit of a giveaway, too.

Mitch had said to be on the lookout for human interest stories, so I watched to see where the car was going. If I hurried, I might see what was going on.

But trying to persuade Rosie to hurry was like trying to herd cats. In the end I settled for the only thing that was guaranteed to make her move, a dog treat held firmly between my fingers, just out of her reach.

Together the dog treat and I, closely followed by Rosie, made our way towards Mill Lane, which was where the police car had been heading.

As we reached the lane, Rosie gave a low growl and stopped abruptly. The police car was across the road, blocking it, the blue light still flashing.

Mill Lane led, not surprisingly given its name, to Gerald Crabshaw's Winchmoor Mill. The police car had stopped right outside.

As Rosie and I approached, I could see two more cars and the post van parked by the entrance to the Mill. A cluster of people stood around. I could also make out the postie a few feet away from them, sitting on Gerald's garden wall, one of those silver blankets that sparkled in the dull morning light wrapped around his shoulders.

Had there been an accident? As far as I could see, the post van looked in pretty good shape.

"I'm sorry, madame, you can't go any further," said the uniformed policeman who'd just got out of the patrol car.

"What's happened?"

"There's been an incident. That's all I can say at the moment."

An incident? A shiver raced down my back. I'd heard that line before. I was right then in thinking it wasn't a road traffic accident.

"Is anyone hurt?"

"There will be a statement in due course," he said. "Now, if you don't mind -"

As he spoke another car pulled up. I recognised the man who got out.

Ben Watkins used to live in the village and had gone to school with us. He'd been in Will's year and had been an awkward, geeky kid back then with a massive crush on Jules.

But he'd grown up and filled out nicely in all the right places and was now a detective constable. He spoke quietly to the uniformed officer, then began to walk towards the Mill.

"Ben?" I called.

He turned back. "Hi, Katie. I didn't realise that was you standing there. How are you?"

"Fine thanks and it's Kat." My response was automatic.

He pulled a face and grinned. "Sorry, I always forget, don't I?"

"You and everyone else in this place," I grumbled. "So, what's going on? And what's the postie doing, sitting there, looking like an oven ready turkey?"

His grin faded and he looked so serious that I took a closer look at the postie. He'd been delivering post to the village for as long as I could remember and always had a cheery grin for everyone, even when he was delivering the Council Tax bills.

No cheery grin now though. His face was the same colour grey as the wall he was sitting on. His eyes had a glazed look like he'd just seen something he was trying to forget.

A sudden flashback knocked the breath out of my body. I remembered sitting like that, shocked and drained, staring into nothingness as I tried to stop seeing something that would be imprinted for ever on my mind.

Another time. Another story. *Another body?*

I tried to get my head back into gear. Tried not to think of the time when I'd sat, like the postie, trying not to think about - or remember - what I'd seen. But the memory of the day Will and I had discovered a body, even though it was now two years ago, filled my head. The horror of it was still as fresh in my mind as if it had just happened.

When I'm stressed, this really bad thing happens to me. My brain switches off, while my mouth carries on like a hyperactive five-year-old who's eaten too many jellybeans.

Instead of telling Ben how I was really feeling, I said the first stupid, inappropriate thing that came into my head. I didn't even know it was in there. But out it popped. Like a rabbit out of a hat.

"Jeez, Ben," I said with a pathetic attempt at a laugh, "Don't tell me Gerald Crabshaw's had his revenge. And that we've got yet another headless corpse in the village."

Ben didn't quite grab me by the shoulders and shake me. But he looked like he wanted to.

"What do you mean by that?" he asked, no trace of his earlier grin now.

I took an instinctive step back and almost fell over Rosie. "Sorry. Forget it. I was being facetious."

The look he gave me was not unlike one of the looks Mum gives when she thinks I'm not telling her the whole truth. "Come on. You must have had a reason for saying what you did. What did you mean by another headless corpse?"

"I'm sorry, Ben. It wasn't meant as a serious remark. It was stupid insensitive thing to say."

"Why should Gerald Crabshaw be out for revenge? Revenge on whom? And for what?"

I sighed and really wished I'd never started this. Would I never learn to engage my brain before speaking?

"Look, it was nothing more than a silly argument between neighbours over a boundary fence that was made a whole lot worse by a stupid article in the paper - which, incidentally, I did not write, even though it had my name on it. Well, sort of my name. But it didn't mean anything. So just forget what I said, will you? "

"I can hardly do that. I might as well tell you. There'll be a statement issued shortly anyway. The postman discovered the body of a man early this morning."

The shock of his words took my breath away. A thousand questions filled my head. But this time I'd learnt my lesson. I didn't say a word.

"So, I'll ask you again, Katie," he said in a very quiet voice. "What did you mean by another headless corpse?" he asked.

I felt like something cold and slimy had just crawled down my back. "You don't mean. the dead man. Please don't say he'd been decapitated."

Chapter Nine

"Well," I prompted when it looked as if Ben wasn't going to answer me. "Was he .... ?" I swallowed hard. "Decapitated?"

He didn't answer. Instead he jingled the loose change in his pocket and looked across to where a uniformed PC was now talking to the postie. "Look, I shouldn't have said anything, although it will all come out soon enough, I suppose. The poor guy -"

He broke off and frowned at me, his eyes dark with suspicion. "Are you still working for The Chronicle?"

"What? Yes. No. Probably not. Oh, I don't know. It's kind of complicated," I waffled. My brain was still stuck on the word 'decapitated' and hadn't yet found forward gear. Then I realised what he was getting at. "For goodness sake, Ben. You don't seriously think I'm going to write about this, do you?"

His long stare suggested he was having to think hard about that one. "It's what journalists do, isn't it? Assuming you are still one?"

I shrugged. "If you must know, my job at the paper is very much up in the air at the moment. There's been a change of ownership and I'm not sure how - or, more likely, if - I'm going to fit in to the new set up. Or even if I want to."

Just at that moment it didn't seem terribly important, not when you weighed it up against the enormity of some poor guy being decapitated.

But who? And why? And, equally important, *by whom*?

"Look, Ben," I said earnestly as I tried my best to look the epitome of discretion and reliability. "I swear this is off the record and not a word you tell me will leave my lips. But you can't leave it like that. Who is it?"

"What did you mean about another headless corpse?" He had that infuriating habit that lots of policeman have of answering a question with one of their own.

"Nothing at all. If you must know I thought you were talking about peacocks."

"Peacocks?" Now it was his turn to look bewildered. "What the hell have peacocks got to do with anything?"

"I'm sorry, Ben, my brain's totally scrambled at the moment." To my horror, I felt the prickle of tears behind my eyelids. *Get a grip, girl*, I told myself sternly. *This is not about you.*

He looked at me without speaking for a moment. Then he said quietly, "Are you ok?"

I gave a quick nod. But, like one of those annoying spots you get on your chin two hours before a hot date, I couldn't leave it alone. But it was worse not knowing.

"So, who is it?" I asked. He'd said 'the poor guy' so obviously it wasn't Fiona Crabshaw. "It's not Gerald, is it?"

Goodness knows, there was no love lost between me and Gerald Crabshaw, but I wouldn't have wished that on him.

He hesitated then said, "We're waiting for a member of his family to make an official identification but we're pretty sure it's Paul McAllister."

"You're kidding." I said. But of course, policeman didn't make those sorts of jokes, did they? Even so, I couldn't believe it. "But I only saw him last night. He was in the pub early on. And you're saying he was murdered? But who would do that? And why? He was such a lovely guy."

"I certainly didn't say he was murdered," he said quickly. "So don't you go spreading that around. It looks as if it may have been just a horrible accident. But we'll know more after the post-mortem."

"An accident?" I couldn't see how it could possibly be. "But you can't decapitate someone accidentally, can you?"

"We're investigating the condition of the fence that runs between his property and Mr Crabshaw's," Ben said. "We thought -" he stopped and looked at me closely as he heard my sharp intake of breath. "What is it?"

It was no good. I had to tell him. If I didn't, someone else would.

"Last night, in the pub. Paul was complaining to Gerald about the poor condition of his fence," I explained. "In fact, that was what they fell out about. He said - oh my god, he - he said it was a death trap and that he cycled down there most days and that yesterday morning he was nearly…" The word stuck in my throat. "I mean, it's horrible. But at least it wasn't deliberate. So was that what happened? He fell and -" My voice trailed away. I couldn't go on.

"I get to ask the questions, Katie. Not you," he said. "And I think I've already answered more than I should. So now it's your turn to answer. Tell me a bit more about this falling out he had with Mr Crabshaw. And where the hell does a peacock come in to all this?"

"Oh, that. It was just a lot of hot air. A falling out between neighbours over a scruffy old hedge that Gerald had so say spent years fashioning into the shape of a peacock. Paul was trimming back the hedge, to make the path between the two houses safer for him, when he accidentally cut the head off Gerald's so-called peacock. At least that's what Gerald claimed. Paul apologised, but Gerald wouldn't accept his apology and was threatening all kinds of things. But I'm sure it was just an accident. Paul didn't seem the kind of guy to do such a mean, spiteful thing."

Ben was writing in his notebook all the time I was speaking. It felt like I was dropping Gerald Crabshaw in it, but he was the one who'd been going around making wild accusations. And there'd been plenty of witnesses to the exchange. Everyone in the bar last night, with the possible exception of Ed Fuller, of course.

As I was talking, I jumped as something cold and wet touched my hand. It was Rosie's nose. The poor dog had been waiting patiently for her dog treat while this conversation was going on but now the nudge to my hand was her way of telling me that her patience was wearing thin. The puddle of drool at my feet was also a bit of a give-away.

I gave Rosie her treat, checked my watch and saw with a start that I needed to hurry and collect Prescott if I was going to get the dogs walked before my lunch time shift at the pub. I couldn't afford to be late again. Not when Miss Welsh Barmaid of The Year was seeking to extend her career path in the hospitality industry. It wouldn't take her long to realise that the Winchmoor Arms was a dreary little road to nowhere but in the meantime the damage to my particular career path - and finances - would have been done.

I was still rattled by what had happened to Paul and was actually quite relieved that my promise to Ben to say nothing meant I didn't have to relive it all over again by telling Elsie.

Although, knowing her, she probably knew already.

***

No-one ever gets to use Elsie's doorbell because as soon as they come within a metre of her gate, her front door shudders under the weight of what sounds like a pack of hell hounds who hadn't been walked or fed for a fortnight.

In fact, the noise comes from Prescott, a small brown and white Jack Russell terrier who bites first and asks questions later. If ever a pair deserve each other, it's Elsie and Prescott. She's a cantankerous old lady with scarecrow hair, a fondness for Homer Simpson slippers and a tongue sharp enough to slice shoe leather. He's a cantankerous dog with hair like an over-used toothbrush and a fondness for ankles, trousers - in fact, anything that comes within range of his snapping jaws.

But, as Elsie insists on reminding me, he did save my life once (even though he probably didn't mean to) which was why I walk him every day. For free.

"Come along in for a moment. Olive and I were just talking about you," Elsie said at the same moment as Prescott shot between my legs and disappeared down the road like a heat seeking missile. Elsie, unconcerned, muttered something about a springer spaniel on the other side of the village.

"Shall I go after him?" I asked although I was in no condition to give chase, not while I had Rosie with me.

"No point," she said. "He'll come back when he's ready."

Rosie did a quick detour into the kitchen where she hoovered up the remains of Prescott's breakfast, which served the little horror right. I left her polishing Prescott's bowl to a mirror-like shine and followed Elsie into the sitting room, where Olive Shrewton, Elsie's neighbour and fellow member of the Grumble and Gossip Group, sat in a high-backed armchair, a half finished cup of tea balanced precariously on its arm.

"Has lover boy popped the question yet?" Elsie, never one for the social niceties, waded in.

She obviously hadn't heard about Paul McAllister. Well, that was a first. But at least I didn't have to listen to her wild theories on who'd done it or why. And what she didn't know, she'd make up. The small matter of the truth was never allowed to get in the way of what Elsie considered a good story. She'd have got on well with Mitch Muckleford. They were out of the same mould.

I didn't bother to tell her that my relationship with Will was none of her business, firstly because there was no point. Elsie thought everything that happened in Much Winchmoor was her business. And secondly, because she asked me the same question every day. And I never answered it.

"If I was you," she went on, "I'd do the asking before someone else does. Like that pretty young vet."

"She's got a boyfriend," I said quickly but should have saved my breath.

Elsie snorted. "So you say. But there's plenty more out there, younger and prettier than you and whose hair doesn't look like a multi-coloured scouring pad who'd jump at a good looking fellow like Will Manning. Not keep him hanging about like a spare part, waiting for you to make up your mind. You should –"

"Talking of hair," I jumped in, keen to stop her going any further down that particular no through road. "Where did you and Olive get those perms done?"

You see, Elsie's a fine one to talk about weird hairstyles. Her new perm made her look more like a mad scarecrow than ever. As for Olive, she always reminds me of one of those gaunt grey herons that hang about garden ponds – only now her new perm was so tight she looked like a gaunt grey heron who'd somehow managed to get a cauliflower stuck on its head.

"We can get our hair done wherever we like. It's a free country," Elsie said defiantly. "We fought a war for that, you know."

"Not you personally, you didn't," I reminded her. "You were still at school during the war. So, come on, spill. Who did your perms? Because it wasn't my mum, was it?"

"If you must know, dear, she's called Crystal," Olive said. "She talks a bit too much for my liking and her skirt's too short for someone her age. And -"

"And then there's the snake," Elsie cackled, her button-bright eyes shining with mischief.

"She has a snake?" I asked.

"It's a tattoo. On her arm. Only Olive here thought it was the real thing when Crystal reached out to shampoo her. Nearly jumped out of the chair. She had a fit of historics at the sight of it."

"Historics?" I asked with a grin. "Don't you mean hysterics?"

Elsie glared at me. "That's what I said. She came over all historical."

Olive tutted. "It gave me a turn, I'll admit. But it was very realistic. And, you know, Katie, her rates are so reasonable -"

"Oh, come on," I cut in. "Mum doesn't exactly charge London prices –"

"And she comes to the house," Elsie chipped in. "She's recently moved into the area and has set herself up as a mobile hairdresser.

"And will this Crystal be doing your hair in future?" I asked.

There was a long silence, which was unusual in Elsie's house. Elsie doesn't do silences, least of all long ones. But she'd found something interesting outside the window that demanded her attention while Olive plucked at the sleeve of her hand-knitted grunge-green cardigan. Neither of them looked at me.

I waited.

Olive was the first to break. "The thing is, Katie, love, I'm – er, I'm –" she cleared her throat and started again. This time the words came tumbling out. "Well, if you must know, I'm not too keen on meeting men in dirty raincoats. I'm not a prude, but I don't think that sort of thing's suitable for our village, do you? Think of all the children, my own grandchildren included, who live nearby. I'd never have believed it of your mum, of all people. I know times are hard and folks have to making a living as best they can these days. But even so...." She put her half-finished cup of tea on the coffee table, stood up and wrapped her cardigan tightly around her thin frame. "I'm sorry, Elsie, but I must go. I've just remembered I've - er, I've left something in the oven."

"Men in dirty raincoats?" I turned to Elsie as Olive beetled out, her cheeks red enough to stop traffic. "Don't tell me she believes that nonsense that's been going around about Mum opening a massage parlour? Have you been winding her up again?"

Elsie shrugged. "Who knows what goes through Olive's head? If you ask me, she's getting those senior dimensions. But never mind her." Her eyes sparkled as they always did when she was on the scent of a bit of gossip. "I heard it was a lively evening in the pub last night. What with Gerald Crabshaw threatening to murder someone, then Ed Fuller knocking Martin Naylor clean out. Sounds like I missed all the fun."

I thought of the police cars outside The Mill - and the grey-faced postman sitting on Gerald's wall. It was certainly not my idea of fun. Nor, I suspected, the postie's.

Rosie was giving Prescott's now empty food bowl one final polish when I dragged her away and headed back. At least I didn't have to walk Prescott now, which took the pressure off a bit.

But I wasn't looking forward to my lunchtime shift at the pub as by now, word about Paul McAllister's death would surely have rattled around the village, even though, by some miracle, it had failed to reach Elsie.

And, indeed, it was every bit as bad as I'd feared. Everyone had a theory about who had done it and why. And nobody wanted to listen to the guy who said he'd heard it was all a horrible accident. To add to my stress, my phone pinged a couple of times. And when I checked caller ID, I switched it off. Because the caller was Mitch.

What if the news of Paul McAllister's death had reached him and he was now asking me to follow up on it? When I'd just given Ben Watkins my word that our conversation was 'off the record.'

But there was something else. Something that had been niggling away at me ever since I'd left Ben. He'd hinted that Paul's death could have been an accident. But I wasn't so sure. Paul knew about the dangerous state of Gerald's fence. Only last night in the pub he'd talked about how he'd very nearly ridden into one of the stakes that morning. I couldn't believe that, knowing that, he'd have ridden into it by accident.

But I was going to keep such doubts to myself. And I certainly wasn't going to write about it. At least, not until I'd thought it through. Which, I know, didn't make me much of a journalist.

But then, I wasn't much of a barmaid or dog walker, either. Suddenly, night-time shelf stacker in a Dintscombe supermarket was beginning to sound surprisingly attractive.

As the lunchtime shift crawled by, the stories of Paul McAllister's death became more and more outrageous, in direct proportion to the amount of beer and cider being consumed. There was nothing like a grisly and as yet unexplained death in the village to get tongues wagging and sending imaginations into overdrive.

I tried once to turn the conversation by asking if anyone knew who this Crystal was who was muscling in on my mum's patch. But that just set them off on another round of outrageous speculation and wild talk about turf wars and massage parlours that I wished I'd not said anything.

The only thing that diverted them was when they moved on to the subject of last night's showdown between Ed Fuller and Martin Naylor - but even that was made to sound like something out of *High Noon* whereas the reality had been more like an episode of *Tom and Jerry*.

As for the speculation as to why Martin hadn't been in to collect his flash motor from the car park - believe me, you really don't want to know the various mad theories flying around about that one.

Two o'clock finally came and my shift was over. I was actually looking forward to covering the Little Drearyfield Fruit and Vegetable show. Normally I found these shows a total yawn, their only redeeming feature being the fact that I got paid a decent amount of linage for including all the names of the prize-winners at the end of my write up. But after all the nonsense in the pub, it would be cathartic to write about the winner of the longest runner bean or the rudest shaped carrot.

But even that small pleasure looked as if it was going to be denied me when I finally got around to turning my phone back on and listening to the messages that an increasingly annoyed sounding Mitch had left for me.

Chapter Ten

"I'm not in the habit of chasing around after my staff," he growled when I finally got back to him.

"I'm sorry," I said. "I do a lunchtime shift at the village pub and there's no phone reception in there."

It wasn't a total lie. Mobile reception was pretty good in the main bar, more the pity. And it had certainly been a lot better at lunchtime without Martin Naylor's annoying ring tone disturbing the peace every five minutes with its phoney Irish accent screaming out insults.

But there were other parts of the pub, the ladies' toilets, for example, where it was impossible to get a signal. So my mumbled excuse was at least a version of the truth.

"I've had a tip off there's been another gruesome murder in your village," Mitch said.

"Poor guy. Yes, it's terrible. Although at the moment it's an unexplained death. According to the police, it could just have been a horrible accident."

"You managed to get an interview with the police?" The surprise in his voice wasn't very flattering. "Well, good for you."

I remembered my promise to Ben that our conversation was off the record and did a bit of hasty backtracking.

"Well, they didn't actually tell me as such." I hoped I sounded a lot more convincing than I felt. "That was the story going around the pub this lunchtime. But you know how it is once people have a couple of beers inside them. Everyone has a different version of what happened, each more outrageous than the last."

"So you didn't actually get to talk to the police? Did you speak to anyone at the scene?" His gravelly voice rasped with barely concealed irritation.

My Gran Latcham always used to say that not telling the whole truth was as bad as telling a lie. But then, she wasn't the one desperately fighting to hang on to a much-needed job, was she?

"I - um - I overheard someone in the bar talking about it. And I couldn't call you - or take your call, because as I've already explained, there's no signal. And I didn't have time to go and check it out when my shift finished because I've got to be in Little Mearefield this afternoon for the Flower Show -"

"Forget the bloody Flower Show," he snapped. "I've already made my thoughts clear in that respect, haven't I?"

"Well, yes, but -"

"As well as spelling out how I feel about 'yes butting'."

"Yes. Right. Of course you did. No 'yes butting'. I'm sorry. It's just that -"

He gave an impatient sigh. "Out with it. Just what?"

"It's just that Trevor Bidwell, the Chairman of the Flower Show, is one of the paper's biggest advertisers. He's the Bidwell of Bidwell's Bespoke Conservatories. You know, the great big advert that's always on the front page. He contacted the paper only last week to check we were going to send a reporter and a photographer to the show as usual. And to talk about his advertising budget for the coming year."

He gave another sigh. This one was marginally less impatient as his business brain obviously started doing the maths.

"No photographer. But you can cover it," he said. "Although I can't guarantee there'll be room to print it. Not with this murder -"

"They don't know it's murder," I reminded him.

"Not with this murder in the village," he carried on as if I hadn't spoken.

"But I don't think -"

"I'm not interested in what you think, sweetheart. And don't worry, I wasn't asking you to cover it. I wouldn't leave an important story like this to someone like you."

He didn't quite say 'a bumbling amateur like you', but I got the message.

"So who is covering it? You?" My heart sank as I thought of the way he'd 'sexed up' the peacock story.

"Not this one," he laughed. "I know my limitations. Remember I said how we've got a new editor lined up?"

"Yes." I didn't say that, as far as I was concerned, he couldn't start soon enough.

"Well, I've been in touch with him. And as soon as I told him there'd been another murder in Much Winchmoor -"

"That hasn't been confirmed."

"As soon as I told him about the yet to be confirmed murder in the village, he was dead keen to start right away."

"Really?"

"He's a real high-flying journalist, made his name as a crime reporter. Been turning out some great stuff for one of my other titles, including a whole series of articles about the murders in this part of the world."

I should have paid more attention to what he was saying. But at that moment, a passing white van ploughed through a puddle at the side of the road and sent a shower of muddy water all over me.

By the time I'd shaken my fist at the driver and wiped myself down, Mitch had ended the call. Now I'd have to waste precious time changing before heading off to my afternoon of fun at the Little Dreary field Flower Show.

I was looking forward to it as much as a turkey looks forward to Christmas.

…..

Was there was any point wasting precious petrol by driving to Little Mearefield when the chances were Mitch wouldn't even print it? I was sorely tempted to ring and say I couldn't make it. But Dilys Northcott, the woman who organised the show, was a poor, harassed creature who crept around apologising for the space she took up and looked as if she was constantly on the verge of tears. The chairman of the committee, Trevor Bidwell, was a bully who made her life a misery and would probably have blamed her for my no show. I couldn't do that to her.

Chances were, though, that by the time I'd written up my

copy and filed it, I'd be out of a job anyway. Just when I was beginning to think things were turning a corner for me and that the bank might start owing me money, rather than the other way around.

I couldn't even rely on the odd shift in Mum's salon, if what Elsie said was to be believed and the rest of her Grumble and Gossip Group were about to defect to this Crystal person.

Then, just to make my black Saturday complete, it started to rain. I mean, really rain. Not the steady drizzle we'd had most of the morning but big fat lumps of the stuff that splatted on the pavement and soaked into my thin jacket in seconds.

I whirled round at the beep of a horn behind me and was prepared to have a real go if it was the white van man who'd soaked me earlier. A mud-encrusted old Land Rover pulled up alongside me and my heart gave a little skip when I saw Will. And not just because he was about to save me a walk in the rain.

"Get in before you get soaked to the skin," he said.

I didn't need to be told twice.

"You look grim," he commented while I brushed enough straw to line a hen house off the passenger seat and scrabbled for the seat belt. "What's up?"

That's the thing about Will. He could always be guaranteed to say the right thing. Not.

I glared at him. "Thanks a bunch. You've made me feel a whole lot better."

"Sorry. I just meant, you look like you've lost a fiver and found a penny. What's wrong?"

I was about to reel off my long list of worries - Norina, Mitch, Elsie and Olive's defection to Crystal - when I remembered Paul McAllister. It put everything else into perspective.

"Did you hear about Paul?" I asked Will.

"Yeah. Dad told me. Some sort of horrible accident, wasn't it?"

"So they say. But I'm not so sure."

He gave me a look. "Katie?" he said in that tone of voice that always reminded me of my mum. "You're not getting involved in this, are you?"

"No way," I said quickly as I remembered the postie, grey faced and shaken. "And I told Mitch that."

"Mitch?"

"The new owner of The Chronicle."

He scowled. "I don't know why you bother writing for that rag. It's getting worse than ever. As for what you wrote about Gerald Crabshaw's hedge, what were you thinking of? You've probably made the whole thing a hundred times worse. And -"

"For goodness sake, Will," I cut in, furious that he, of all people, could have thought I was responsible for that rubbish. "You don't seriously think I wrote that stupid piece, did you?"

"Well, it had your name on it."

"And since when did I mis-spell my own name?"

"I just thought it was a typo."

"How could you even think I'd write something that crass," I hissed as I unclipped my seatbelt and reached for the door handle. "And don't bother with the lift. I can walk."

"Course I didn't," he said - and let me just say that Will is a very unconvincing liar. But I was too tired to argue. Besides, the rain was hosing down and I didn't fancy getting wet through to my underwear. Not when I had to turn around and go straight back out again.

"Ok," I muttered and clipped on the seat belt again.

"So who did write it?"

"Mitch. The new owner. He's sacked Mike and appointed himself acting editor. Only now he's brought in a new editor, which is something to be thankful for, I suppose. Anyway, Will, why aren't you off counting your sheep or whatever?"

"I finished early so thought I'd pop in the pub for a swift half - and to see you of course," he added quickly as a better-late-than-never afterthought. "Only when I got there the place was shut."

"I dare say Norina kicked everyone out. I left on the dot of two o'clock because I'm off to cover the Flower Show at Little Mearefield this afternoon. I don't suppose you'd drive me out there, would you? I'd get soaked on the scooter."

I gave him my sweetest, most beguiling smile. But it was

totally wasted on him.

"Sorry." He shook his head, looking anything but sorry. "I've got things to do this afternoon. But I'll see you tonight."

"Only if you're planning to spend the evening in the pub. I'm working."

He looked disappointed. "Can't you change your shift? Dad's out this evening. We'll have the place to ourselves for a bit."

"Tempting," I said, relishing the thought of the chance of some rare time alone with Will. "But I daren't. Norina's making noises about her niece from Wales, who is apparently just dying for the chance to leave the bright lights of Pontypridd and bury herself in the middle of nowhere."

Before he could answer, I realised the significance of what he'd just said. "What do you mean, your dad's going out tonight?"

After Will's mum, Sally, died a couple of years ago, John Manning went on a bender for several months and only sobered up when he found himself in a police cell, accused of murder. He was innocent, of course, and was released when the real murderer was discovered. But he'd been almost a recluse ever since which worried me.

He was a gentle, kind man and I was very fond of him. It bothered me to think of him, shutting himself off from everyone. So it was great to hear he was actually going out. "Is he going on a date?"

Will didn't appear to share my delight at the prospect. "Of course it's not a date," he growled. "Just someone he met up with in Glastonbury the other day. An old schoolfriend of Mum's by all account."

"So it's a woman?"

"Yes." His voice was clipped.

"Well, I hope it is a date." I reached across and took his hand. I held it for a moment between mine. "He needs to get out more, Will," I said gently. "It will be good for him. Your mum would have wanted him to. Have you met this woman?"

Will shook his head and pulled his hand away.

"Not interested," he said flatly and started the engine. It was a pretty effective way of ending a conversation. His old Land Rover was so noisy and rattly it was impossible to hear yourself think, least of all talk.

…..

Mum was sitting at the kitchen table, surrounded by tottering piles of paper, when I got in. She'd already heard the news about Paul McAllister.

"What a terrible thing to happen," she said. "A shocking accident."

"If it was an accident," I said.

"Katie!" She had exactly the same look as Will had earlier. Her words were almost identical too. "You're not getting involved, are you?"

"Of course I'm not." I said indignantly.

"I'm glad to hear it. Glad, too, that you're back early because I have a little job for you."

"Sorry. But I should have been at Little Drearyfield - I mean, Little Mearefield ten minutes ago. I told you this morning. The annual Flower and Vegetable Show. Remember?"

I hurried upstairs, did a quick change and grabbed my bag and notebook. Mum was still sitting at the table and the tottering piles of paper were now strewn all across it.

"You're not going out in this, are you?" she asked. "You'll get drowned."

I pulled a face as I looked out of the kitchen window where the rain was beating down on the wasteland that was all there was to show for what would one day be the sun terrace for Mum's new salon. Although at that moment it resembled a small swimming pool. Maybe she was thinking of adding mud therapy to her list of treatments on offer.

"I don't have much choice," I replied. "I made a big thing to the new boss about how important it was we should cover it. I can hardly turn around and say I didn't go because it was raining, can I?"

"You'd best take my car then," she said as I shrugged into my raincoat and reached for the pink sparkly helmet that I'd inherited, along with the scooter, from Shane's younger sister.

I turned around, slowly. The last time I borrowed Mum's car I managed to reverse it into a metal gate. And the car had come off worst. She'd vowed that was the last time I'd have her precious car. And, despite numerous times when I'd begged, pleaded and grovelled, she'd kept that vow as strictly as a Trappist monk.

And now she was offering me use of her precious car without me even asking? *Why?*

"On one condition -" she went on as my heart sank. She was going to ask me to work full time in the salon, wasn't she? Or pick out one of the meringue wedding dresses she'd been sighing over for the last six months.

"You're good with words, Katie." She pushed the papers to one side. "Better than me, that's for sure. I've just been told by the bank that I need to draw up a business plan before they'll even talk to me..." She waved her hand across the scattered papers. "I don't even know what a business plan is, least of all how to write one."

No wedding dresses or shifts in the salon, then. Words I could manage. Words were my thing.

"I'd love to," I said and really, really meant it. "We only need to Google 'business plans'. There are bound to be plenty of help on the internet. But do you mind if we leave it until tomorrow? I'm working this evening, remember?"

"You work too hard," Mum said. "It's not good for you. Everyone needs a little bit of down time and a social life. You never even have time to see Will these days."

"I saw him just now. As well you know, seeing as how you watched us draw up. I saw you twitching the curtains."

She gave me one of her looks. "Don't be silly. If the curtains twitched, that was because I was straightening them. I'm not in the habit of spying on people."

Her tone was as snippy as her look and I could see the offer of the car being withdrawn at any moment. Time, I reckoned, for a hasty change of subject.

"Will's Dad has got a date tonight," I said, hoping to divert her attention.

It worked. "Really? Who? Anyone we know?"

"According to Will, she's someone who used to go to school with Sally." I made a mental note to ask Elsie about it. "She'd moved away but has recently returned to the area. John bumped into her in Glastonbury apparently. Will didn't sound too happy about it."

Mum sighed. "He should be pleased his father is picking up the pieces of his life again."

"That's what I said," I said as she handed me her car keys. "Or words to that effect."

I didn't think she needed to know my actual words. She thought the sun shone out of Will and would always take his side against mine. Even the time he tied my plaits to the back of my chair on my first day at primary school. She said I shouldn't have pinched his rubber and should have handed it back when he asked for it.

"It would be good to see John happy again, wouldn't it?" she said, and I couldn't argue with that. "It would make things easier for Will, too."

"In what way?"

"Well, there would be nothing to stop you and Will getting married, would there?"

I stared at her. Sometimes, I wondered what planet my mother was on.

"John isn't stopping me and Will getting married," I said and realised, too late, I had walked into her trap.

"Then what is?" she asked.

I looked up at the kitchen clock. "Is that the time? I must go," I said. Before she could press me for an answer to a question that I didn't dare ask myself.

Least of all answer it.

Chapter Eleven

Little Mearefield, (or Little Drearyfield as I now thought of it) Annual Fruit and Vegetable Show was a total wash out in every sense of the word. The torrential rain had slowed to a steady drizzle, leaving everything soaking underfoot. I was so grateful to Mum for the use of her car, even though the journey to get there had been very much a 'heart in the mouth' experience.

It's a six-mile drive from Much Winchmoor to Little Drearyfield, across a stretch of dead flat moorland, criss-crossed by willow fringed, ruler-straight roads with right angle bends.

It's part of a stretch of land known as the Somerset Levels and Mum thinks it's beautiful. She's always banging on about the bird life and stuff and there are plenty of artists and photographers who agree with her. But to my mind, the moor is, at best boring and, at its worst, like now, quite scary.

The single-track road was lined with ditches (or rhines as they're known locally and pronounced to rhyme with beans) on either side. They're filled with brackish water deep enough to swallow a car particularly one as small as Mum's. There was also a distinct shortage of passing spaces along the single-track road, which didn't exactly make meeting oncoming traffic a fun experience. Especially if, like me, you're a bit rubbish at squeezing your car into tiny gateways.

The whole area is prone to flooding and in the winter months Little Drearyfield has been known to be cut off for weeks at a time. I drove slowly and carefully, horribly conscious that on either side of the road, the rhines were full and looked as if they were going to spill over at any moment.

The journey took much longer than I'd anticipated, and I began to worry they'd have all packed up and gone home by the time I got there. Particularly in view of the weather.

When I finally arrived, the field that had been designated as a car park had turned into a mud slide so that the few people who'd braved the conditions (and they were mostly those who'd entered things in the show) were having trouble getting their cars out and were having to wait while the local farmer towed them out with his tractor.

I parked Mum's car on the road and made my way to the almost empty show ground. I was looking for Dilys Northcott who would, hopefully, have the results ready for me. Every year her neatly typed lists of prize-winners made my job a doddle and earned me lots of lovely linage for very little effort.

"Excuse me," I called to a man with an unhappy looking Dalmatian on a lead. "I'm looking for Mrs Northcott."

"Over by the tea tent, love," he said. "In the white jacket."

The tea tent was a cheery orange gazebo, bedecked in home-made bunting. At least that's how it had looked in previous years. This year, after a couple of hours of continuous heavy rain, the cheery orange had faded to sulky salmon while the bunting hung, limp and forlorn, like dead leaves clinging to the branches of a tree in winter.

No wonder I hadn't recognised her. The Dilys Northcott of previous years wore long baggy cardigans and had lank mousey hair cut in a severe bob. But now her mousey hair was the colour of a well pickled red cabbage and she wore a smart white linen jacket and navy trousers.

"Hi, there," I said. "I didn't recognise you for a moment."

She looked blankly at me but was obviously too polite to say that she didn't know who I was either.

"I'm Kat Latcham. From The Chronicle. I've come for the results if they're ready."

"They're a bloody fix, that's what they are," grumbled the man with the Dalmatian. The dog at least was looking a bit more cheerful now he'd found a discarded burger bun to snaffle. His owner, not so much. "My runner beans beat everyone else's by a country mile," he went on. "But did they win? Of course not. But you can guess who won the sweet peas.... again! Can't you?"

"Really, Joe. I don't think you want to go around saying things like that. Especially in front of a member of the press." Dilys Northcott turned to me. "I wasn't expecting you in view of the weather. Isn't the road flooded?"

"Not yet. Although the rhines are looking pretty full. But if we get any more rain, they'll soon overflow."

"Oh dear." She bit her lip and looked as if she was about to burst into tears at any moment. "I thought - when you didn't come either, that the road to the village was flooded again. And that was why...." Her voice trailed away.

"It's not flooded at the moment. But it's looking increasingly likely. So I'd prefer not to hang around longer than I have to, if it's ok with you."

"What?" She gave me a blank look as if, for a moment, she'd forgotten I was there. "Oh yes, of course." She turned towards the tea tent. "I left the results in here for safe keeping. I'll just go and get them."

She disappeared inside the now empty tent and soon emerged carrying a neatly clipped pile of papers. But as she stepped outside there was a huge gust of wind and the sulky salmon gazebo gave a heave and a shake, the way Rosie does when she's wet. In doing so, the rainwater that had collected in the sagging top spilt out and emptied itself in one giant whoosh all over Dilys. And all over her carefully collated results list.

"Oh my god," someone shouted as Dilys screamed and let the soggy sheets of paper fall to the muddy ground. "She's bleeding."

I ran up to her. "Are you hurt?"

"Just - just startled," she managed to say when she'd caught her breath, while the red stain on her jacket got bigger and bigger. "And more than a little damp."

"But you're bleeding." I rummaged in my bag and took out a packet of tissues which I handed to her. "It's your face."

She took one, dabbed it to her face, then looked in horror as it came away red. Her hand went to her head. She smoothed her wet hair, then looked down at her palm.

"Oh no," she wailed.

"I'll call an ambulance" someone said.

Dilys looked more panicked than ever. "Oh no. No. Please don't. It's nothing, really."

She looked around the small crowd that had now gathered. Her eyes darted from side to side, like a trapped animal.

"No ambulance. I'm fine. It's just..." She looked down at the soggy results sheets now buried in the mud and her eyes filled with tears. "Oh no, I'm so sorry."

"Don't worry about it." I took her arm and led her gently away from all those curious eyes. Because I knew only too well what the problem was.

Not blood. But a temporary hair colourant. You know, the sort you spray on for an evening out, then wash out the next day. Wash out being the operative word here.

"Come on then," I said to Dilys as I handed her the rest of my tissues. "Let's get that lovely jacket off before it's completely ruined and then I'll run you home."

"That's so kind," Dilys was saying as we picked our way across the muddy field. "I really appreciate -"

She stopped abruptly in front of my mother's car and gasped.

Now, Mum's car often gets commented on, usually disparagingly. It is bright bubblegum pink, with *Chez Cheryl, Your Hair, Our Care*, picked out in silver sparkly letters all down the side. Mum's idea of getting the message 'out there' which would be fine only the car never went further than ten miles from Much Winchmoor, so 'out there' didn't extend very far. A bit of a marketing fail, that one. But at least there was no chance of the car getting stolen by boy racers.

"This is your car?" Dilys asked.

"It's my mother's," I said. It was still raining, only not quite so heavily, and I thought it was a bit off of her to be so choosy about her mode of transport.

Dilys' hand flew to her mouth. "You're Cheryl's daughter? Cheryl from Chez Cheryl? Oh no. Oh dear, no." She shook her head and backed away.

"Look, if you're worried about getting the seats wet, it doesn't matter. Mum will understand..." I began, my fingers crossed firmly behind my back as I wasn't at all sure Mum would.

But Dilys continued to shake her head. "No. It's all right. I'll walk, thank you."

"But you're soaked through."

"Then a bit more rain isn't going to make any difference, is it? And I only live up the road there, just past the church. You've been so kind. So very kind. I - I didn't realise - I'm so sorry. I really, really appreciate your kindness. And I'll get that results list to you as soon as possible. It's just that - oh dear, nothing's gone right for me today." She wasn't really talking to me anymore but muttering away to herself. "This is all my fault. I should have known he wouldn't - I've been so stupid -" She bit her lip then turned and scuttled away, still muttering.

Talk about a waste of an afternoon. I'd left my shift early and incurred Norina's wrath and all for nothing. Dilys wasn't the only one having a bad day. Although at least my hair colour (I'd gone for a rainbow of pastel shades that day) had stayed in place.

But my black afternoon did at least end on a slightly upbeat note. Or two if you count the fact that it had finally stopped raining at last as one. The second one was a run in with Gerald Crabshaw.

As I was driving back along the High Street, I saw him. He was on foot and had just turned into Mill Lane. The blue and white police tape was still across the entrance to the path between the two houses and it fluttered and rustled in the stiff breeze that had sprung up.

I got out of the car and called after him. "Gerald? I wondered if you'd be interested in giving me a statement in the light of this morning's tragedy. Would you like to take back what you said about your neighbour? Or do you have anything to add to the account you gave me last week?"

He whirled round, his small piggy eyes narrowing as he saw me. "I've nothing to say to you."

"That's a bit different to last week, isn't it?" I said. "Then, you couldn't stop talking."

"That was before I was all but accused of murder," he

snapped. "And it's all your fault. Twisting my words like that. I've had the police on my back all morning. But I managed to convince them that Paul - God rest his dear soul - and I were on excellent terms and that you'd made the whole thing up to sell your wretched newspaper."

The idea of Gerald having the police on his back all morning gave me the kind of warm, fuzzy glow I usually only get from a couple of glasses of Prosecco.

"So you now admit he wasn't the one who vandalised your hedge, do you?" I allowed myself the luxury of a small smirk. "Can I quote you on that? And do you have any idea who did then?"

He glowered at me without speaking while his face went the colour of Dilys' hair before the deluge. Then he snarled. "The sooner the Chronicle building is demolished and turned into a housing estate, the happier I'll be."

With that, he stormed off. I hadn't really expected him to have anything useful to say and, in truth, was only winding him up. So I went home, stripped off my wet clothes and stood under the hot shower, trying to wash away the disappointments of the day.

I'd have given anything to have spent the evening with Will, just the two of us and was really not looking forward to another deadly dull evening stuck behind the bar, watching the hands of the clock inch their way with agonising slowness towards closing time.

I was thankful that Gino had banned Martin Naylor. At least things would be better without his annoying presence. And his even more annoying mobile phone.

***

The talk in the bar that evening hadn't moved on very far from lunchtime's main topic. Only this time the stories were more and more outrageous, and I half expected to hear that the latest theory being chewed over was that Paul had been abducted by aliens.

Gerald Crabshaw didn't come in for his usual early evening

drink. He probably couldn't face the thought of the third degree he'd get from the regulars. Some claimed he'd been taken into custody. But I didn't bother to put them right.

The one thing the 'incident' had done, however, was to boost the number of customers as word got around the village and surrounding area of another as yet unexplained death in Much Winchmoor, the so called 'murder capital of Somerset'.

Even my dad, who'd defected to the Black Swan along with the rest of the skittles team, was back in his customary place at the far end of the bar.

"Here, there was someone in here earlier looking for you, Katie," Shane said as he came up to the bar for another pint. The two Neanderthals were, as always, hovering around.

"Said he was looking for Kat Latcham," Neanderthal One said. "We told him, the only cat around here is called Pitbull."

"And he's been missing for over a week now," chirped Neanderthal Two, pushing his empty glass hopefully in Shane's direction. "Maybe we should set our Miss Marple here on the case. Here, do you reckon Pitbull's been murdered as well?"

I ignored them as did Shane. He also ignored their outstretched glasses. He'd been caught by them too many times.

"Did he leave his name? Or say what he wanted?" I asked Shane.

If he was asking for Kat Latcham then it had to be something connected with the paper. I wondered if it could be Runner Bean man, ready to spill the beans (I couldn't resist the pun there) on Sweet Pea-gate.

"No. He did say he'd be back later, though."

The bar was suddenly filled with strains of *Are You Lonesome Tonight* as the door from the kitchen swung open and Gino bustled in, his round face wreathed in smiles.

"Is very busy tonight, Katie *bach*" he said as he handed me a jug. "This make Norina very happy. And if she happy, then I am *molto* happy. Kitchen going flat out. She need more beer."

"Really?" I laughed as I filled the jug. "Last time I looked, she was drinking gin and orange."

He shook his head. "Is not for her to drink, is for the fish."

"You're feeding beer to the fish?"

"Now I know you tease," he said with a smile. "You know well is for batter for cooking fish. Everyone wants fish and the chips tonight." He raised his eyebrows. "You English and your precious fish and the chips."

"Norina does make very good fish and chips." I said, trying not to think about how little I'd had to eat that day.

"She also make very good pasta." He sighed. "She get very frustrated always cooking the fish and chips."

"Well, anyway, it's good to see the pub busy. And good to see you smiling again, Gino," I said as I handed him the jug. "And, of course, singing."

"Ah yes, the singing." His smile faded for a moment. "What he said, it wasn't true."

"Sorry? What who said?"

"That Martin Naylor. His wife came in this afternoon to fetch his car. And to pay his bar bill. And she ask me if I was coming to choir rehearsal on Wednesday." He beamed. "She'd hardly do that if she thought my singing was terrible, would she?"

"Of course she wouldn't," I said. He looked so pleased with himself, like a little boy who'd just come first in the egg and spoon race that, without thinking, I reached across and patted him on the hand.

I was happy for him. Although not so sure about what it would mean for the fledgling Much Winchmoor choir. His singing could verge on the over enthusiastic side at times, but as long as Suzanne avoided any Elvis songs (his absolute favourite) they should be all right.

"That's totally awesome, Gino." I gave his hand a squeeze just as the kitchen door swooshed open. Gino leapt back as if he'd been stung by an angry wasp.

"Gino! In here with that beer now!" Norina snapped while the look she gave me said, "I'll deal with you later."

Gino scampered after her so quickly he was in danger of spilling most of the beer before it reached the kitchen. As he disappeared into the kitchen the door from the car park opened and a tall, slim man in faded jeans and a white linen shirt came in.

"Hello again," Shane said to him then turned to me. "This is the guy I was telling you about, Katie. And I've just remembered what he said his name was. It was -"

"Liam." I said. "His name's Liam."

His eyes were as bright a blue as I remembered. His hair a little longer. And he still had the same slightly crooked smile.

"Hello, Kat Latcham," he said softly. And his voice - oh, his voice. It had that soft musical lilt that makes you think of gentle Irish rain falling on emerald fields. Liam O'Connor could read the back of a cornflakes packet and make it sound like a poem.

"What are you doing here, Liam?" I managed to ask, even though my heart was thudding so violently it was threatening to choke me.

"Well, first off, hoping for a drink. That's what people usually come in a pub for, isn't it? What do you have here that's remotely drinkable? And please don't say the cider."

"Hardly," I said. "Ferrets' Kneecaps is good tonight. It's a fresh barrel."

"I'll have a pint of that then please."

"So what brings you to this part of the world?" I asked, as I pulled on the handle of the beer pump. "Or are you just passing through?"

"I'm not passing through. I've got a job. In Dintscombe."

I stared at him. "But last I heard, you were in London. Why Dintscombe?"

I knew the answer before he told me. There was a sick feeling in my stomach as I waited for him to confirm it.

"Did you not know? You're looking at the new editor of the Dintscombe Chronicle, so you are."

Chapter Twelve

There are times when I'd have been delighted to be proved wrong. This was one of them.

The last time Liam and I had spoken had not been a happy occasion. A few weeks prior to that, he'd asked me to give him an on the spot account of my encounter with a murderer - and when I said no, that I didn't want to talk about it, he made it all up anyway. And printed something I'd told him in confidence that he'd assured me was 'strictly off the record' to add insult to injury.

Liam was as trustworthy around what he considered a news story as Rosie the Labrador was with an unguarded plate of sausages.

I'd been furious with him over what I considered a betrayal of my trust. The sharp exchange that followed had ended with him saying, "Call yourself a journalist? I wouldn't employ you if you were the last person on earth."

Given the stressful circumstances I was pretty pleased with my retort that if I was the last person on earth, there would be no need for journalists.

Pity he didn't stay on the line long enough to hear it.

And now, this guy who'd vowed he wouldn't give me a job if I was the last person on earth was about to become my boss? I stared at him without moving for several long seconds.

"Well," he said with that little twisted smile he was so good at. "Are you going to give me my pint - or am I going to wear it?"

"Sorry," I handed him his pint and took his money. I turned my back on him as I went to the till, thankful for the chance to pull myself together.

It took several goes to get my head in gear enough to pick out the correct change.

"So-" My voice, I was surprised to hear, sounded cool and steady, and I had to stop and think for a moment if it really was me speaking. "You're the 'ace crime reporter' Mitch was talking about when he said he was bringing in a new editor. But I thought you hated this part of the world and couldn't get away quick enough?"

"And why would I be saying something like that?"

Because I beat you to a story once and you never got over it? I could have said. Instead I just shrugged as I counted out his change.

"Besides," he went on, "Mitch is a very difficult man to say no to, in case you hadn't noticed."

"Yeah." I met his eyes and there was a momentary connection between us as we shared the same thought. "I know what you mean."

"I wasn't due to start for a couple of weeks. Was planning to nip across to Ireland to see the folks. But when Mitch said there'd been yet another unexplained death in Much Winchmoor, that did it for me. What is it about this place? Must be something in the water." He looked down at his pint then added, "Or the beer."

He gave a wry smile and lifted an eyebrow, in a way that I remembered way too well. "Then when I learnt that you were still here," he went on, "Well, I couldn't stay away, could I now?"

I wasn't about to point out that the last time we'd spoken we hadn't exactly parted on the best of terms. If he'd forgotten, I sure as heck wasn't going to remind him.

"If you're referring to Paul McAllister's death," I said, "The police are pretty sure it was nothing more than a tragic accident."

"That's not what I heard." He picked up his pint and took a sip. "Hmm, that's not bad at all."

"What did you hear?" I asked. "Have the police now realised it couldn't have been an accident?"

He looked across at me, his eyes an intense blue. "Do I take it from that then you don't think it was accidental death?"

I was about to tell him how the idea of Paul's death being an accident didn't sit right with me and my reasons for thinking that. But then I remembered who I was talking to. "I wouldn't know, would I? The police wouldn't tell me anything."

I turned away to serve another customer. When I'd finished Liam beckoned me over.

"When I was in here earlier, I was told there'd been a bit of aggro between the deceased and one of the locals. I couldn't believe it when I heard that the guy he'd fallen out with was none other than our good friend, the disgraced ex-councillor Crabshaw."

"You should know better than to listen to pub gossip. But then," I added, unable to keep the bitterness out of my voice, even though I'd promised myself I wasn't going to have a dig at him. "You've never been one to let the truth stand in the way of a good story, have you Liam?"

He gave me a long, level stare. Then he grinned, picked up his glass and took a long, slow drink.

"I think we need to have a little talk about whether or not you and I are going to be able to work together, Kat Latcham, don't you?" he said softly as he leaned across the counter towards me, so close I caught the faint, citrussy tang of his cologne.

I flushed and stepped back. "I'm busy," I said, as I saw Norina glaring at me through the little diamond shaped window in the kitchen door.

"I didn't mean now. How about tomorrow? I hear there's a half decent coffee shop in Dintscombe now. Or would you rather meet up somewhere for lunch? My treat. On expenses."

"Coffee will be fine. I assume you mean Pickwicks, on the High Street? Just down from the Post Office. Or, at least, from where the Post Office used to be."

"Probably." He tossed back the rest of his pint and placed the empty glass back on the counter. "Tomorrow it is, then. About eleven?"

Without waiting for my answer, he turned and headed for the door. As he reached for the handle, the door swung open and Will came in. The two men exchanged glances that were far from friendly.

"Wasn't that- ?" Will began.

"Liam O'Connor." I said.

His scowl deepened. "Not that smooth talking Irishman who nearly got you killed?"

"Yes and no."

"Meaning?"

"Yes, it's that smooth talking Irishman and no, he didn't nearly get me killed."

"You've got a short memory," he muttered. "What's he doing here? I thought we'd seen the last of him."

"He's back working for The Chronicle. He's going to be my new boss, apparently."

From the look on his face, I could see Will was as unhappy at the prospect as I was. "For pity's sake, Katie. Tell me you're not getting mixed up with him again."

"I said he was my new boss, not my new best friend. The usual?" I asked, as I reached for a glass and swiftly changed the subject. "So, did your dad go on his date? Where was he going?"

He shrugged. "Haven't a clue. All I know was that he was all spruced up and wearing a shirt I'd never seen before. It looked like he'd bought it especially."

"Well, I for one hope he has a good time. And so should you."

By the time I'd served a customer down the other end of the bar, Will had taken himself off to the table in the window where Shane was sitting. Rosie was pressed against Shane's leg, on high alert, her eyes focussed with laser like precision on the open packet of crisps on the table in front of them. It was like she thought she could move them from the table to her mouth by sheer power of thought.

"Do you fancy a trip to the coast tomorrow morning?" Will asked later when he came up for a couple of pints for him and Shane and more crisps for Rosie. "We could go to the beach cafe for lunch. The weather forecast's looking better and Dad owes me some time off."

I sighed. "I'd love to, Will. But I can't. I'm supposed to be meeting Liam in Dintscombe for coffee and what he calls 'a

86

little chat' about my future tomorrow morning, which sounds ominous. And Mum wants me to help her write a business plan for the bank manager so that's the morning sorted. But we could go there for the afternoon."

"Forget it," he muttered with a frown. "It was a dumb idea."

"No. It was a great idea and I could -" but before I could finish, someone rapped on the bar to get my attention. As I did so, Will picked up the drinks and the crisps and went back to Shane and the ever-hopeful Rosie.

I didn't get the chance to talk to him again until we were walking home, after closing time.

I took his hand as we walked along. "I'm really sorry about tomorrow, Will."

"It's ok," he said. "We can do it another time."

As we walked past the village pond, he stopped and turned towards me. The earlier rain had now passed, and the cloudless sky was studded with stars. It was so clear that the moon's reflection spread like a ribbon of silver satin across the almost still surface of the pond.

"Katie - I mean, Kat," he said quickly before I could interrupt. "You and me - we are good, aren't we?"

I stood on tiptoe and brushed my lips against his cheek. He didn't need expensive citrussy cologne to smell good. He smelled of grassy meadows and clean, fresh air, even when it was overlaid, as now, with the scent of a couple of pints of Ferrets' Kneecaps Best Bitter.

"We're good." My voice came out as little more than a husky whisper as he turned his face towards mine, so close that I could feel the warmth of his breath on my lips.

He gave a little groan, bent his head and kissed me. As he did so everything in my world, that had seemed so out of kilter and upside down, suddenly righted itself.

It didn't matter what Liam was going to say to me tomorrow. It didn't matter that Norina was probably going to sack me the moment her niece arrived from Wales. It didn't even matter that no one, apart from Shane, wanted to pay me to walk their dogs.

All that mattered was that Will and I were 'good'. And, oh

yes, did I mention that he was, without doubt, the best kisser on the planet?

As we reached the end of our road, a car drove past, gave a little peep of the horn and slowed down.

"That's your dad, isn't it?"

"It is." Will waved to say that he didn't want a lift and John Manning drove on.

"I hope everything went all right for him this evening."

"Believe it or not, so do I," Will said. "It's not that I don't want him to be happy because of course I do. Or that I can't bear the thought of someone replacing Mum."

"Then what is it?" I asked gently.

"It's that woman. She's not right for him, Katie. Tottery high heels, tattoos, leopard skin skirt that just about covers her decency. Made up to the nines. He couldn't have picked someone more different to Mum if he'd tried."

"Perhaps he did just that," I suggested. "And you shouldn't judge people by their appearance. You never know. She might be very nice."

Will shrugged.

I looked at our house, in total darkness. "Looks like Mum and Dad have gone to bed," I said as I smiled up at him. "Would you like to come in? For a ..." I paused and stepped closer to him. "For a coffee? Or something?"

"Or something sounds good to me," he said as he wrapped his arms around me.

And it was. 'Or something' was good. It was very good.

***

The sun was streaming in through my bedroom window when I woke next morning, still glowing from the memory of Will and the 'or something' from last night.

It was, I decided, a perfect morning for a run, unlike the day before. My happy mood dipped though when I realised that, this morning there was no chance of a cheery exchange of greetings with Paul McAllister out on his morning bike ride.

When I got back, Mum and Dad were already up. Dad was

working away in the new extension while Mum was in the kitchen, papers strewn across the table yet again.

"You were in late last night," she commented, as she reached for the biscuit tin. Things were obviously not going any better for her if she was still on the Chocolate Hobnob diet.

"The pub was packed. Nothing like a sudden death to drag people away from their tellies." I looked down at the paper strewn table and her precious little blue book, where she keeps all her customers' details, open in front of her. "Have you made a start on the business plan?"

"I'm doing my accounts. It doesn't matter how many times I add it up, the answer still comes out the same. It doesn't make pretty reading, that's for sure. I don't know what's happened." She flicked through the pages of her book. "I've been through every page. People are cancelling left right and centre. I'm losing customers by the day. It can't just be a coincidence."

I reached for the biscuit tin, only to find it was empty.

"Oh, sorry, love." She pushed her chair back and went across to the cooker. "I took the last biscuit, I'm afraid. I can make you some scrambled eggs if you like?"

"No, it's fine." I wasn't that hungry. Mum's the only person I know who can scramble a couple of eggs and make them look and taste old socks. She sat back down, and I took the chair opposite her. I wasn't looking forward to what I was about to tell her.

"Mum, what you said just now about all those cancellations not being a coincidence. I was talking to Elsie and Olive yesterday -"

"Did you mention it's time for them to come in for their perms?"

"No. Because -" I swallowed. She wasn't going to like this. Not one little bit. "Because they've already had their perms. By a mobile hairdresser called Crystal. She comes to their house and is, according to Olive, cheaper than you."

Mum stared at me in astonishment. "A mobile hairdresser? Here in Much Winchmoor? Who is she?"

"They said she'd recently moved to the area from up north

somewhere. They didn't say where exactly. Mind you, that could be anywhere in the country. 'Up North' to Elsie and Olive means anywhere north of Bristol."

There was a time when Mum would have smiled at this. But not that morning. She looked seriously worried. "So how much did this Crystal person charge?"

"They didn't say that either. But I have to say, I didn't think much of her handiwork. Olive looked like an overstuffed cauliflower while Elsie's hair looked like a Brillo pad that's been plugged in to an electric socket."

It's a measure of how distracted Mum was that she didn't pull me up on my less than flattering descriptions.

"And talking about weird hairdos," I went on as I suddenly remembered poor drenched Dilys from Little Drearyfield. "Is Dilys Northcott one of your customers?"

"From Little Mearefield. Yes, she is." Mum bit her lip. "Or should I say was?"

"Well, I don't know whether Dilys has defected to Crystal or if she went in for a bit of home colouring, but she got caught in the rain yesterday - no, that's not quite right. She got a gazebo full of rainwater tipped over her head. And the colour from her hair poured out and all over her clothes."

Mum looked thoughtful. "Poor woman. She must have been using that spray on temporary stuff. Even a home hair colourant wouldn't have run like that. Not if it was applied properly. Anyway," she said briskly as she closed her little blue book with a decided snap. "It's no good crying over lost customers. What I need, as you so rightly said the other day, is new ones. When my new spa is up and running, the place will be buzzing, you'll see. Your dad's nearly finished the interior and if that young Ed Fuller finally gets round to keeping his promise to do the sun terrace, it's all going to look amazing. Once the word gets around, people will be flocking here."

I glanced up at the kitchen clock. "I've got to go into Dintscombe in a minute. I'm meeting -" I stopped. I didn't want to tell her that I was meeting Liam. Her reaction to the sound of his name would probably be similar to Will's. "I'm meeting The Chronicle's new editor."

"On a Sunday? That doesn't sound right to me."

I shrugged. "He's the boss. And then, of course, when I get back I'm going to have to clean your car. The roads around Little Drearyfield were a bit muddy, by the time the tractor had been up and down a few times. Unless, of course...?" I paused.

"Why do I have the feeling I'm not going to like this?" Mum asked.

"I was only going to say, why don't I take your car in to Dintscombe and put it through the car wash?"

"And here's you always telling me how hard up you are and yet you're willing to waste money on a car wash," she grumbled. "When there's a perfectly good bucket and sponge in the garage."

"Well? I should be an hour at the most in Dintscombe and it means that when I get back, I'll have time to work on your business plan. I've already had some thoughts I'd like to run past you."

Which was why, after years of not being allowed anywhere near my mum's pink glittery car, I found myself in the driving seat for the second consecutive day.

Only this time I wasn't scared as I drove across the almost flooded moor. This time I was more scared about whether or not I was about to lose my job.

Chapter Thirteen

The queue for the car wash was a mile long so I had to give up on that. Did people have nothing better to do on a Sunday morning, I wondered, than sit in a queue for a car wash?

Liam was already in the coffee shop when I arrived. He was sitting at a table in the window, his long legs stretched out into the aisle.

"I see your parking hasn't improved any," he said in an unfair reference to what I'd thought had been a pretty neat bit of parallel parking - if you don't count the front nearside wheel being slightly on the pavement, that is.

But before I could think of a suitable retort, he went on. "I can't believe your mum still has that car."

I thought back to the day when the two of us had sat in it, Liam's long legs scrunched up, so that his knees were almost touching his chin.

I'd been so eager to impress him that day. So keen to show that I was a smart, going somewhere journalist. It felt like nothing had changed since then.

Apart from the fact that now I didn't trust him farther than I could throw him, of course.

"So, what'll you have?" he asked.

"A straight black Americano, please."

He raised an eyebrow. "Funny. I'd have you down as a cappuccino girl," he said as he got up to go to the counter. "Anything to eat?"

As soon as he mentioned it, I realised I was starving, and Mum had taken the last Chocolate Hobnob. "Could I have a chocolate brownie please?"

"Not watching your weight then?" He grinned.

"Why?" I was instantly on the defensive. "Do you think I should be?"

"God, no. Of course not. You look as lovely as ever, Kat Latcham. I see you haven't lost your –" his glance lingered on my hair. "- your penchant for the unusual."

Dilys' failed experiment with spray on hair colourant had inspired me to brighten up my own hair. The pastel rainbow was, I reckoned, a tad subdued. And I didn't want to be seen as subdued. Not today. I needed to come across as confident and out there. So I'd added a stripe in shade of green so vivid it would have made Kermit the Frog envious. It looked pretty cool, although I made a mental note to avoid walking anywhere near waterlogged gazebos.

I watched Liam as he crossed the room, and I noticed I wasn't the only one to do so. A couple of girls on the next table stopped staring at their phones long enough to eye him up.

They were still doing so as he came back with the brownie and coffees - black Americano for me, cappuccino for him. They looked across at me as if trying to work out what on earth a hot bloke like him was be doing with a green haired weirdo like me.

He pushed the brownie across to me and sat down opposite.

"So," he said, stirring the froth into his cappuccino. "Here we are again, Kat Latcham. Who'd have thought it? I thought you were as keen to get away from this place as I was?"

I shrugged and put my fork into the brownie. It was a good one, soft and squidgy in the middle, slightly crispy on the outside. Exactly how I like it. As the rich dark chocolate melted in my mouth, I felt some of the tension begin to slip away. Chocolate does it for me every time. It even made me forget, just for a moment, that I was probably about to lose my job. And instead allowed me to make out like we were two old friends, catching up on old times over cake and coffee.

"Yeah, well, things don't always turn out the way you want them to, do they?" I looked across at him then gestured at my plate. "This is really good. Want some?"

He shook his head. "I'm good, thanks. So you've been working for Mike North all this time? But I see you're still freelance. No chance of a staff job then?"

My heart leapt. "You offering?" I asked quickly.

"Not at the moment. Mitch is keeping us all on a very tight rein for now. But if we can make a go of things, get the circulation up to decent levels, then who knows?"

I liked the way he said 'we'. I liked it very much. It made it sound like we were a team and gave me a warm glow. I took another forkful of chocolate and shot a smug glance at the two girls on the next table. But they'd already gone back to their phones.

When I'd arrived, I thought it was to be told he didn't want me on his 'team'. But now, it was beginning to look as if things might, just might, work out after all.

"I'm seeing Mitch tomorrow morning," he went on. "And one of the things he wants us to do is go through all the freelancers. Check out which ones we'll hang on to and which we'll let go. You're in luck, Kat, with this latest murder, there's going to be plenty to write about. It's come just at the right time for us."

His attitude hit a jarring note, but I reminded myself that he hadn't known Paul.

Nevertheless, I couldn't stop myself from commenting. "It was anything but the right time for Paul McAllister."

He paused in the act of putting his cup to his lips and carefully put it back on the table as he looked at me, a challenge in his eyes.

"Are you saying you don't want to cover the murder?" he asked.

"So he was murdered? Do you know that for sure?"

"It would appear so." He lowered his voice and leaned into me. He was wearing the same citrussy cologne he'd been doing the night before. "They've found evidence that points definitely towards murder."

I dropped my fork with a clatter. It gave me no pleasure to discover I'd been right after all.

"What sort of evidence, do you know?" It was a struggle to keep my voice at a whisper and not shriek so the whole coffee shop could hear.

"This isn't for general release so I'm relying on you to keep it to yourself. But they found that a trip-wire had been deliberately rigged up across the path. It caught in the spokes of his bike as he rode along and that was how he came to fall off. As he did so, he fell on to one of the metal posts from the broken fence. It caught the poor fellow right in the throat. According to my source, it all but decapitated him."

I stared at him in horror. No wonder the poor postie had looked so green around the gills. I pushed my half-eaten brownie away. Suddenly, my gills felt pretty green too as my appetite deserted me. My chocolate induced feel good factor had completely vanished.

"Do they know who put the wire there?" I asked.

"Do you?" He turned the question back on me. "Tell me about the row between him and Gerald Crabshaw. I read your account of it."

"I didn't write that," I said quickly.

"No. I didn't think you had." He gave a quick grin. "It had Mitch's killer touch all over it. But I was talking to a couple of fellows in the pub last night who told me that Crabshaw had nearly come to blows with Paul McAllister over this silly hedge."

"Who was that? I didn't see you talking to anyone."

"That's because you weren't there at the time. I went in earlier, spoke to these fellows, who were really quite chatty after I'd bought them a pint of cider each -"

"I can guess who you were talking to, then," I said. "And you don't want to believe everything they say. No. Forget that. You don't want to believe *anything* they say."

"Anyway, they said you'd be in later, so I thought I'd go around and have a look at this hedge myself. But I couldn't get that close though as the police still have it cordoned off. That's when I realised that there really was a story here."

"I never thought it was an accident," I said and told him how Paul McAllister knew about the dangerous spike and would never have ridden into it accidentally.

"So, from what I hear, Gerald was threatening all sorts of things," Liam said. "They said you were there when it all kicked off."

"I was," I admitted. "And yes, he was pretty pumped up.

But you must remember what he's like, Liam. He was just showing off to the rest of the people in the bar. Playing the hard man."

"Sounds like he wasn't playing, though," Liam said. "The police are pretty damn sure they have some evidence. They won't say what, obviously. But my source said they're pretty confident they'll be making an arrest soon."

"They've got evidence against Gerald?" I couldn't believe it. But Gerald himself had told me the police had him marked down as a suspect. And he had been very angry with Paul. But would he kill him over something as trivial as a peacock-shaped hedge? It seemed a tad extreme, even for him.

"My source didn't name him. But who else could it be? He was heard to make threats."

I shook my head. "Even so, I can't really see Gerald doing a thing like that. He's all mouth and trousers."

Liam looked mystified. "He's what?"

"All mouth and trousers. Don't they say that in Ireland?"

He shook his head. "Not the bit where I come from, that's for sure."

"It's what my grandmother used to say." I smiled as I remembered her describing a certain politician that way. She had a few other, even more colourful things to say about said politician, but that was another story. "It just means someone who's all talk and no action"

But then, as I was saying this, I thought back to Friday evening, in the bar. After he'd had the set-to with Paul. What was it he'd said? Something about, "if he fell off that damned bike and I found him dead in a ditch I'd step right over him." And then he'd preened, tweaked his so-called regimental tie and muttered something vaguely threatening.

I'd thought it was just Gerald and his nonsense, nothing more than a bit of hot air, because Paul had dared to stand up to him. Coming on strong to save a bit of face.

Was that really what had happened? Had Gerald found Paul dead in a ditch? Or had he put him there? I couldn't see him squaring up to Paul, face to face. But setting a trap for him, stretching a tripwire across the path, knowing that he wouldn't see it and fall off. That was certainly his style.

And he hadn't exactly contradicted the Neanderthals when they'd said how he'd been trained to kill, had he? Just smirked and muttered something how people shouldn't mess with him. I'd thought it was just another of Gerald's stories. But suddenly, I wasn't so sure.

Certainly he had motive and, of course, opportunity.

But even Gruesome Gerald, no matter how wound up he was, wouldn't kill someone because of a hedge. Would he?

But what if it hadn't been about the hedge? What if the thing with the peacock had been the final straw, the one that finally pushed him over the edge?

What if this had been about Mill Cottage with its four good sized bedrooms? He'd made no secret of the fact that he was furious with Paul when he'd decided to live in the cottage after his father died instead of selling it, as he'd promised to Gerald who'd been planning to use the cottage to expand their Guest House.

With Paul out of the way, the cottage would go back on the market. And this time, presumably, Gerald would be able to buy it.

"Well?" Liam asked. "I can see from your face that you're beginning to have second thoughts. Do you think our favourite ex-councillor has gone too far this time?"

"I can't believe it would have been him." I hoped I sounded more convinced than I felt. Because he had been very, very angry with Paul. Angrier than I'd ever seen him.

"But if it wasn't him, then who was it?" Liam asked. "You must hear things, working in that bar. People say all sorts of careless things, particularly when they've had a few. And they never really notice the barman - or, in your case, the barmaid, listening. Although, I have to say, in your case and in that blue sparkly thing you were wearing last night, you're pretty hard to ignore."

I flushed, unable to work out if he was paying me a compliment or not. I liked the fact that he'd noticed what I was wearing though. Will wouldn't notice if I turned up in a crinoline and wellington boots.

"I'll bet they tell you things, don't they?" he went on. "Things that probably, when they're sober, they wish they hadn't."

"Believe me, Liam," I said wearily, "Most of the stuff I hear behind the bar is total rubbish, I promise you. And most of it they won't remember saying the next morning anyway."

"They might not remember. But you would, wouldn't you?"

"Yes. But I wouldn't write about it," I said with a flash of anger. "I don't put words in people's mouths. Unlike you."

There was a long pause. "You're still on about that, aren't you?"

"You printed things I'd told you in confidence." The memory of that awful piece he'd written in one of Mitch's more lurid publications, still smarted. *"How I outwitted not one but two murderers, while the police looked on" says plucky local girl in Somerset's notorious murder village.*

People in the village cold shouldered me for weeks after that, apart from Elsie Flintlock, of course, who'd thoroughly enjoyed the whole thing. The effect it had had on my dog walking business was nothing short of disastrous when the vicar refused to let me walk his Cockerpoo anymore, no doubt worried I would corrupt the poor creature.

As for Grandma Kingham, she claimed she'd almost had to resign from her bridge club due to the shame of it all. That's my mother's mother, of course. My other grandmother, Gran Latcham, would, like Elsie (the two had been great friends) have thoroughly enjoyed the whole thing if she'd still been around.

"Have you any idea how difficult it was for me to face people in the village, after that came out?"

"I'm sorry," he said, although he looked as sorry as Rosie does when she's snaffled the contents of the kitchen bin. "I didn't realise you still lived in the village when I wrote that. You told me you couldn't wait to leave the place."

"But that shouldn't have made any difference. It was still betraying a confidence."

"I'm really sorry if I caused you any problem. I'd like to make it up to you. We're a good team, you and I, Kat.

Remember?"

"Until you accused me of pinching 'your' story," I reminded him.

A flicker of annoyance darkened his eyes. Then he smiled. "That was just a professional difference of opinion. This time, we're on the same side, aren't we? Unless, of course, you want to see The Chronicle closed down and a housing estate built on the site."

"Of course I don't."

"I didn't think so. So, all I'm asking you to do, Kat, is use your local knowledge. Ask around. Give me some background stuff on Paul McAllister and Gerald Crabshaw. I would certainly like a bit more detail about this interview you did with McAllister. You did interview him, didn't you?"

"Of course I did. I'm not in the habit of only giving one side of a story. It's just that Paul was adamant he didn't want to be quoted."

He shrugged. "Well, that's hardly going to bother him now, is it? Go back to your notebook -" he broke off and gave me a searching look. "You did take notes, didn't you?"

"Of course!" I said indignantly.

"That's fine, then. You should have plenty of material. So I'll look forward to seeing what you come up with. As soon as possible, please."

He picked up his cup and took a sip of coffee, all the time never taking his eyes off me. I felt like he was testing me. Seeing if I was up to the job.

Was I? This was my chance to put the record straight as far as Paul was concerned, to write up the interview as it had really happened.

After I'd spoken to Elsie Flintlock, of course. She was, after all, my go to source when it came to local gossip and I was hoping she'd fill me in on Paul McAllister's background.

Chapter Fourteen

I drove back home via the car wash, which was now a lot quieter than it had been earlier. It was almost lunchtime when I finally parked Mum's shiny clean car outside the house.

Dad was already part-way through his lunch when I came in. He didn't look very happy which was hardly surprising as he was manfully ploughing his way through a grey/green sludge that looked suspiciously like something Will feeds to his chickens.

"You're in luck," Mum said. "There's enough in the pot for you."

"What is it?"

Her face lit up. "It's this new recipe I found on the internet. It's chock full of superfoods. Just what you need with all that running you do. It's very tasty, isn't it, Terry?"

Dad didn't answer, but the pained look he sent me told me all I needed to know.

"I'm due at the pub, remember?" I said. "I'll grab something there, thanks."

"I might be in a for a swift one later," Dad said. "But if I don't and you see that Ed Fuller, you tell him I'm not happy with him. Not happy at all."

"What's he done now?" It was obviously Ed's weekend for upsetting almost everyone he came into contact with.

"He promised me faithfully he'd make a start on the patio -"

"You mean, the sun terrace," Mum corrected.

"The sun terrace," Dad said with a sigh. "I was going start the plastering this weekend, but didn't because I'd promised Ed I'd give him a hand. I didn't want to start and then have to break off when he arrived."

"And, I take it from what you're saying, he didn't?"

"No. And he's not answering his phone either. What is it with young people today? When you say you're going to do something, that should be it. Your word is your bond, that sort of thing. I'd have got someone else in to do the patio -"

"Sun terrace," chimed Mum.

"Sun terrace, if I'd known he didn't want the job. I only agreed to let him do it because I felt sorry for the lad and I know how hard up him and Julie are. Not hard up enough, obviously, if he can afford to turn his back on a cash in hand job. Probably more important that he has his Sunday morning lie in."

"Well, I know their youngest is still giving them trouble at night," I said.

"And, from what I heard last night, he made a right fool of himself on Friday night with that new guy who's moved into The Old Forge."

He meant Martin Naylor, of course, who has lived in the village for almost six months now. But my dad is one of those people who will call anyone 'that new guy' until they've lived here at least five years.

**

But Ed wasn't in the pub that lunchtime so that I could pass on Dad's message. Elsie and Olive were, though. They'd come in for Sunday lunch and a good gossip washed down by a couple of glasses of port and lemonade.

In fact, Elsie was so busy sharing her theories on Paul McAllister's murder to anyone and everyone I was surprised she managed to find the time to put away a large roast beef dinner (with extra roast potatoes) followed by a generous helping of apple crumble ('none of that foreign tira-me-what's-it for her, thank you very much!') and half of Olive's Sticky Toffee Pudding as well.

As Elsie worked her way through the amount of food that would probably have fed a family of four, she and Olive had almost everyone in the village marked out as the murderer.

First on Elsie's list was Gerald Crabshaw. Because she had "never liked the fellow who was far too uppity even though he'd been sacked from the council," and had once called her

Prescott "an annoying little rat of a dog," which, I thought, was probably the only sensible thing Gerald had ever said.

Olive thought the murderer might be the man who delivered the free newspaper every other week because he looked like Boris Karloff. Or she thought, maybe, it was Martin Naylor. Because he was a newcomer, had a swearing phone and wore his trousers too tight for a man of his age.

Finally, they both settled on the postie.

"Surely not," I protested as I remembered the poor guy's shocked face.

"Inspector Morse is always suspicious of whoever finds the body," Olive said.

"Not only that," Elsie chipped in. "He always stops for a cup of tea with that flighty piece from Number 12."

"What?" I couldn't resist it. "Inspector Morse and the flighty piece from No 12?"

She gave me a withering look. "I was referring to the postman, of course. Besides," she added. "He has sandy eyelashes. Never trust a man with sandy eyelashes, that's what I always say. But then again, it could have been the vicar."

"The vicar? Now you're really scraping the barrel," I said. "Why do you think it's him?"

Elsie shrugged. "I've never taken to him. He's a cold fish. And his eyes are too close together."

"What is it about you and eyes?" I laughed. "So all Avon and Somerset Police have to do is look out for a guy with sandy eyelashes whose eyes are too close together and the crime rate will be halved overnight."

Elsie scowled. "Eyes are windows of the soul. And there's no need for you to be sarcaustic, young lady."

I had been going to ask her if she knew anything about Paul McAllister's background. But figured I'd better leave that until tomorrow when I could talk to her quietly. And when she didn't have a couple of port and lemonades inside her. That always made her opinions more extreme and unreliable.

"Did you enjoy your lunches?" I asked them as they came up to pay.

"It was acceptable," Elsie said. "But you can tell that

Normalina -"

"It's Norina, Elsie," I tried to say but she ignored me.

"That Normalina that she cooks a pretty good bit of beef. For a foreigner."

I was surprised. Praise from Elsie was a rare thing.

"Well, thank you, I'll pass that on," I said. "She'll be -"

"However-" Elsie stopped me with a raised hand as if she was directing a taxiing plane. "Her Yorkshire puddings are soggy. You can tell her from me that if she used proper beef dripping and got her tin smoking hot before adding the batter, she'd find a great improvement. You make sure you tell her that mind."

Tell her that? Not if I valued my job I wouldn't. Norina would brook no criticism of her cooking. Although Elsie was quite right, Norina's Yorkshires' bottoms were so soggy they'd have had Mary Berry reaching for the smelling salts.

"Here, I've been thinking about that Crystal person," Elsie went on as she watched me count out her change with all the intensity of a cat outside a mouse hole. "Trying to remember where she said she'd come from."

"Where?"

"Manchester," Olive suddenly butted in. "I'm sure it was Manchester."

"And I'm sure it wasn't," Elsie said.

"Well, it was somewhere up north, beginning with M." Olive said sharply. "Or was it N?"

"Be quiet, Olive" Elsie said. "I can't think straight with you going on. That and thinking about those soggy bottomed Yorkshires. It was -"

She broke off, a smile creasing her small pointy face. "Yorkshire. That was it," she cackled. "She came from Liverpool."

I stared at her. "But that's not in Yorkshire. And it doesn't start with an N. Nor an M."

"I never said it did. That was Olive. She gets things muddled." She leaned across and said in a whisper loud enough to be heard in the next room. "She does my head in sometimes. I'm sure she's got those senior dimensions, you know."

"I heard that," Olive said indignantly. And I could hear the pair of them, still bickering away at each other, all the way down the High Street.

***

Elsie and Olive were the last to leave, as always. So I wasn't far behind them. I decided to go home via Jules's house to see if Ed was around and to pass on Dad's message.

They lived on a small estate on the edge of the village that had been described, when it was being built, as a set of executive family houses. They turned out to be houses fit only for executive families of mice. Their tiny two bedroomed house was cramped enough when they only had Kylie, but as soon as the baby came along, the place burst at the seams, much of which had spilled out onto the pocket handkerchief sized (or easy maintenance in estate agent speak) front garden.

I stepped over a sugar pink bike, a miniature sit on tractor complete with a trailer full of gravel from the path and an upturned dolls pram before I reached the front door.

But before I could knock, it swung open and Jules stood there, looking even more harassed than usual.

"Oh my god, Katie, thank goodness -" she gasped, although I barely managed to hear her above what sounded like a dozen screaming banshees running riot in her kitchen.

"Jules. What's happening?" I shouted, as I thought about dialling 999. She said something that I didn't catch above the noise. I shook my head and mimed not hearing. "Sorry?"

"Hang on." She turned back into the house. "Shut up!" she yelled at the top of her lungs.

Personally, I thought she was just adding to the noise but to my surprise, it stopped as suddenly as if someone had thrown a switch.

"What's going on?" I asked.

She looked up and down the road then beckoned me inside.

"Thank goodness you came along," she said. "I'm at my wits end."

"What is it?" I was beginning to get worried for her.

"It's Ed –" she began and, to my astonishment, her eyes filled with tears. "He's -"

Now I felt really worried. Jules never cried. Or at least, the last time I'd seen her do so, she'd been about nine and her hamster died. She didn't even shed a tear when we were about fourteen and One Direction broke up. I, on the other hand, cried for a week.

I thought about the last time I'd seen Ed. And how awful he'd looked. I'd imagined at the time it was nothing more than a well-deserved hangover from hell. But now -

"Oh no," I whispered. "Ed. He's not -"

I couldn't finish the sentence.

She looked at me, her eyes brimming, the tears running unchecked down her pale cheeks.

"He's been arrested," she said in a broken whisper. "For Paul McAllister's murder."

Chapter Fifteen

I stared at her. Stunned. Of all the things she could have said Ed had done - or, as was more often in Ed's case, had not done - being arrested for murder was the one I hadn't seen coming.

Ed Fuller was all sorts of things, most of them bad. But a cold-blooded murderer? No way. He hadn't appeared anywhere on Elsie and Olive's list of suspects. And for a very good reason.

He was incapable of killing anything, even wasps. Jules was forever grumbling how she always had to deal with them while he flapped around like a wet hen. As for committing murder, the ultimate act of violence, I remembered how ineffectual he'd been when he'd tried and failed to hit Martin Naylor.

"They've got the wrong man, surely," I said.

"Well, of course they have," Jules snapped with a touch of her old spirit.

"When did this happen?"

"This morning. Early." Her voice shook as she wrapped her arms around her body. "We'd just finished breakfast and he was saying how he had a job to do for your dad today when there was this knock on the door and these two great big policemen stood there. Said they were arresting him in connection with…" She shook her head like she still couldn't believe it. "With Paul McAllister's murder. I didn't even know at that point that Paul had been murdered. I thought they said it was an accident."

"Apparently not. They found some evidence at the scene that convinced them it was murder."

When Liam had told me that I'd thought at the time they meant Gerald, to be honest. (I'd discounted Elsie's theory about the postie and his sandy eyelashes).

"So this - this murder... it happened Friday night, right?" Jules asked.

"I imagine so. The postie found him early on Saturday morning. I saw him. The poor guy was sitting on Gerald's wall. Looking pretty awful."

"And that was Saturday morning? You're sure?"

"Yes, of course."

"Right then." She picked up her car keys from a hook by the door and grabbed her bag. "I'm going down there."

"Where?"

"Bridgwater. They were taking Ed to Bridgwater Police Station. I asked don't they have a station closer, but they said that's where their Major Crime Unit was based. Major Crime, my Ed. I ask you."

"They've got the wrong man, obviously," I said.

"Course they have. And they'll have to let him go when I tell them he was here all Friday night and Saturday morning, won't they?"

I was about to say how I'd seen Ed early on Saturday morning but at that moment, the baby - whose name I could never remember - set up a howl that made my ears ring. He was strapped in a highchair which had been pulled up against the kitchen table. He was squirming against the straps, his small round face scarlet with rage.

"Hush, Zack," Jules said distractedly. "And Kylie, stop teasing him. Give him back his iPad."

"He has an iPad?" I stared at her. What was the world coming to when little kids who couldn't hold a spoon had an iPad?

"Not a real one," she said. "It's a pretend one. He loves it."

Kylie handed the pretend iPad to Zack but not before she'd pulled a face at him. Zack quietened down, but it looked like the truce was only temporary.

"But if you're going to Bridgwater, what's going to happen to these two?" I asked.

"I've been trying to ring Gran to see if she'll come down and look after them. But she's not answering."

"I'm not surprised." Jules' Gran was Elsie's partner-in-gossip, Olive Shrewton. "She and Elsie were in the pub lunchtime, washing down their roast beef with a couple of glasses of port and lemonade."

"A couple? Each?"

I nodded.

Jules groaned. "No wonder I couldn't get an answer, then. Gran goes out like a light after a couple of those. She'd sleep through an earthquake. I don't suppose you would?"

I glanced across at the children. Zack had obviously decided the make-believe iPad was not to his taste after all and had hurled it across the room, narrowly missing the cat as he did so.

The cat then, very wisely, made a swift escape through the cat flap and I was beginning to wish I could follow him.

"But I'm no good with children," I said.

"I know. But you're my last hope."

"What about your neighbour?" My voice came out in a panicky rush. "The one you share child minding with. Surely she -"

"They went off on holiday to Cornwall yesterday. Lucky things. We had a holiday planned but had to cancel. Thanks to my idiot husband." Her eyes hardened. "Look, I've got to go. I can't just sit here waiting. I've got to do something. You do see that, don't you?"

"Yes, but -"

"Great. Thanks a lot. I owe you big time, Katie -"

"Kat."

"Kat." She jingled her keys. "I'll keep trying Gran, to see if I can wake her. And you could try as well, if you like. But they'll be no trouble, I promise you."

Before I had chance to say anything else, my one-time best friend, who after this I'd probably never speak to again, grabbed her bag. Then she waved at the children, told them to 'be good for 'Aunty Katie' and hurried out the door, leaving the two children silent - an unusual state for them - as they stared after her.

"Where's Mummy gone?" Kylie asked, her big blue eyes wide, her bottom lip trembling alarmingly.

"Mummeee?" echoed little Zack, as he, too, stared at the closed door.

"She's - um, she's had to go out." My over-bright voice sounded as sincere as the host on one of those afternoon TV game shows Elsie watches, even though she always complains that they're rigged. "I'm going to look after you for a while. Won't that be fun?"

My face ached with the effort of plastering on a big smile for their benefit. But neither Kylie nor Zack made any attempt to return that smile.

"But Mummy was going to plait my hair into braids," Kylie said.

"Mummmmeeee!" moaned Zack, who, even with my limited experience of children, I could tell was about to kick off again.

"Braids? With beads? And ribbons?" For the first time in my entire life I blessed the fact that I was a hairdresser's daughter. "Would you like me to do it for you?"

She looked at my hair - it was still green, short and spiky - and frowned. "Can you do braids?" she asked, her big blue eyes full of doubt.

"You bet I can," I assured her. "Go and get your stuff."

She nodded, still looking doubtful, but hurried off upstairs.

"Mummmeee!" Zack's moaning was shaping up to become a full-on eardrum-perforating screech as he saw his sister vanish as well as his mum and some weird green haired stranger appear in their place. He looked pretty upset and I couldn't blame him.

I tried Olive's number but, like Jules, didn't manage to raise her. I cursed that second port and lemonade I'd served her.

Zack's cries were making the kitchen windows rattle by the time his sister came back with a box containing beads, ribbons and a small pink sparkly hairbrush.

I looked around the room and at the large flat screen TV that took up most of the far wall. "Do you want to watch a DVD?" I asked.

"Zack likes Peppa Pig," Kylie said.

"Great." A huge wave of relief swooped through me.

"Peppa Pig it is then."

"But I don't." Kylie said as the wave of relief sank back into the pool of despair. "It's for babies."

"Look, let's get Peppa Pig going for young Zack here, shall we?" I said. "And then, I'll see about doing your braids."

Sometimes in the salon, Mum had those magazines that are full of advice on parenting. I didn't often read them. But I knew from the snippets I'd seen that it was wrong to bribe children. That it was something I would never do. That people shouldn't use a screen, whether it was a phone, tablet or TV, as a babysitter. That we'd never had things like that when I was small, and it had done me no harm.

But now? Now I couldn't get that TV on fast enough. Or, to be strictly accurate, ask Kylie to do it for me.

She nodded and went across to the TV. Their downstairs was one room. Estate agents called it open plan, but the truth was there was nothing much planned about it. And not much open either. It was nothing more than a not very big kitchen squashed on to a not very big living room to make one not very big room.

Thankfully, Kylie knew how the TV worked and, in a moment, the plinky plonky music filled the room and Zack fell miraculously silent. I moved his chair closer to the TV for him and then went back to the table, sat Kylie down and began the long process of weaving her silky blonde hair into beribboned and beaded braids.

"Are you allowed to wear braids to school?" I suddenly asked, knowing from experience that it took almost as long to unbraid the hair as it did to braid it. Jules would thank me for that on a Monday morning. Not.

Kylie giggled. "There's no school tomorrow. It's the holidays." She picked out a purple ribbon and a handful of pink and green beads. "I'd like these please."

There was something almost soothing about standing there, weaving and plaiting her baby fine hair, while Peppa Pig pranced about in the background and little Zack stared at the screen, transfixed. Gradually, my panic began to settle, and I dared to start to believe that maybe I wasn't quite so rubbish at this baby-sitting lark after all. And Kylie's hair was looking so cool, I was beginning to regret that mine was too short to braid.

Kylie, too, had obviously decided that someone who could braid hair as well as I could ("Much better than Mummy," were in fact her exact words) could be trusted after all and she began to prattle away, telling me all about her BFFs (that's Best Friends Forever) and how annoying the boys in her class were.

I can remember feeling exactly the same when I was her age, and the boy that annoyed me most had been Will, the man I now loved - even though he still annoyed me as much as ever sometimes. Although he stopped tying my plaits to the chair some years ago.

"Shall I tell you a secret?" Kylie whispered.

I bent towards her, expecting her to name one of the annoying boys who was, perhaps, slightly less annoying than the others.

"Daddy has a pot of gold," she whispered. "He said he's going to buy me a new bike and Mummy will have a new dress. And Zack -" she waved her hand vaguely. "Zack will get something."

"That's nice," I murmured. Ed was always good at telling fairy stories. It was, according to Jules, one of the few things he was good at.

"Would you like to see it?" Kylie asked.

"Yes please." I went along with her game.

She slipped off the chair and led me into the small utility room that opened off the kitchen. There was a faded old rucksack with a broken strap hanging on the overfilled coat rack.

"It's in here," Kylie reached up and slipped her hand into the rucksack. She grabbed something then held it out towards me.

But it wasn't a pot of gold. It was a wallet. Butter soft tan leather. With a distinctive Mulberry logo. And it certainly wasn't Ed's. I knew exactly who it belonged to - and where I'd last seen it.

It belonged to Martin Naylor. He'd been flashing it around the pub on Friday night.

"Look," Kylie said as she handed it to me. "Look inside. It's got money. Lots of money. Enough, Daddy says, for a new bike and -"

"Does Mummy know about this?" I asked.

The beads of Kylie's new braids clicked together as she shook her head.

"No," she whispered. "And you must promise not to tell her. Daddy says it's going to be a surprise and it will be spoilt if she knows about it."

Oh, it was a surprise all right. I held the wallet in my hand, and it felt as if it was burning a hole right through my palm.

Oh Ed. What have you done? You stupid, stupid -

Before I could think what to say or do, there was the sound of a key in the lock and the front door opening. Kylie ran out into the hallway while I stayed in the utility room, trying not to panic.

"Granny!" I heard her shout and, without stopping to think about it anymore, I stuffed Martin's wallet into my jeans pocket where it sat, like a lump of lead.

I needed time to think.

"My life, sweetheart," Olive was saying to Kylie. "Don't you look the pretty one."

"Katie did it. She let me choose the colours and I chose pink and purple. And some green. Do you like it? The purple ones are my favourite. Look Granny, they make a clicking sound when I turn my head. Would you like Katie to do yours?"

I heard Olive laugh. "I don't think they would look as good on me as they do on you," she said - and she wasn't wrong there. There wasn't enough room on her Crystal tight perm for a single bead, least of all a ribbon.

"So where is Katie?" I heard Olive ask.

"She's -"

"I'm here, Olive," I said quickly as I went back into the kitchen. I didn't want Kylie explaining to Olive what we were doing going through Daddy's rucksack.

"Thank you so much, my lovely," she said. Kylie was hanging on to her hand and Zack looked up from Peppa Pig long enough to coo at her as she bent down to kiss him. "This was so kind of you to step in like this. I hope they haven't given you too much trouble. I know they can be a handful and it was so good of you to offer to step in. Julie is so grateful."

Well, I didn't exactly offer, Olive, I wanted to say. *As for trouble? They've given me a lot of trouble, at least Kylie has, with her daddy's secret 'pot of gold' and I don't know what to do about it.*

***

"So that's why Ed didn't turn up to do your patio this morning," I explained to Mum who was staring at me, her eyes wide with shock.

"Ed arrested," she murmured. "I can't believe it. The police have made a mistake, of course."

"Of course they have. Goodness knows what they think they have on him."

On the way back from Jules' house I'd transferred Martin's wallet from my jeans pocket to the very bottom of my bag, buried beneath tissues, dog treats and poo bags. (Empty ones, of course. It's my dog walking bag, in case you're wondering)

I couldn't help thinking, though, that it was a good job it was Paul McAllister who'd been murdered and not Martin. Naylor. (Although not from Paul's viewpoint, obviously.) That would have made things look very black indeed for Ed after the very public set to he and Martin had had. And now, he had Martin's wallet. But how had he come by it? Had he stolen it?

But I couldn't think of him as a thief any more than a murderer. Having said that, he and Jules were always hard up. And Martin had owed him a lot of money. Which Ed was dead unhappy about.

Had Ed found the wallet somewhere and intended handing it back to Martin - after taking what was owed to him, maybe? If only Ed hadn't been arrested, I could have talked to him, asked him what the hell he thought he was doing. Made him put it back.

And that was when the idea came to me. I could take it back. Say it had been found in the bar slipped down the side of the settle where it had obviously fallen during the spaghetti incident.

It hadn't, of course. But how - and when - had Ed come by it? I took a deep breath. The longer I put off returning it, the worse it was going to be for him.

I picked up my bag and headed for the door. But before I reached it, Mum called me back.

"Not so fast, young lady," she said. "You owe me, remember?"

"Sorry?"

"You promised we could sit down and brain drain some ideas for my business plan, remember?"

"Are you sure you don't mean brainstorm, Mum?" I grinned.

"You see? It's what I said. You're the one who's good at words. Not me. So come on, sit down and let's make a start. I've sketched out a few things I want to say. It's up to you to find the right words."

I know better than to argue with my mother when she has that look in her eyes. And besides, she did let me borrow her car. She was right, as usual. I did owe her.

We'd almost finished putting together what we both agreed was a pretty good business plan when there was a knock at the door. Mum sighed, then got up to answer it. When she came back, she was followed in by a policeman. Not friendly Ben Watkins, more the pity. This was his less than friendly boss, Detective Sergeant Miller with whom I'd had a run-in before.

"Would you like a cup of tea, Sergeant?" Mum asked but to my relief he shook his head. I could feel his cold grey eyes boring into my bag, as if any minute he was going to reach in and pull out Martin's wallet.

"No thank you, Mrs Latcham." He turned to me. "I understand you witnessed an altercation in the Winchmoor Arms on Friday night?"

"Well, yes." Me and half a dozen others, I thought. "But it

was only a bit of handbags."

"Handbags?"

Oh dear! I wished I hadn't mentioned that word as I tried not to look in the direction of my own handbag. "You know, a lot of huffing and puffing. Posturing. No real harm done or intended."

He looked down at his notebook. "And this was between Edward Fuller and Paul McAllister?"

"No. It was -" I was about to say it was between Ed and Martin. But perhaps he didn't know about Ed's pathetic attempt to floor Martin and I was about to make it worse for him.

"I understand there were threats uttered to Mr McAllister," he said. "We have a couple of witnesses. Can you corroborate that?"

"Well, Gerald Crabshaw and Paul had a few words, certainly," I said. "It was all to do with a boundary hedge that Gerald claimed Paul had vandalised."

He nodded. "And Edward Fuller?"

"I don't think he had anything to do with the hedge," I said. But I was playing for time and he knew it.

"Did you hear Edward Fuller threaten Paul McAllister?" He spoke slowly and carefully as if to a not very bright child.

"Well, I don't think he said anything at all to Paul. After all, as far as I know he didn't even know the man. Why would he? He said -"

"Go on." DS Miller said, his sharp eyes never for a moment leaving my face.

"Ed was pretty drunk," I said. "And didn't know what he was saying. I think he thought he was talking to Martin Naylor - Paul was sitting with him. But this was all going on over the other side of the bar and I couldn't see or hear clearly. Besides, he was slurring his words so much it was difficult to make out exactly what he did say."

"And after that?"

"After that, he went and sat down and Paul left. But later Ed had another exchange of words with Martin," I didn't feel he needed to know that the exchange of words had been accompanied by a flailing right hook. "And then, Gino suggested they both leave as they'd both had plenty to drink. And Ed went home. This would have been about half past nine."

"Did anyone see him go home?" he asked.

"I don't know. I didn't. I was working until gone 11.30. I assume he reached home safely."

"Thank you." He put his notebook away and handed me a card. "There's my number. If you remember anything else, please call me."

"You've got the wrong man, you know," I said as I opened the door to let him out. "Ed is incapable of hurting anyone."

He turned and gave me a piercing look. "Who knows what anyone is capable of, given the right circumstances, Miss Latcham? Thirty years as a policeman has taught me that."

"Well," Mum demanded as we heard his car drive away. "Are you going to tell me?"

"Tell you what?"

"Whatever it is you're hiding. You might - or might not - have fooled that policeman. But not me. I always know when you're being shifty. "

"Of course I'm not being shifty," I said with as much indignation as I could muster.

She gave me a look. "You're not thinking of getting yourself involved in this murder, are you? Because you know what happened last time. If that little dog hadn't been around -"

"Talking of Prescott," I said quickly as I grabbed my bag and edged towards the door. "I promised to walk him this afternoon. I'd better go and do it before Elsie starts phoning to see where I am."

"But it's Sunday," Mum called after me as I scuttled off down the path.

Indeed it was. It was turning into one of the longest Sundays of my life. And it wasn't over yet.

Chapter Sixteen

Martin and Suzanne Naylor lived in the Old Forge, one of the oldest and largest cottages in the High Street. When it was originally built back in the days when Judge Jeffreys went on his rampage around Somerset it had been a simple one up, one down dwelling with a blacksmith's forge (hence its name) on one side. Over the centuries, it had bits and pieces added to it so that inside, it was a bit of a rabbit warren, while outside, the uneven roofline told the old place's history.

Before Martin and Suzanne moved in, the interior of the house had been gutted. Builders swarmed all over the place, blocking the High Street with their vans, disturbing the peace with their power tools and radios and generally not doing anything to endear the newcomers to the other residents.

I'd always fancied seeing inside and hoped they hadn't done too much to wreck the ambience of the old place.

But that morning I had things other than interior decor on my mind. I took a long steadying breath before lifting the old-fashioned iron knocker which, I was happy to see, they'd retained. Was I doing the right thing? The more I thought about it, the more I managed to convince myself that Martin's wallet had indeed fallen during their little scuffle and that Ed had picked it up, intending to return it.

The sound of the heavy iron knocker was loud enough to scare a pigeon that had been scratching around in a bank of laurel bushes that grew alongside the path between the house and what I assumed was now the garage. The pigeon, in its turn, scared me as it flapped and crashed around in the bushes in a panic before flying off.

My heart rate had only just returned to normal when the door opened. I was relieved to see Suzanne Naylor standing there. I hadn't been looking forward to explaining to Martin how his fancy designer wallet had ended up in my dog walking bag.

I'd interviewed Suzanne a couple of weeks earlier when the village choir gave its inaugural concert in the old people's home (this was the interview Mitch had chosen to spike and had described as 'boring snoring').

She was in her mid-twenties although she dressed a lot older, in a long line grey cardigan over a heavy tweed skirt. She was one of those naturally pale people. Her skin was almost translucent, her eyes a strange silver colour. Her fine light blonde hair was fashioned into a chin length bob that swayed like a silk curtain as she moved her head.

At that time of the interview she'd been animated, happy, her eyes shining as she talked about her plans for the newly formed choir. Now they were red-rimmed and the dark shadows under them that stood out so sharply against her pale skin gave her the look of a startled panda.

"Mrs Naylor, I don't know if you remember me, but I'm -" I began.

"Oh yes. Yes. You're the girl from the paper." She stepped back and looked as if she was about to shut the door in my face. "I've got nothing to say," she said briskly.

"No, please." I had to resist the temptation to put my foot in the door. "I'm not here to interview you."

She gave me a long hard stare. "Then why are you here?"

"I've come to see your husband. Is he in?"

Something flashed in those strange silver-grey eyes. "Why do you want him?" Her voice was wary. Suspicious.

Me? Want him? I suppressed a shudder. I wanted Martin Naylor as much as I wanted a bout of what Elsie calls 'new-monials'.

"I - I've got something that belongs to him." I swallowed hard, reached in my bag and took out the wallet. "Do you recognise this?"

She gave a sharp intake of breath. "Of course I do. It's Martin's. I gave it to him for his birthday." She moved forward and all but snatched it out of my hand. "Where did you find it?"

"It was in the pub." I crossed my fingers behind my back. It was, after all, only a little white lie. And, for all I knew, maybe Ed had indeed found it in the pub. The fact that he didn't remember doing so was neither here nor there.

"Then how come you've got it?" She was still very suspicious. And who could blame her?

"I work there."

She frowned. "I thought you worked for the newspaper?"

"I have more than one job," I explained. "In fact, I have three jobs, if you count my dog walking business. Your husband's wallet must have fallen down behind the settle in the bar and has only just been discovered. I imagine he's been looking for it?"

"What? Oh yes. Yes." She looked around vaguely, while her long, thin fingers plucked at the wallet. "Yes, of course he has."

"I - I hope it's all there," I said, although she made no attempt to open it. Just stood, holding it between both hands, as if it was a bouquet and she a bride.

"I'm sure it is." She flashed me a quick smile. "Well, thank you so much for this. I'm sure Martin will be very grateful. As am I, of course."

"You're welcome." I was just happy to be shot of it and began to walk away when she called me back.

"Look, I'm sorry," she said. "I'm afraid I can't quite remember your name."

"It's Kat. Kat Latcham."

"Yes, of course it is. And ... I thought.... Did- did you say just now that you have a dog walking business?"

"I do. Do you have a dog that needs walking?"

"We do. Martin's away on business at the moment and I am ..." There was a funny little pause, like she'd forgotten what she was about to say next. I'm quite used to Olive doing it, but it was kind of weird from someone who was only in her mid-twenties.

"Are you asking me to walk your dog?" I prompted when it looked like we were going to stand there on her doorstep forever while she dithered around.

"What? Oh yes. Yes please. That would be lovely."

"Could I meet the dog?" I asked.

She looked startled. "No. Not at the moment. It's not convenient. Can you start tomorrow morning?"

"I can. But first would you like to see my references?" I asked, swinging into businesswoman of the year mode. "And here," I rummaged among the dog treats and poo bags and handed her one of the leaflets I'd prepared back in the time when I'd been sure the world would be beating a path to my door and I'd be turning people and their dogs away. "Here's the list of my charges."

She took it and, without looking at it, said, "Yes, that's fine. Shall we say about 11? I could -"

She broke off as from somewhere inside the house a phone began to ring. With a muttered excuse me, she closed the door in my face and hurried off to answer it.

***

Next morning, my to do list for the day was a mile long, not helped by the fact that I had to do two separate dog walks, Suzanne's first and then Prescott and Rosie. I was packing my bag with extra supply of dog treats when my phone rang. It was Jules.

"I just wanted to let you know that Ed's home," she said. "Thanks so much for stepping in like you did. I really owe you one, Kat."

"No problem," I assured her.

"Gran said the kids were as happy as Larry when she arrived." She had the cheek to sound surprised. "And Kylie's thrilled with her hair. At least I can hear her coming now, clicking away."

"So how are things with Ed?"

"When I told the police he was with me all Friday night and Saturday morning, they had to let him go, didn't they?"

"And was he?" I asked gently.

"Of course he was," she said. And even if I hadn't seen Ed coming out of the barn early Saturday morning, I would have known Jules was lying. I could always tell.

Lying to me was one thing. She did it all the time. But lying to the police was something else. Jules was playing a dangerous game. But then again, so was I.

"So where's Ed now?" I asked.

"At work, of course." She sounded surprised I should ask. "Where do you think he'd be on a Monday morning?"

"Yes, of course. So where's he working today?"

"Why do you want to know?"

"No reason," I said airily. "You know how nosy I am. Want to know the ins and outs of everyone's business. I've been spending too long with Elsie Flintlock, that's my trouble."

She laughed. "You're even beginning to sound like her. But if you must know, Ed's working on that new housing estate in Dintscombe. The one where the Red Lion used to be. Do you remember that night we -?"

"I certainly do," I cut in quickly, before Jules lost herself in memories of what we used to get up to before we were legally old enough to drink. "Sorry, Jules. I've got to go. I've got a new client for my *Paws for Walks* business. I'd best not be late."

I ended the call, promising I'd pop in later for a coffee and a catch-up and hurried off to The Old Forge.

Suzanne must have been waiting for me because she was much quicker opening the door this morning. She still looked pale but at least her eyes weren't as red rimmed this morning. And she was still wearing the same baggy grey cardigan - unless she had more than one of them, of course.

"Good morning, Kat," she said with a smile. "I'm so pleased you're here. Come along in and meet Finbar."

"Finbar?"

"The dog. He's a real sweetie."

She led me down a narrow hall, its wooden floor the colour of pale honey. A vase of dahlias stood on an oak console just inside the door, the flowers' vibrant red a startling contrast to the elegant dove grey walls.

She opened the door into a large, open plan kitchen. Here again, the monochromatic theme continued. Sleek white units were topped with black granite worktops, polished to a mirror like finish. White walls, glossy black crockery artfully arranged on an open shelf. The whole thing looked like something out of the pages of the glossy magazines that Mum leaves around the salon's waiting area.

It was all a little too perfect for my taste.

She walked through the kitchen and, to my surprise, out into a small courtyard. Immediately in front of us was the stone building that had once been the forge but was now converted into a large garage, part of which had been partitioned off to make what was obviously a utility room, although it was a far cry from Jules' chaotic one.

A washing machine, tumble drier and chest freezer took up one wall but there were no towering piles of laundry, or overflowing coat racks. Instead, there were more ranks of shiny white units. In the far corner was a large wicker dog bed, so big it looked as if it should be hanging beneath a hot air balloon. And filling the giant basket almost to overflowing was a small horse.

Not really a horse, of course. But as close to a horse as a dog could get without actually sprouting hooves and a mane, or if horses came with bristly fur and folded down ears. He stood up as we approached, his long feathery tail gently waving, as if he wasn't quite certain of what he should be doing.

"This is Finbar," Suzanne said, and the sound of his name set his tail wagging slightly faster.

"He's -" I swallowed hard and tried to sound a lot more confident and knowledgeable than I felt. "He's very big for a ...."

I paused, reluctant to let her know that I didn't have the faintest idea what sort of dog it was.

"For an Irish Wolfhound?" Thankfully, she finished the sentence for me. "Do you think so? I must confess I don't know much about dogs. He's my husband's dog really."

"And he usually walks him?" I asked.

"Yes, but he's, um - like I said yesterday, he's away on business at the moment."

I felt a pang of disappointment. So this wasn't to be a regular job, then. And this for a customer who hadn't quibbled when she'd seen my charges.

"How long is he likely to be away for?" I asked.

"I - um, well..." For a moment I thought she wasn't going to answer the question and that she was going to drift off again. Then, "It's hard to tell. It depends on - well, he's in property development, you see. And you can never tell how long a particular job is going to take. But.."

"Right," I said when I realised she wasn't going to finish that sentence either. "Does Finbar get on with other dogs?" I asked

She looked blank. "I'm sorry. I don't really know. But he's very placid. I'm sure he does. Certainly, Martin's never said anything about having any trouble."

"OK. I have other dogs to walk but I thought this morning I'd take Finbar on his own, to see how we get on. "

"He's a real gentle giant," she said. "If you could give him about an hour, that would be great. It's what Martin does. Look, I've got to pop out for a bit. If I'm not back, I'll leave the back gate and this door unlocked. You can just put him back in here when you're done, leave him with some fresh water and he'll be fine."

I thought of Prescott and how he had his own armchair in Elsie's overcrowded sitting room - and woe betide anyone who was foolish enough to try and sit in it.

"Finbar doesn't live in the house then?" I asked.

Her shake of the head sent her blonde bob swaying. "No. Martin doesn't like dogs in the house."

As if he could understand what she'd just said, Finbar gave a long sigh. I sympathised with him. Why on earth own a dog if you were going to keep him in the outside shed? OK, it was a very posh shed. But still a shed.

"How do you want to be paid?" Suzanne's tone suddenly became brisk and business-like. "By the day or at the end of the week?"

My heart gave a little skip of joy. "You want me to walk him every day?"

"Of course. I thought that was understood. I haven't got time to walk him myself."

"In that case, pay me at the end of the week," I said, whilst I tried to do a quick mental calculation of how much that would be.

"That's fine," she said. "The dog's lead hangs on that hook by his bed, if you'd put it back there when you come in."

Above Finbar's basket was a window into the garage part of the building. As I went across to get his lead from the hook I glanced in and saw to my surprise that Martin's fancy red car was in there.

"Your husband didn't take his car on his business trip then?" I said.

She stared at me, her expression so fierce I thought she was going to tell me to mind my own business.

"I'm sorry." I said quickly, desperate not to upset her. "I didn't mean to pry."

"No, it's ok. Martin took my car," she said. "He... he didn't want to leave his own car in a railway station car park. "She glanced at the slim gold watch on her wrist. "Now, if you'll excuse me, I have an appointment -"

She handed me the lead and opened the gate that led from the small courtyard garden and on to the High Street.

Finbar and I hadn't got very far when there was the sound of a powerful engine roaring into life. I turned and looked back as Suzanne drove along the road in a series of jerky movements. She looked absolutely terrified and obviously didn't get to drive Martin's powerful car very often. She made no attempt to return my wave as she and the big beast of a car bunny hopped past.

I hoped the panicky pigeon from yesterday wasn't still hanging around. The noise of Martin's over-revved car would have given the poor bird a heart attack.

Finbar was, indeed, as gentle and easy to handle as Suzanne had said he was. Unlike Prescott, he didn't pull my arm out of the socket when he spotted something to chase, or, in Rosie's case, caught the scent of a litter bin. His long loping strides made me have to step it out as well and I really enjoyed the change of pace.

There is a network of lanes around Much Winchmoor that lead out on to the moor. I decided to take Finbar along Back Lane, where Jules' grandad's barn was. Further along the lane is a ford where the river Winch that flows through the village crosses the road. In a dry spell, the water across the road isn't very deep and easily passable but after the weekend's heavy rain, the ford would be so deep as the river ran faster that it would only be passable by tractors.

This meant the lane would be traffic free - unless, of course, Will took the opportunity to go roaring around on his tractor. The round trip took about an hour at a brisk walking pace which would be perfect for Finbar. It was one of my go to routes for my morning run if I was pushed for time. I couldn't help thinking sadly that it was also the route favoured by Paul McAllister.

I realised with a guilty start that in all the upset over Ed's arrest, I hadn't done what Liam had asked and checked out the notes I'd made when I interviewed Paul and Gerald. As soon as I got back, I promised, I'd move it straight to the top of my mile long to do list.

I was busy rewriting the notes in my head as Finbar and I walked along. We'd set up a nice easy rhythm, so it came as a shock when he suddenly veered off the path and into a gateway, dragging me with him as he did so.

It was the gateway that led into the field where the old barn was. Finbar pushed his long grey muzzle against the five-bar gate and whined.

"Come on, boy," I said, in my best 'dog walker who stands no nonsense' voice. "Nothing to see here. Come on. NOW."

But he didn't move. Just whined some more and tried to stick his large head through the bars of the gate. I had visions of him getting it stuck and tried to pull him away. No chance.

I reached in my bag and took out my never fail dog training support - a handful of dog treats. I waved them under his nose, but he didn't even look at them. What sort of dog was immune to dog treats, for heaven's sake? I thought with the beginning of a mild panic attack. What would I do if he refused to move?

If it came to a show of strength between us there was only ever going to be one winner and it wouldn't be me.

"Finbar!" I shouted, more in desperation rather than expectation. "Come here NOW!"

To my astonishment, he pulled away from the gate and we were able to continue our walk back into the village, although he looked backward every now and again. His sad, wistful face looked sadder and more wistful than ever and I found myself apologising to him.

***

Suzanne was still out when Finbar and I got back to The Old Forge. I let myself in the back gate and through to the courtyard.

I let myself in to the utility room, wiped Finbar's paws, then filled his water bowl. He lapped half-heartedly, like he was only doing it to be polite then got in his basket and settled down with a long, sad sigh.

I felt mean leaving him there and was tempted to take him with me when I walked Rosie and Prescott. We'd passed a couple of dogs on our walk that morning and he'd show only a polite interest in them, so I was pretty sure they'd all get on.

I hoped it wouldn't be too long before Suzanne came back.

"See you tomorrow," I told him as I went to shut the door. But he gave such a long, mournful sigh that I turned back. He was looking at me with those big sad eyes.

I couldn't bear the look on his face. It said that he didn't fancy being shut in this soulless room with only the washing machine and tumble drier for company. And I couldn't say I blamed him.

"Come on, then." I'm a sucker for a sad face. And Finbar's was as sad as a dog could get. He jumped up and came towards me, his tail wagging.

"Don't blame me if you don't get on with Prescott," I warned him. "Although I'll level with you. Nobody does."

I clipped his lead back on and was about to walk away when we both stopped dead as a volley of curses suddenly

126

erupted from inside the house.

I'd know that noise anywhere. The curses got louder and the angry Irish voice got angrier and more Irish.

It was Martin Naylor's phone. The one he never went anywhere without.

Chapter Seventeen

"Pick up the phone, you eejet"

Who in their right minds would think a volley of Irish curses, which got louder - and more sweary - the longer the phone went unanswered, would make a good ringtone? Obviously the same guy who thought wearing clothes a size too small and two decades too young would make him look cool. Yeah, right. That worked. Not.

Finbar waited patiently by my side as I stood by the back door, listening and wondering. Why hadn't Martin taken his phone with him if he was away on business? I got what Suzanne had said about why he left his car behind and took hers instead. But his phone? Every time I'd seen him it had been welded to his person like his right hand had morphed into a flipper.

Something about this set-up didn't feel right. I thought back to the shifty way Suzanne had reacted when I'd asked her about Martin. Had he done a runner? Was that what had made her behave so oddly? But why leave his phone behind? And, if he had done a runner, then why? It couldn't be because of financial problems, not if the way he was flashing the cash in the bar was anything to go by.

Not running away from his creditors, then. But what if he'd been running away from something far more serious? Like murder.

What if Martin had been the one to set that trip-wire for Paul McAllister and had now run off to avoid being caught? Certainly the two of them were involved in something judging by the way they'd huddled together last Friday. But whatever it was they were talking about, it didn't look particularly angsty. Yes, Paul had seemed a bit agitated when he'd first come in. But Martin had calmed him down and they'd been on pretty friendly terms when they parted.

I wished I'd tried harder to find out what they'd been discussing. But whatever it was, Martin definitely hadn't wanted me to overhear. Not that that in itself was significant, though. He liked to play the big cheese, acting like he was auditioning for the Businessman of the Year Award as he arranged important and terribly hush-hush deals. At the same time, flashing the cash like he was minted.

Cash that had somehow ended up in Ed Fuller's possession which made no sense whatsoever. There was obviously bad blood between Ed and Martin. And if the postie had found Martin's body instead of Paul's lying on the path, then things would indeed have looked very bad for Ed.

Or, should that be, even worse for Ed? I had to see him, tell him what I'd done and try to find out what exactly was going on.

I decided that as soon as I'd walked the dogs, I'd go into Dintscombe to see if I could catch Ed at work. I couldn't risk waiting until he came home. I didn't want Jules or anyone else in the village to be around when we talked.

Finally, the cursing phone went silent. Either whoever was calling had rung off or someone had answered it. I listened for the sound of footsteps inside the house but there were none, so I gave up. I texted Suzanne to say that I was giving Finbar an extra hour (free of charge) then Finbar and I headed off to Elsie's to pick up Prescott.

I knocked on Elsie's door and stood back, ready for the onslaught. As she opened the door, Prescott hurtled out, only to screech to a halt at the sight of Finbar in a true Tom and Jerry moment.

"What is that?" Elsie demanded as Prescott proceeded to walk, stiff-legged and wary, around Finbar, who stood quiet and still as Prescott continued his inspection.

"This is Finbar," I said. "Martin Naylor's dog. I'm walking him, while Martin's away on business."

Elsie's bristly eyebrows crinkled together in a suspicious frown. "What sort of business?"

"Suzanne didn't say. He's a property developer so I assume

it was to do with that. But then," I couldn't help adding, "you probably know more about him than I do. After all, he and Suzanne have been in the village for all of five months now. Plenty of time for you to have found out his life history."

She scowled. "He's a mystery that one. That's for sure."

"Really? You mean he's the one who got away? You must be slipping."

"There's no need for that, young lady," she huffed. "The way you talk, anyone would think I was one of those nosy old biddies with nothing better to do with their time than pry into other people's lives."

That was exactly what I thought.

"He was pretty chummy with Paul McAllister the other night. I didn't even know they knew each other," I said.

"Paul McAllister managed the estate agents in Dintscombe, and they handled the sale of The Old Forge so I daresay that's how they came across each other. "

"I didn't know there was an estate agent in Dintscombe anymore. Every other business seems to be closing."

"It's in the main street opposite where the Full Moon pub used to be before they converted it into flats for folks with more money than sense," Elsie gave a toss of her Brillo pad hair. "As for what they've done to the building that used to be the Co-op - how on earth they got planning permission for that, I'll never know. Talk about corrupt planning officials. That's what you should be writing about in that rag of yours, young lady, not messing about with a load of local tittle-tattle."

That was rich, coming from the queen of local tittle-tattle, but I let it pass.

"You were saying about Paul McAllister's estate agency?" I asked, hoping to head her back on track.

"It's just him and that woman who used to moon around him like a lovesick heifer. She must have really fancied her chances with when he got divorced."

"Who are you talking about?"

"That Dilys Northcott as she chooses to call herself although I remember her when she was plain Dilly Finch who

130

worked on the bacon counter in the Co-op before it closed. But she started putting on all sorts of airs and graces when she began working for Paul McAllister."

"She works for Paul McAllister? I didn't realise that. I met her last weekend. She lives in Little Drearyfield - I mean, Little Mearefield."

Elsie gave a snort of laughter. "You were right the first time. Little Drearyfield's a good name for the place."

"No wonder she was so snippy with me, then. If she'd read the piece in The Chronicle."

"I bet Gerald regrets shouting his mouth off now," Elsie chortled. "Wouldn't surprise me if the police have him pegged out as suspect number one. I heard they let Ed Fuller go."

"Of course they did. Ed's all sorts of a fool but he's no killer. So what do you think was the connection between Paul McAllister and Martin Naylor? They were certainly deep in conversation in the pub on Friday night."

"No idea, I'm afraid. But I did hear that the Naylors paid way over the odds for that place. And then spent a fortune doing it up. They've got those fancy laminny-dated floors all the way through, for a start."

"Laminated?" I ventured. Elsie's vocabulary could be a challenge at times but in the eighteen months or so I'd been seeing her regularly I'd got pretty good at interpreting it.

"Whatever it's called, it cost a pretty penny. Some people have more money than sense. What was wrong with that lovely Axminster carpet old Mrs Marsh had laid all through the ground floor when she was living there? Treated herself, she did, when she won some money on the Lottery. She even had the downstairs toilet carpeted, if you ever heard anything like it. And that Axminster had years of wear left in it. Yet there it was, chucked in the skip by those builders. Shocking. No wonder there's all this globular warning going on, with folk like them chucking out perfectly good things."

By the time Elsie had finished describing all the other things the Naylors had so wantonly discarded when they were doing up The Old Forge, (Elsie had obviously spent way too much time inspecting the skips) Finbar and Prescott had reached an agreement about which one of them was top dog. Prescott was - no surprise there - and the two dogs and I set off to collect Rosie who greeted the newest member of the gang with her usual affability.

The three dogs got on well, in spite of the fact that Finbar didn't share Rosie's enthusiasm for litter bins or Prescott's obsession with barking at anything that moved.

As we went past The Old Forge, the garage doors were open. Suzanne had returned and had just put Martin's car away.

She glanced at her watch. "You've been longer than an hour."

"I gave him an hour on his own," I explained. "Then decided to try him with the other two. Didn't you get my text?"

She patted her pocket and took out her phone. "Sorry. I don't have it on when I'm driving."

"I wanted to see how Finbar got on with the other dogs. And, as you can see, they're all fine. Don't worry," I added as I saw her frown. "I won't charge you any extra and the other dogs have both had all their vaccinations and treatments in case you're wondering."

"I - no, I wasn't really," she said vaguely.

"Look, now I've got him, he might as well tag along for the rest of the walk, unless you want him back now, of course?"

"No, that's fine," she said. "To be honest, I don't think he likes me very much. I'm not really a dog person."

Oh really? I hadn't noticed. And I'm not surprised that he doesn't like you very much, I wanted to say. Not if you keep the poor boy shut up in the utility room all day.

I wanted to say that. But I didn't. Not to my best paying customer.

Suzanne must have been looking out for me when I brought Finbar back for the second time. Before I could ring the front door bell the side gate opened and she beckoned us in and opened the door to the utility room.

"Does he spend all this time in there?" I asked, not trying too hard to keep the disapproval out of my voice.

"He doesn't seem to mind it. And Martin doesn't like him in

the house. His claws mark the oak floors."

Oak floors? Not lamminy-dated then. Elsie had got her facts wrong for once.

I led Finbar in, topped up his water bowl and watched as he settled in his bed. It still didn't seem right, leaving him there but at least I'd given him a morning full of company and I reckoned he was ready for a good long sleep.

"By the way," I said to Suzanne as she closed the door on him. "I heard your husband's phone ring earlier."

She froze, her hand on the door handle. "You couldn't possibly have," she said quickly. "He has it with him all the time."

"It's just that - well, he's got a pretty distinctive ring tone, hasn't he? Unless, of course, you've got the same one?"

She stared at me for a second, her expression panicky. Then, "Yes, that's it exactly. That was my phone you heard. Martin thought it would be funny if we both had the same silly ring tone. I must get round to changing it."

As if on cue, the Irish curses started up again and with a muttered 'excuse me' she hurried indoors.

But how could that be her phone ringing from inside the house when I'd just seen her take hers out of her pocket to check for my message?

***

I changed out of my dog walking gear, got my scooter out and drove into Dintscombe to find Ed Fuller. He was not, as Jules had thought, working on the building site that used to be the old Red Lion, but was now 'Paradise Gardens, 'an exciting development of exquisite quality homes for the discerning buyers' which is housing developer speak for 'let's cram as many houses, the size of shoeboxes (although not quite so well put together) into as small a space as possible'.

Instead I tracked him down to the site that used to be the White Hart pub but was now being transformed into 'a mews development of tasteful town living for today's discerning family', more developer speak but this time for upended shoe boxes that looked more like seaside beach huts than proper grown up houses.

Dintscombe was losing its pubs faster than my mum lost socks on washing day. But it wasn't because the residents of the town were losing their taste for alcohol. It was more to do with the never-ending demand for new houses and the lack of suitable land. And maybe a touch of what Elsie called 'dodgy dealings in the planning department'.

I stood in what used to be the entrance to the pub car park and looked across a muddy wasteland. A makeshift road wound its way around teetering piles of breeze blocks, roof trusses and concrete lintels. Right at the far end was a line of almost completed upended shoeboxes which was, I'd been told, where Ed was probably working.

By the time I reached it, I was not in the best of moods after completely ruining my favourite pair of boots squelching through sticky mud where construction traffic had ploughed up and down the so-called road.

"Katie?" Ed came out of one of the half-finished houses. He looked at me in astonishment as I bog hopped across what would one day be someone's front garden toward him. "What the hell are you doing here? If the foreman sees you, I'll get sacked."

"I tried to ring you. Why aren't you answering your phone?"

He kicked at the muddy ground with the toe of his work boot. "Forgot to bring it, didn't I?" he mumbled as he bent down to pick up a roll of cable. "Look, I'm in enough trouble with the boss as it is. I'll see you later, right?"

"OK. If that's what you want, I'll come round yours after work, shall I?" I said as I turned to walk away. "Only I thought you might prefer to keep this between you and me. It's about Martin Naylor's wallet. I figured you might be wondering where it is, seeing as it isn't in your rucksack anymore."

He looked at me with wild, worried eyes, his face ashen. "I don't know what you're talking about," he muttered.

Ed always was a rubbish liar. And this time was no exception.

"What were you doing with it, Ed?"

He started getting stroppy then. "Damn it all, Katie, you've got no right coming here and accusing me -"

"Kylie told me all about your little pot of gold. That's what you called it, didn't you?" I cut in and watched as his flash of defiance collapsed like a leaking balloon. I could almost have felt sorry for him if I wasn't so damn mad with him.

"Kylie told you?"

"She did. Said you promised her a new bike."

He groaned, sat down on a pile of breeze blocks and put his head in his hands.

"You've got yourself in a bit of a mess, Ed, haven't you?" This time I did feel sorry for him, even though it was a mess of his own making.

He nodded. "I didn't mean to say anything. But she's bright as a button is Kylie - obviously gets that from her mother."

"Obviously." I couldn't help but agree with him there.

"She saw me take the wallet out of my pocket and put it in the rucksack. And when she asked what it was, I told her, stupid like, that it was the answer to our prayers. Like the story we'd been reading a few days ago. A pot of gold, as she said. And while I was trying to think how I was going to talk myself out of this one, she started on about having a new bike. I hadn't said a word about it. I was still trying to work out what to do about the damn thing."

"I take it you mean the wallet, and not Kylie's new bike? So where did you find it?"

He shrugged. "I dunno. It found me."

"Oh yes, of course it did. It jumped out of Martin Naylor's pocket and into yours, didn't it? Maybe it really is a magic pot of gold after all, disguised as a very expensive wallet."

Ed picked at his fingernails. "If you must know, I woke up in the barn Saturday morning and there it was, on the ground in front of me. I don't know how it got there. I don't remember finding it, but then I was pretty wasted Friday night and don't remember much."

"So what do you remember?"

"It's all a bit..." He dragged his hand down across his face. "I remember going home and not being able to find my keys.

And Jules refusing to let me in. That's how I ended up in the barn, I suppose, although I don't actually recall..."

"Do you remember earlier, in the pub, throwing a punch at Martin?"

He shook his head. "The police asked me that and all. And the answer is no," he added with a quick grin. "Although I wish I did remember. I bet I enjoyed it."

"Jeez, Ed, I hope you didn't say that to the police."

"Course not. What sort of fool do you take me for?"

"Do you really want me to answer that? Anyway, I just wanted to let you know that I returned the wallet to the Naylors this morning."

"You did what?" His mouth gaped like a baby starling's as he stared at me.

"I returned the wallet to the Naylor's this morning. I thought-"

"What the hell did you do that for?" he demanded, his voice harsh, his eyes blazing. "You interfering old cow. How bloody dare you. Of all the stupid -"

This was not any version of Ed I knew. His large hands balled into fists as he leapt to his feet and came towards me. I stepped back and instantly regretted it as my boots sank into the deep, sticky mud. I would have fallen if I hadn't grabbed a nearby concrete post, scraping my hand across its rough surface as I did so.

"Hang on a moment, Ed -" I began but he cut across.

"No, damn it. You bloody hang on. I've had it up to here with people getting on my case. Jules, my bloody sisters, the police - and now you. Do you have any idea what you've done?"

"I've got a feeling you're going to tell me," I said as I nursed my sore hand.

"My fingerprints will be on that wallet. And I'm in enough trouble with the police as it is. They'll be fitting me up for the murder, you'll see."

"But why would the police be interested in Martin Naylor's wallet?" I asked. "He's not the one who's been murdered."

All the fight drained out of Ed. He sat back down on the

136

breeze blocks and rubbed his hand across his face.

"Sorry I shouted at you like that," he muttered. "My head feels like it's about to explode and I don't know what day of the week it is."

"You've been under a lot of stress lately." This maybe wasn't the right time to point out to him that getting blind drunk on Abe's Headbender cider on Friday night hadn't done anything to help the situation.

"I wasn't going to take all the money," he said. "Only what was owed me. Jules went ballistic when she found out I hadn't been paid for all the work I'd done."

"Then why don't you take that up with his wife? Martin's away on business at the moment so I left the wallet with her. She seems a very nice, approachable person."

He shrugged but didn't say anything. I could tell he was still mad with me. And I didn't blame him, really. I'd acted with the best of motives, but I should have spoken to him first. He was quite right. I was an interfering cow, although I drew the line at the old bit.

"But I don't get it," I went on, still trying to make sense of it. "Why didn't he pay you? Goodness knows, there was enough money in that wallet to have paid you and ten others like you. I didn't count it, but it was more money than I'd ever seen in one place."

He shrugged. "Earlier in the week he said if I came in the pub on Friday night he'd pay me. Only when I got there, I told him I wasn't happy about the condition of one of the retaining walls at the back of the property and that it would need someone who specialises in that sort of thing to put it right. He didn't like that one little bit. Told me to mind my own bloody business. Then he said he'd changed his mind about paying me. Said the work I'd done hadn't been up to scratch but that was a complete lie. I did a really good job given the shocking state of the site."

"So where was this site? In Dintscombe?"

"Nah. Some run down old houses in Bristol. Talk about a mess. Best thing you can do here, I told him when I first saw it, is bulldoze the lot. But he just laughed and said people

137

would pay good money for them once he'd 'tarted the places up' a bit. His words, not mine. Couldn't see it myself. I earned that money, fair and square, you know." He jabbed his finger at me, as if the thought had just occurred to him. "Anyway, how do you know he didn't have a change of heart later and pay me?"

"Because when he left the pub after you took a swing at him, he looked like the only thing he was likely to give you was a punch on the nose. Added to which, if he'd had a change of heart, he'd have given you the money, not his uber-expensive designer wallet as well, wouldn't he?"

"Yeah. I suppose. When I woke up and saw it lying on the ground beside me, I thought maybe he'd changed his mind and that I'd forgotten."

"I'm really sorry if I've upset you, Ed," I said. "But when I saw the wallet in your rucksack, I panicked. At the time you were still at the police station. What if the police had searched your house and found it? How were you going to explain that on top of everything else?"

"Yeah, you're probably right."

"Did the police say why they carted you off yesterday?"

"They kept asking me what I was doing on the path between Gerald Crabshaw's house and Paul's. I told them over and over again that I'd never been there. Then, they showed me my keys. Said they'd found them on the path, near Paul's body. I couldn't deny they were mine, because they had a picture of my kids on it."

I stared at him, a thousand questions zipping around inside my head. Ed had been on the path where Paul's body was found? But when? And why?

"So, what were you doing there, Ed?" I asked.

Chapter Eighteen

Ed flushed and looked away. "Must have lost them when I went round to his place. He wanted a quote to replace that ramshackle old fence that's between his place and the Crabshaws'."

"You went to Paul's house."

"That's what I said, didn't I?"

"When was this?"

He shrugged. "Can't remember. Some time last week."

"And you've been without your keys all that time?"

He shrugged again. "Must have been."

"But you just said you told the police you'd never been to Paul's place."

He sighed. "Yes. No. Oh, I don't know. I told them I didn't know how my keys got there because at the time I didn't. I was confused, still hungover from Friday night and they were doing my head in. Only now I've had time to think about it, that's what must have happened. I must have dropped them the day I went round to give him the quote."

"And now that you have remembered, are you going to tell them?"

He shook his head. "No way. I'm not going back there again. They get you to say whatever they want you to say by going on and on, asking the same question over and over again. I'd probably still be there now if Jules hadn't said I was home with her all night."

"But that wasn't true, was it?" I said as gently as I could, not wanting to risk setting him off on one again. "I saw you coming out of Jules' grandad's barn, remember?"

He glared at me. "How do you know I hadn't gone in there during an early morning walk?"

"Because you didn't look in any fit state for an early

139

morning walk. You'd spent the night in the barn, hadn't you? You lost your keys (or so you've just told me) and Jules wouldn't let you in."

He swore and looked as if he was about to explode again. "What is this? The third bloody degree? You're worse than the plod."

"I'm right though, aren't I? You did spend the night in the barn."

He sighed, scuffed at the ground with the toe of his boot and nodded. "You going to tell them?"

"Not if they don't ask me. So, you don't remember losing your keys and you don't remember finding the wallet."

"They didn't know about that, thank goodness."

"Let's keep it that way, shall we?"

He gave a short, bitter laugh. "Well, I shan't be telling them any time soon."

"I told Suzanne the wallet was found in the pub, by the way. Down the side of the settle. Martin Naylor was as drunk as you were on Friday, so he probably won't have a clue what he did with it. I think the most likely thing is that he dropped it somewhere. In the Gents. Or maybe in the car park. And you found it and picked it up."

Ed looked doubtful. "I may have done, I suppose. I'd have thought I'd have remembered."

"Like you remembered taking a swing at Martin?"

He pushed his hand through his already tousled hair and scratched the back of his head. "Yeah, ok. You're probably right. Thanks, Katie. And I'm sorry I went off on one. I know you were only trying to help."

"It's Kat - and you owe me a new pair of boots," I said pointing down at my mud encrusted boots.

There was a glimpse of the old Ed as he laughed. "In your dreams. If you're daft enough to go traipsing across a building site in them ..."

As I turned to pick my way back across the muddy swamp that passed for a road, he called me back.

"Tell your dad I'm sorry about Sunday," he said.

"It's ok. He knows you were... otherwise engaged."

"I suppose the whole damn village knows that and all."

"Of course. And what they don't know, they'll make up."

He sighed. "Sounds as if some of them certainly have been making things up. The police kept asking me why I threatened Paul McAllister Friday night. I couldn't make sense of it. Why would I do that? Like I said, I hardly knew the bloke."

"I think I know what might have happened. Paul was sitting at the table by the fireplace with Martin. Do you remember that?"

He frowned. "Can't say I do. It's all a bit of a blur after the second pint -"

"Second pint? Ed, you were on your fourth by that time. And as you staggered back to your seat, you passed their table. In fact, if I remember right, you all but bounced off it. Then you muttered something about money. You sounded pretty mad. From where I was standing behind the bar it looked as if you were talking to Martin. But maybe someone else in another part of the bar heard it and thought you were talking to Paul."

He looked at me blankly. "Don't remember saying anything to either of them. But then, I don't remember drinking four pints of Headbender either." He shook his head slowly. "Jeez, no wonder I've still got a hangover."

"Indeed. But if it's any consolation, you didn't drink much of the fourth pint. Most of it went on the floor when you staggered back to the table with it."

As I turned to go, he called me back again. "Look, with a bit of luck I'll be finished here in an hour or so. I could make a start on your mum's patio this afternoon."

"That would be good, although Mum won't be in. She's off to Taunton to see her mother and Dad will still be at work. But I should be there."

"Doesn't matter," he said. "Your dad showed me where all the stuff is. So I'll just crack on. The sooner I start, the sooner I finish. See you later."

Once safely back on terra firma in what used to be the pub car park I was balancing on one leg, trying to scrape at least some of the mud off my boots when my phone rang.

It was Liam. No doubt to ask about how far I'd got locating my notes on the interview with Paul and Gerald. A question I wasn't ready to answer yet.

I went back to my mudscraping when the phone pinged. Liam again. But this time, a text.

"Do you have Ed Fuller's number? Or know where I can get hold of him?"

My answer to both questions was yes. But there was no way I was telling Liam that.

.....

"The police had him in for questioning over the weekend," Liam said when I returned his call. "I'm surprised your village rumour mill missed that one. I wanted to ask him what that was all about?"

"Oh that." I gave what I hoped was a convincing laugh. "For pity's sake, Liam, don't go down that rabbit-hole. It was all a total misunderstanding. Someone had said that Ed had a fight with Paul in the pub, but they'd got it wrong. It was Martin, not Paul, that Ed had fallen out with. It was all to do with payment (or rather, non-payment) for some work Ed had done for him. Even then it was nothing more than a lot of posturing and exchanges of insults. They were both pretty drunk. I should know. I was there."

"A non-story then?"

"Yeah. Nothing to do with Paul at all. Added to which, Ed's wife confirmed that he was with her all Friday night. At which point they let him go."

"Fair enough. How are you doing with the background stuff on McAllister and Crabshaw I asked for? I was going through your story about the Headless Peacock this morning and I definitely think it might be worth rattling Crabshaw's cage a bit. He was making some pretty wild accusations."

"My story? Don't you mean the one Mitch so tastefully 'sexed up'?"

He laughed. "That's the one. I'd be interested in seeing those notes you promised to let me have. Remember? The ones you assured me you'd taken at the time? It might give me something useful before I go and see Gerald Crabshaw."

Before I could think what to say, he went on. "I'm just wondering why every time I mention those notes, I come up against a wall of silence. So, I'll ask you again. And I want an answer. When you interviewed Gerald Crabshaw and Paul McAllister, did you take any notes?"

"Well, not in any great detail." I wasn't going to tell him that the only thing I'd written on the page headed with Paul's name had been the words 'sweet peas'. "I've got pages of notes from Gerald. He insisted on it. Actually dictated some of them. But Paul didn't want to be interviewed so we just had a very informal and off the record chat. But I can remember, almost word for word, what he said."

"Nothing's off the record when you're talking to a journalist," he said sharply.

"I had noticed."

I heard him give a long, irritable sigh. "How about we call a truce on that one?"

"How about letting me cover something more interesting than rained out Flower Shows and choir outings?"

He laughed. "I'll say this for you, Kat Latcham. You don't give up, do you?"

No, I don't, I thought to myself. Particularly when you were thinking of hanging a friend of mine - or at least, the husband of a friend of mine- out to dry, just to fill a few column inches. If Liam got hold of Ed, he'd end up confessing to kidnapping Shergar, carrying out the Brinksmat robbery and would probably put his hand up to being Jack the Ripper as well.

"Talking of Flower Shows," I went on, wanting to deflect him from Ed, not to mention my non-existent notes. "I'm in Dintscombe right now. And I know the woman who worked for Paul. She's also the secretary of Little Mearefield Flower Show and I was talking to her on Saturday. In fact, she promised to let me have the show results. How about I pop in there and see if I can get some background stuff about Paul McAllister? She might even be able to shed some light on a link between Paul and Martin Naylor. They certainly looked as if they were up to something on Friday night and Martin was very edgy when he thought I might be able to overhear them.

Got me wondering."

That, at least, gave me a breathing space as far as my non-existent notes were concerned and he rang off, but not before reminding me to keep him in the loop.

I gave up on getting my once lovely boots any cleaner and headed off towards the High Street to see what Dilys Northcott, who was once known as Dilly Finch from the bacon counter in the Co-op, could tell me.

......

Dintscombe High Street was such a sorry sight even the pigeons looked depressed and the empty shops stood out like missing teeth. At one time the occasional gap was soon filled as another popped in to take its place but now the units remained forlorn and unwanted unless a charity shop took one on.

And the once thriving Nag's Head pub in the Market Place which used to be packed to the rafters on market day had closed and been converted into apartments for 'the discerning homeowner looking to enjoy all the advantages of town centre living.' Even the bank had gone and was, according to the board outside, waiting for someone eager to take advantage of this 'exciting retail opportunity'.

You'd be forgiven for thinking Dintscombians had experienced some sort of epiphany. That they'd seen the light, gone teetotal and started hiding their money under the mattress, donating all their worldly goods to charity shops and had given up shopping in a bid to save the planet by avoiding excessive consumerism

But the demise of Dintscombe High Street had less to do with the change in people's shopping habits and the rise of the internet and more to the fact that, owing to some skulduggery in the council's Planning Department a few years earlier, the new 'out of town' retail centre wasn't exactly out of town. It was, in fact, on the site of what used to be a cheese processing factory at the top of the High Street.

Once the not-exactly-out-of-town retail park opened, the High Street died with astonishing suddenness. These days it only lacked a bit of tumbleweed bowling down the middle of the road to complete the picture of a ghost town.

Dintscombe Estate Agents would at one time have occupied a prime location, situated between the Nag's Head and the Post Office. But since the Post Office relocated to a small corner of one of the stores in the not-exactly-out-of-town retail park, passing trade had stopped passing and most of the shops had stopped trading.

The window of Dintscombe Estate Agents was festooned with cards advertising 'elegant bungalows in need of updating' (estate agent speech for total wrecks). I peered in between the cards and spotted Dilys Northcott, seated at a desk, staring intently at the screen in front of her.

As I went in, she looked up with a half-smile that vanished the moment she recognised me. She certainly looked a lot drier than the last time I saw her and her hair had calmed down several tones from its original pickled cabbage red to a weird muted orange that would have had an orangutan reaching for the colour charts.

Her face was as pale as ever and there was no sign of the vivid crimson lipstick she'd been wearing Saturday. It was obvious from her red rimmed, puffy eyes that she'd been crying.

"I've nothing to say to you," she said tersely. "Your paper's done enough damage."

"I'm not here about the paper, Mrs Northcott," I said. And I really meant it, whatever I might have said to Liam. All I wanted at that moment was to get her to talk to me.

"Ms Northcott," she corrected me coldly. "So, are you looking for a property?"

The look she gave me suggested she knew all too well the sorry state of my finances.

"Not exactly. I was wondering if you'd mind talking about Paul McAllister. I understand you worked for him."

"I'd hardly be sitting here if I didn't, would I?" she snapped. "And if you think for one moment I'm going to talk to you about him, so that you can write some more of that disgraceful nonsense you did last week -"

"Look, I know you probably won't believe me, but I didn't

write that rubbish. I spoke to Paul about Gerald Crabshaw's ridiculous accusations and he declined to comment. He said that it was one of those things where the least said, soonest mended. As it happened, I agreed with him and respected his decision."

"You're so right. The accusations were indeed quite ridiculous, weren't they?" Her voice softened and her shoulders sagged as if her anger had been the only thing holding her up. "He - he was a wonderful man. One of life's true gentlemen. I can't believe he's gone."

Her swollen eyes swam with tears as she fumbled in her desk drawer and took out an almost empty box of tissues.

"I thought you'd like to know Gerald Crabshaw is now flatly denying there was any rift between him and Paul," I said. "And that the whole story had been blown out of all proportion by the unscrupulous new editor of the paper, who Gerald is threatening to sue."

She frowned. "Are you saying Mr Crabshaw didn't say all those terrible things about Paul? I know Paul said he wasn't the easiest of neighbours."

"I'm saying Gerald Crabshaw is backtracking like crazy because he doesn't want the police to finger him as suspect number one."

"A suspect?" She stared at me, her eyes shocked and wide, the hand holding the tissue stopped halfway to her eyes. "But Paul's death was a horrible accident. Wasn't it?"

"The police are treating his death as suspicious."

You hear about people's faces going white when they've had a terrible shock, don't you? But, until that moment, I'd never actually seen it. Although Dilys' face didn't go white, so much as the same colour as that gloopy grey porridge my mum makes.

"Suspicious? That means. Oh my God. That means he was murdered, doesn't it?" Her voice rose to a squawk as the porridge-like grey gave way to a flush of red-hot anger. "And I know exactly who did it."

"You do?" I asked. Then, when she didn't answer, prompted, "Who?"

"That woman," she hissed. Her eyes, which I'd thought of as a washed out sludgy green suddenly flashed like emeralds in firelight. "She took him for every last penny, but even that wasn't enough."

"Do you mean his wife?"

"His ex-wife." She spat the words out, as if they left a foul taste in her mouth.

"But why would she do that?"

"Why? To get her greedy, grasping hands on Mill Cottage, of course. It was the only thing the poor man had left. She'd taken everything else."

"But how could she get her hands on the cottage? I thought they were divorced?"

She tossed her head. "She wouldn't let a simple thing like divorce come between her and what she considered her money. I tell you, she's completely ruthless when it comes to getting what she's set her mind on. She'll stop at nothing."

Nothing? Would that include murder? I wondered. "Where can I find her?"

But it was a question too far. She'd obviously suddenly remembered she was talking to a journalist.

"I can't give you that sort of confidential information," she said primly. "Why do you want to know anyway?"

"Because the police have a friend of mine in the frame," I said. Ok, Ed wasn't exactly a friend of mine, but Jules was. "And I know he couldn't possibly have done it. So do you have any evidence that Mrs McAllister was involved?"

"I don't need evidence," she retorted, tossing the crumpled tissue in the waste bin and reaching for another one. "I know her and what she's capable of. And what she put that poor man through. He confided in me, you know."

The tears, which were never far from the surface, now flowed over and trickled unchecked down her cheeks.

I felt so sorry for her and wanted to offer some words of comfort. I thought back to the conversation I'd had with Paul. The one I didn't record in my notebook.

"You do realise he intended going to the Flower Show on Saturday, don't you?" I said softly.

"I had hoped... and then when he didn't turn up, I thought it was - was because –" she said between hiccups. "I expect you think I'm all sorts of a fool, don't you? Thinking a man like him could be interested in someone like me. Getting all dressed up to the nines, just in case. I think now that he had no intention of going to the Flower Show, that he only said he might to be kind."

"But you're wrong. He had every intention of going. In fact, he told me he was going because you'd asked him to."

Her head came up sharply, her eyes brimming with tears - and a shimmer of hope. "Because of me?"

"He said someone had persuaded to enter his sweet peas in the show and while he didn't for a moment think they were in with a chance of winning, he was going to the show because it was someone he couldn't say no to. And," I added "From the way he smiled when he spoke, it looked as if it was someone he didn't want to say no to. In fact, I remember thinking to myself at the time that he looked like a man who was looking forward to a date. It was you who persuaded him to enter, wasn't it?"

She nodded, the tears spilling over again and I felt at a loss to know what to say to her. I seemed to be making things worse rather than comforting her.

"I'm so sorry for your loss, Ms Northcott," I said quietly, and placed a hand over hers.

"Please call me Dilys." She gave a watery smile. "I used to hate my name, you know, but Paul told me I should be proud of it. He said it's Welsh for perfect. And so I am proud of it. No one's ever called me perfect before. Even if he was just saying it to make me feel better. I was pretty low when I first came to work here after my marriage broke up."

"I didn't know Mr McAllister very well, Dilys," I said. "But I liked him. He didn't deserve what happened to him."

"He didn't, did he?" Her puffy eyes began to well up again. "He was very kind to me. I'd just split up from my husband, and, well, he was very understanding. And patient, while I learned the job. I'd never done anything like this before, you see."

She looked up at me, her thin nervous fingers shredding the tissue she'd been holding. Now the rush of anger was past, her eyes had lost their emerald fire and had reverted to dull, sludgy green.

"Thank you for telling me," she went on. "Knowing Paul intended coming on Saturday means more to me than you'll ever know. I should have had more faith in him. It's just that I couldn't quite believe it when he said he'd be there. And while we're talking about last Saturday," she took a deep, steadying breath and looked me straight in the eye. "I was rather ungracious after you were so kind to me. I meant to contact you earlier to apologise for my behaviour - and of course give you the copy of the results sheets I promised you - but the terrible news about Paul just drove everything else from my mind."

"Hardly surprising. So, let me guess, when I offered to drive you home last Saturday you saw my mother's name on the side of the car and realised who I was, didn't you?"

She flushed and I knew I was right. "Could you tell me why you don't use her salon anymore? I understand if you'd prefer not to. After all, it's a free country and you're perfectly entitled to change your hairdresser. It's just that Mum can't understand what's happening."

Dilys touched her weird orange hair. "I wish I'd kept my regular appointment with Cheryl. But she phoned to say it had been cancelled."

"Mum did?"

Her cheeks went as red as her hair had been last Saturday. "No. This Crystal person. She said Cheryl was giving up hairdressing and she was taking over her client list. In fact, she said she'd bought your mum out as Cheryl was going to turn her place into a spa and massage parlour. And, I'm sorry, you're going to think me terribly old fashioned," her cheeks began to burn again, "But I'm really not into that sort of thing."

I sighed. Obviously the fake news had reached Little Drearyfield as well.

"Mum's not giving up hairdressing. She's building as

149

extension on the back of the present hair salon which she's turning into a beauty salon. She's going to offer facials, manicures and pedicures and that's it. No full body massages and definitely no men in dirty raincoats," I couldn't help adding, suppressing a smile as I remembered Olive's burning cheeks. She and Dilys could have lit up both sides of a zebra crossing.

"Oh dear," Dilys murmured. "I've been a bit silly, haven't I? But Crystal was very convincing."

I was beginning to get seriously annoyed with this Crystal person. Who was she - and why was she deliberately trying to ruin my mum's business?

Chapter Nineteen

A bit of healthy competition was one thing but to work her way through Mum's customer list while telling lies about Mum giving up hairdressing was something else. Where had she got the customers' details from anyway? Mum was usually so careful with things like that.

"Anyway," Dilys was saying. "I paid the price for my vanity, didn't I? I wanted to look my best for the Flower Show. And, of course, for..." her voice wobbled and she cleared her throat. "...for Paul. I've sort of let myself go since my divorce and I felt this was my chance, like it was a new beginning." She frowned at the shredded tissue in her hands, as if trying to work out where it had come from. "Then while I was wondering how to go about it, this Crystal rang, saying she'd taken over from your mother and was doing home visits. Well, I thought it would be good to cover some of my grey hairs and she assured me it would look lovely. Only it didn't. Instead of being the beautiful auburn colour like it showed on the box, it came out like this." She tugged at her strange coloured hair. "Not exactly Captivating Copper, is it?"

Captivating Copper? It was more like Revolting Rust.

"Then when I complained to her at the way it had turned out, she said the colour hadn't taken because I had too much grey, which you'd have thought she should have known, wouldn't you? Anyway, she gave me this temporary colourant that you spray on, just to tide me over. And it looked ok, if a bit on the bright side. But she didn't warn me what might happen if I got caught in the rain. I nearly died when I saw how the colour had run all down my lovely new jacket. My only consolation was that Paul hadn't been around to see it. Silly really, as things turned out."

"Look," I felt my way as gently as I could as I didn't want

to embarrass her any further. "I know my hair isn't a very good advert for Mum's salon and I've had more bad hair days than you've had hot dinners. But I promise you, I'm the one who experiments with the colours, not her."

"So I see," she murmured, as she looked at my blue and green hair. "But you're young and pretty. You can carry it off."

"And, on the many occasions when things have gone very wrong for me, Mum's brilliant at putting it right. I once mixed up some colours that I thought were going to give me a lovely plum shade but it ended up like -" I paused, remembering how Will had laughed and said it looked like I was wearing a cow pat on my head. But I thought that maybe Dilys wouldn't think that was funny. Any more than I had. "It looked a mess. But Mum soon sorted it."

"Yes. Thank you, dear. I'll give Cheryl a call," she said as she threw the remains of the shredded tissue in the bin and straightened her chair. "Well, if that is all, I'd better get on. I have a stack of things to do today. Especially with Mr Pinney from Head Office due back any moment."

But I had one last question for her. "Paul was working on something with Martin Naylor. I heard them talking about it in the pub. I don't suppose you've any idea what that might have been?"

She looked thoughtful. "Do you know, I wondered if -" she began but broke off.

"Do you think they were involved in something iffy?" I prompted when she didn't continue.

She straightened up and the emerald fire returned to her eyes. "Of course not. Paul would never do anything 'iffy' as you choose to put it."

"And yet, you started to say something."

She bit her lip. "I did, didn't I? And, to be honest, it's been bothering me. There was one project. He was very secretive about it, which was most unlike him. If I came into his office while he was working on it, he'd hurriedly close it and put it in his desk drawer."

I glanced towards the office at the back. "And where is it now?" I asked.

"I - er..." She took a slim folder out of her desk. "Mr Pinney from Head Office turned up this morning. He's been asking all sorts of pointed questions about Paul and what he was doing. So when he popped out just now I went in and got it. And -"

She broke off as the front door opened and a tall, thin man in a dark suit came in.

He hardly looked at us as he headed towards what used to be Paul's office. As he did so, Dilys shoved a stack of particulars of bungalows 'in need of modernisation' in my hand and assured me that I'd be sure to find exactly what I was looking for in there.

As the one on the top of the pile was in Crabshaw Gardens, just opposite Elsie and next door to the man everyone called Creepy Dave (for very good reasons), I doubted that very much. I might be desperate for somewhere to live, away from my mum and dad and their passion for *Antiques Roadshow* and endless repeats of *Midsomer Murders*, but not that desperate.

But I took the papers and, in response of the desperate appeal in her eyes, stuffed them in my bag.

"I'll take these and have a think about them. Thank you. You've been very helpful," I said as I left.

***

Mum was staggered to learn about Crystal and the rumours she'd been spreading. And even more worried by the fact that it looked as if she'd somehow got hold of a list of Mum's clients and their contact details.

"Who is this Crystal?" she asked. "And where's she based?"

"Nobody seems to know. She's only recently moved into the area. Dilys didn't have her phone number. She asked her for it but somehow Crystal changed the subject and didn't get around to giving it to her. Pretty weird way to do business, if you ask me. Don't call me. I'll call you."

"And that's what she's doing, is it? Working her way through my client list?"

"That's what it looks like. But where could she have got it

153

from?" I asked.

"I've absolutely no idea. I'm always so careful about my customer records. You know I always -" She broke off and looked down at the stash of papers I'd just taken out of my bag. "What on earth are you doing with details of a bungalow in Crabshaw Crescent?"

But it wasn't the flowery descriptions of the bungalow's 'cosy sitting room' or 'panoramic views' that made me gasp.

Tucked in among the papers was a slim manila folder, stamped with the logo of Dintscombe Estate Agents.

It was surely the file that, according to Dilys, Paul had been so secretive about. Was I about to find out what he and Martin had been getting up to? And could that have something to do with Paul's death?

But the excitement I felt as I opened the folder ended in a whoosh of disappointment. There was nothing in there except a slim book with a dull sepia coloured cover and a small folded over leaflet.

"What have you got there?" Mum asked.

"Just some research material I've got for something Liam wants me to do."

"*The History of Somerset's Hidden Villages.*" She read the title of the book and raised an eyebrow. "Not something The Chronicle would be interested in, I wouldn't have thought."

She wasn't wrong there. Although Liam, like me, would well wonder why Paul McAllister was. And why he'd been so secretive about it.

I flicked through the book. It featured a number of obscure Somerset villages, one of which was, not surprisingly, Much Winchmoor which is about as obscure as you can get.

It looked like the section on Much Winchmoor had a whole heap of stuff about the Monmouth Rebellion and not much else, which just goes to show that nothing worth talking about had happened in the village since the seventeenth century.

Unless, of course, you counted the odd murder or two. But they weren't mentioned in the book anyway.

My interest quickened when I saw a yellow sticky note marking one of the pages. I flicked it open, hoping I was going to find something significant scribbled on it. Maybe, a cryptic note that would explain why Dilys was so anxious for me to smuggle it away before Mr Pinney saw it.

But it was blank and had obviously just been used as a bookmark. The interesting thing, however, was that it marked a page about the history of Winchmoor Manor.

The Manor House stood, set back from the road behind a cloak of ancient beech trees, on the outskirts of the village. It had been empty for the past twelve months or so while there was some sort of legal wrangle over who actually owned the place.

It was, so the book said, built in the 16th century, although it had been much added to over the centuries, so that it looked more like a collection of random buildings stuck together than a single dwelling. What, I wondered, was Paul's interest in it? Chances are it was no more than the mild curiosity of a newcomer to the village wanting to find out about what was one of the oldest houses in the village.

But it was the other thing in the folder, the leaflet, that caused my heart to quicken.

"What's that?" Mum asked.

"Just a load of bumf from Historic Buildings England," I said as I put it away from Mum's all-seeing eyes.

Now what, I wondered, did Paul McAllister want with an application form for Listed Building Planning Consent form?

I put the file back in my bag and turned to go upstairs to my room, away from Mum's prying eyes. "I'd better get on. I've got loads to do."

"Before you do, there's a couple of things I need to talk to you about."

I hated it when she did that. The look on her face that told me that, whatever it was, I wasn't going to like it.

"First off," she said. "I've got an appointment with the bank manager next week. To discuss the business plan we put together. And I wondered, seeing as you were such a help, whether you'd come with me? It's all sounding very positive."

"Of course I will," I said quickly, relieved it was nothing worse.

155

But my relief was short-lived.

"Then there's Will," she went on. "Look, Katie, I know this is none of my business. But I'm very fond of Will. But I've got the feeling that things don't seem to be going that well between you lately. Is everything all right?"

Not going well? She must have been deeply asleep on Saturday night when Will walked me home after my shift at the pub and came in for a coffee... 'or something'.

"Yeah, we're good," I assured her and was very tempted to say that, for once, I agreed with her. My love life was, indeed, none of her business.

But I'd never been able to keep things from Mum for very long. And besides, the whole 'me and Will' thing was beginning to get me down.

"Mum, how did you know? I mean, when you met Dad, how did you know it was... it was the real thing?"

Her eyes softened as she smiled. "I knew from the first time I saw him. It was at Wells Carnival. I was still living with Mum at the time but a friend from work lived in Wells and persuaded me to go to the carnival with her. The town was absolutely packed and I'd never seen anything like those amazing floats. During the evening we met up with a group of my friend's mates, one of which was your dad. And there was something about him. We didn't just click - it was more like fireworks going off."

I shifted uncomfortably and hoped she wasn't going to go into too much detail about the 'fireworks'. There are things about your parents, you just don't want to know, aren't there?

"But we were both seeing other people at the time," she went on. "And, at the end of the evening, we parted, and I thought we'd never see each other again."

"But obviously you did."

"Obviously. Without telling each other, Terry finished with the girl he'd been going with and I finished with James, much to my mother's fury as he was the son of a friend of hers. I don't think my mother has ever forgiven your dad."

"She certainly hasn't," I said wryly. Grandma Kingham was a snob of the first order who'd always thought her daughter had married 'beneath her'. "You'd think she'd be pleased that you and Dad are still so happy together, wouldn't you?"

"That's what she's like, I'm afraid. But I'm not like her. All I want, sweetie, is for you to be happy." She placed her hand over mine and gave a gentle squeeze. "You've kept Will hanging on for such a long time, haven't you? If you're not sure…"

How could I tell her? Any more than how could I tell Will? I loved him. And yes, there were fireworks every time he touched me. But were the fireworks enough to make up for me giving up on my dream of leaving Much Winchmoor?

I couldn't ask Will to leave the village. There were probably Mannings farming up on Pendle Knoll Farm back when the foundation stones were being laid at Winchmoor Manor. He was as much a part of Much Winchmoor as the village pond, although he smelt a whole lot nicer.

I wished we'd stayed just good mates. In a brother and sister kind of way. Wished too we'd never had that first kiss. Because that was when the fireworks started. And fireworks, as we all know, can be very dangerous if used carelessly.

"You should tell him," Mum said. "It's not fair on him."

And, of course, she was absolutely right. It wasn't fair. But I didn't know what to say to her, least of all what I was going to say to Will.

I was spared having to respond though because the salon phone rang and she hurried to answer it. I stayed long enough to ensure it wasn't someone else calling to cancel, then escaped to the safety of my room.

I took Paul's folder out of my bag and forced myself to focus on it. If only to stop my head from going round and round, thinking about Will.

What was the significance of the Listed Buildings Consent leaflet and form? Did that mean Winchmoor Manor, which was almost definitely a listed building given its age and historical importance, was on the market? I checked on several websites, including the one for Dintscombe Estate Agents but there was no mention of it.

Dilys, of course, would know but I didn't want to ring the

number on the website, in case the call was answered by Mr Pinney. Instead I searched through my contacts and found her mobile number under Little Mearefield Flower Show. She sounded very wary as she answered.

"Just a small thing, Dilys," I assured her. "And one I'm sure you can answer. Is Winchmoor Manor on the market? And if so, are you the agents?"

There was a long pause.

"Dilys?" I prompted. "Is it difficult for you to speak? Can we talk later?"

"Yes," she said clearly. "That will be fine. I'm sorry the property wasn't what you were looking for. Is there anything else I can show you?"

I grinned. "Well, I don't think one of the old folks' bungalows in Crabshaw Crescent was quite what I had in mind. Can we speak later?"

"That'll be fine," she said smoothly. "I'll see what else I can find that might appeal to you. Thank you for calling Dintscombe Estate Agents."

I had to hand it to Dilys. For an ex-bacon slicer from the Co-op, she had an excellent telephone manner.

I ended the call, turned back to the Listed Buildings leaflet then smiled as I heard voices from downstairs. Mum's was one. The other was Will's.

My heart gave a little lift as it always does at the sound of his voice and I hurried downstairs to see him, trying to put all thoughts of fireworks out of my mind.

***

"There you are," Mum said. "Will was just enjoying one of my home-made energy bars, weren't you, Will?"

I loved Will for a lot of things. I loved him for the way his hair sticks up making him look like he's just got out of bed. I loved him for the crinkly white lines in the corners of his eyes that he's got from spending all his life outdoors and refusing to wear sunglasses, which, he says, are for posers.

I loved him for the way he moans and grumbles all through

a rugby match and always insists that the ref 'hates Bath' (that's the rugby team, you understand, not the bit of bathroom kit, nor even the beautiful Georgian city) and always gives decisions against them when other teams get clean away with it.

But most of all, that day in my mum's kitchen, I loved him for the resolute way he was chewing his way through Mum's hideous home-made energy bars that could have been used to shore up the sea defences at Burnham-on-Sea. He was probably thinking he could safely feed it to his cattle as it would keep them occupied for hours when they were shut up in the barn during the long winter months.

"Very nice, Mrs Latcham," he eventually managed to say.

"William Manning," Mum gave him one of her looks. Had she finally rumbled that Will was only pretending to like her energy bars to be polite? "How long have we known each other? And how long have I been asking you to call me Cheryl?"

He was spared from answering by the ping of the salon door. "Oh, that'll be Mrs Bixon," she said. "I'd better go while I still have any clients left. And then I'm off to see my mother. Are you sure you don't want to come, Katie?"

I was sure. Very sure. Visits to my grandmother were things to be endured. Or, better still, avoided.

"I'm busy," I said. "I've got a couple of things that Liam is screaming for. I'd better stay here and get on with it."

I didn't mention that Ed might be around to start on the patio. Ed wasn't the most reliable person on the planet and I didn't want to get Mum's hopes up. And, if he did turn up, then that would be a nice surprise for her when she got back. After spending the afternoon with her mother she'd probably be ready for it.

"Now Katie, make sure you offer Will another energy bar. I can see how much he likes them. And they're really healthy too. You should have one as well. There are plenty there. I've made them for your dad's lunch box, but he won't mind sharing them."

Too right he wouldn't. As Mum left the room I offered Will

the tin, but he shook his head. "Thanks, but one is enough," he said.

"One is more than enough," I said firmly. "Don't you know by now not to ever, ever accept anything that Mum says is 'home-made'? And what are you doing here anyway? Why aren't you up on the farm, watching your cows grow?"

"Ha, ha. Very funny," he said but he wasn't laughing. Instead, he looked very serious. "I had to get away, Katie -"

"Kat," I reminded him.

"Sorry. Kat. She's up there again. Standing at the stove where Mum used to stand. Baking a cake. Acting like she's already moved in."

"Who? Your dad's new lady? What's her name?"

"Tina. But, honestly, Katie- Kat, she's doing my head in. She's loud, brash - and, like I said, she's all wrong for him. Anyway, I've got the afternoon off. Seems I'm superfluous to requirements when Tina's around. It's a pity we don't do dairy anymore. I'd love to see her in the milking parlour, mucking out in her leopard print skirt and dangly earrings."

"What are you doing instead?"

"I wondered if you fancied going to the Queen Vic at Priddy for a pint and a bite to eat? My shout. I just need to get away from this village for a bit."

I knew that feeling only too well. I needed to get away from the village most of the time. I thought of the notes I'd promised Liam would be on his desk that afternoon. Then I thought of the Queen Vic, one of my favourite pubs right up on top of the Mendips. And of the great ham, eggs and chips they served.

No contest. I'd catch up on work later.

A quiet table for two, a nice pub lunch and a bit of Dutch courage in the shape of a pint of Butcombe and I'd be ready to have that 'little chat' with Will.

Chapter Twenty

The ham, eggs and chips were as good as ever, but the pint of Butcombe wasn't doing much for the Dutch courage department so I told myself I'd do the 'little chat' after we'd finished eating. The thick, sweet-salty ham, the rich sunshine yellow eggs and those incredible chips - crisp on the outside, light and fluffy inside - were too good to spoil by getting angsty.

`Instead, as we ate, I gave Will a carefully edited account of my visit to Dintscombe that morning and my encounter with Dilys. I left out the bit about seeing Ed. That information was on a need to know basis and Will didn't need to know.

Not that it mattered. It was obvious from the distracted way he was pushing the food around on his plate that he hadn't heard a word I'd said.

"Do you want to talk about it?" I asked, as I stole a chip off his plate.

"You can have them." He pushed his plate towards me. "I'm not really hungry."

I looked at him in alarm. The only time I've ever known Will to leave food - and that even includes my mother's concoctions - was when he had chicken pox when he was seven. I peered closely at him, looking for spots but could find none.

"Are you ill?"

He shook his head. "No. Just - just -" he began, then shook his head and reached for his pint.

"Is this about Tina?" I asked.

"Yes. And no."

I waited for him to elaborate. But he didn't. Which again is not like him. He's usually pretty quick to offload his problems on me. Not to mention his (usually unasked for) opinions.

"Ok, then," I went on. "But you're going to have to give me a bit of a clue here if we're going to get a conversation going. Because I've been talking to myself for the last half hour. So, come on, Will. Out with it."

He picked up a beermat and tore it in half. Then he looked across the table at me, his expression so serious that I thought for one scary moment he was going to tell me he'd found someone else. Or that he had some terrible illness.

"Will," I leaned closer to him, my voice low. "You're freaking me out here."

"Sorry. I didn't mean to." He looked down at the shredded beer mat. "The thing is, Katie, I've got to get away."

"Why? What have you done?" I was seriously worried now and did what I always do when things are getting a bit stressy. I make silly remarks that are meant to lighten the situation and lessen the tension but usually have the opposite effect. "Robbed a bank? Forgot to file your Tax Return?"

He didn't laugh. Just went on tearing the beer mat into ever smaller pieces. "This place," he said eventually. "It's stifling me. I've got to get away."

"What do you mean by this place? Not the pub, surely?" The lunchtime session was nearly over and the bar almost empty. A warm breeze came in through the open door. "Because, if so, we can go and sit outside."

"Course I don't mean the pub. I mean, Much Winchmoor. It's time I left. Moved on. Made a life for myself away from the village."

Now this might not sound any big deal. People move away from the place where they were born all the time. It is, after all, what I did. But it wasn't what Will did. Or so I'd always thought.

My heart stood still. This was what I wanted, what I'd hoped for. It would solve all my problems if Will came with me. If we left Much Winchmoor together I could have the life I've always wanted and have Will as well. Who says a girl can't have it all?

But then, to my dismay, I heard myself saying, "You don't really mean that, Will. This is about your dad and Tina, isn't it?"

He shrugged. "Yes. No. Oh hell, I don't know. But this whole Tina business had made me stop and think about what I really want. Certainly if she moved in there's no way I could stay."

"Have you spoken to your dad about this?"

"I tried to talk to him about her the other day and he cut me dead. Said it was none of my bloody business. I said it was very much my business as it involved the farm. And he said that it wasn't my farm yet. And I shouldn't count my chickens."

In the nick of time I stopped myself saying that, last time I looked, they didn't have any chickens on the farm, and didn't he mean count his cows?

Instead, I settled for "That doesn't sound like your dad."

"Not the man he used to be, certainly," Will growled. "But he's changed since he's taken up with her."

"Nonsense. Nobody changes that much. You just caught him on a bad day, I dare say. Of course you'll inherit the farm. If nothing else, it's what your mother would have wanted."

Will gave a bitter laugh. "Do you know, I actually caught Tina in the sitting room the other day and she was measuring up. Said something about the piano having to go. Mum's piano."

"What did your dad say about that?"

"He wasn't there. She was talking to herself and looked pretty embarrassed that I'd overheard her."

"Oh Will, that's just awful." I wanted to put my arms around him and give him a big hug. But Will is a bit old fashioned that way. He doesn't do PDAs. Not that ever he'd call them that. He might not know that PDA stands for public displays of affection, but he certainly didn't go in for what he called 'messing around in public.'

"Look, I'm sure it will all sort itself out," I said as I scooped up the tiny pieces of shredded beer mat and placed them on his now empty plate. Had I really finished off all those chips? Stress might have made Will lose his appetite, but it never worked that way for me. Quite the opposite. "So don't go

163

doing anything stupid like telling your dad you're leaving, will you?"

He stared at me, his eyes intent. "But I thought that was what you wanted?"

"What?"

"I thought you wanted me to leave Much Winchmoor and that I was the only thing keeping you here."

Now, the voice inside my head urged. Now is the time to tell him. Tell him he's right.

But I couldn't do it. Not when he was feeling so down. I was pretty sure this thing with his dad would blow over. They've had their differences before and have always sorted things out in the end.

"I don't think you're in the right frame of mind to make any sort of decision like that at the moment, Will. Come on," I said. "Let's head back, shall we? I really do have a stack of things to do this afternoon."

We were almost the last people to leave the pub and when we got to the car park, the only other car was a sleek silver Jaguar, a real old classic. I felt quite embarrassed that Will's muddy and battered old Land Rover was parked next to it.

On our way back, we were driving down a narrow lane when something in the hedge caught my eye.

"Will, Look. Over there." I pointed to where a sheep had somehow managed to get itself wedged, half in, half out of a dense blackthorn hedge that a mouse would have a job getting through. Least of all a rather plump ewe. "We've got to help her."

Will pulled into the gateway. We clambered over the gate and made our way across the field, wet and muddy from all the weekend rain, towards the panicking animal.

When we reached her, she tried to push herself further into the hedge but was stopped going any further by a small branch covered in lethal looking spikes that was firmly embedded in the poor creature's ear and fleece.

"I've got some clippers in the Land Rover," he said. "I'm going to have to cut her out."

He hurried back to the Land Rover and returned with the

clippers. He approached carefully and spoke in a calm quiet voice to the frightened animal.

It must have worked because she quietened down enough to let him cut through the spiky branch then stayed reasonably still as he gently disentangled it from her ear and her fleece.

"Hang on to her," he said while he worked away with the clippers. "And when I've cut the last bit, we'll pull her back into the field. We don't want her launching herself even further into the hedge."

You have no idea just how difficult it is to get a hold on a slightly wet, very upset sheep who doesn't seem to get that just because the hole she's attempting to squeeze herself into will take her head, it doesn't mean that the rest of her body will follow.

But after a certain amount of pushing, pulling and cursing, the hedge finally gave up its prize and the sheep shot out, knocking us both into the muddy field as she did so. She raced across to join the rest of her flock without a backward glance.

I, on the other hand, was lying face down in the mud. But, do you know what? I was so relieved that we'd got her free I didn't care.

Will pulled me to my feet. He brushed some of the mud off my face with a gentle hand. I was expecting him to laugh, which is what he usually does when I take a prat fall. But he didn't.

"You ok?" he asked, his voice husky.

"Nothing that a hot shower and a complete change of clothing won't cure. I'm just glad we got her out."

"I'll make a farmer's wife out of you yet," he said, still holding my hand and suddenly looking very serious.

"Was that a proposal?" I said with a laugh, trying to lighten things up a bit. "If so, it was a pretty rubbish one."

I'd done it again. Said something light and jokey at a time when I should have been deadly serious. Because, you see, I realised Will's outburst in the Queen Vic was merely him letting off steam after an argument with his dad. Nothing more. His threat to leave the farm - and Much Winchmoor - was an empty one.

I saw the way he was with that sheep. Firm yet gentle. Talking to it all the time he was freeing it from the blackthorn's death grip. He was in his element.

He'd said he'll make a farmer's wife out of me yet? But I didn't want to be a farmer's wife. Not now. Not ever.

I opened my mouth to say something but before I could do so Will laughed and said, "I suppose you'd want me to go down on one knee, with violins playing and someone flinging rose petals all over the place?"

I pulled a face and pretended I thought he was joking. "Nah. That's not me. I can't stand violins. How about you stand in the middle of the pond, in your underpants, with a rose between your teeth? That would be more my style. Now, come on, let's go home. I need to get out of these filthy clothes and have a shower."

"I could help you with the first bit," he said. "Especially if your mum is still out."

"Sounds good to me," I grinned as we reached the Land Rover.

Before he started the engine, he leaned across and kissed me. He smelt of mud, freshly cut hedge and not so fresh sheep. But then, I did as well, so who cared?

"Thank you so much," he said. "You've no idea how you've helped."

"I just stood there. You did all the work."

"I didn't mean the sheep. I meant listening to me while I sounded off. And you're quite right, of course. I need to sit down and talk quietly and calmly to Dad. You always put things into perspective for me. I'd better get on back although -" he added with a wicked smile that sent a shiver of anticipation down my spine. "I've probably got time for a quick shower."

But when we got home, I was really disappointed to see that, for once in his life, Ed Fuller had been as good as his word and was halfway through laying Mum's sun terrace.

I watched as Will and Ed went into a deep and serious discussion about Bath Rugby's latest signing and how it was going to make a couple of the existing players up their game.

While they were doing that, Mum came back. Grandma Kingham, it seemed, was not in the mood for visitors that afternoon.

I said goodbye to Will, thanked him for lunch and went up for my shower. Alone.

.....

I'd just finished drying my hair when my phone rang. It was Dilys.

"I'm so sorry I couldn't answer you properly earlier," she said. "As you may have guessed, Mr Pinney was hovering. He's been doing it all day, driving me mad with his incessant questions. You were asking about Winchmoor Manor?"

"Yes. I don't know if you looked in that folder you slipped in among the property leaflets for me?"

"I didn't have time to. I just grabbed it when I heard Mr Pinney was coming. Was there anything -" she hesitated.

"Anything that incriminated Paul?" I finished the question for her. "No. It was just an old booklet about the history of a few Somerset villages, Much Winchmoor included. There was a bookmark on the page about Winchmoor Manor. Also in the folder was a leaflet and an application form from Dintscombe council about listed building consent. I just wondered if Winchmoor Manor had come on the market. I know there was a bit of legal wrangling over who actually owned the property."

"It's strange you should ask. We were approached a few months ago by the vendor - can't remember who it was, offhand - and I was really looking forward to writing up the description of it. That's my job, you know, writing up the property descriptions and I love it. Paul says - said -" her voice broke a little. "Paul said I had quite a flare for it. I've always been fascinated by the Manor and so I was quite disappointed when Paul said it wasn't necessary. I assumed the vendor had changed his mind. Maybe put off by the fact that it's a Listed Building and you have to go through so many hoops before you can do anything."

"You don't think that was the project Martin and Paul were working on, do you?"

167

"Buying Winchmoor Manor?" She laughed. "Good heavens no. The asking price was well over a million pounds. Paul certainly didn't have that sort of money, not after *she* had finished with him. And, as far as I remember from when the Naylor's bought The Old Forge, they didn't either."

But I wasn't so sure. The Naylors had spent an awful lot of money doing up The Old Forge. Elsie could probably tell me the exact amount. And the flash car in the garage would have probably cost the same amount as a small two-bedroomed cottage so they didn't look as if they were short of a pound or two.

Besides, Martin Naylor struck me as the sort of guy who, even if he didn't have the cash himself, probably knew a man who did.

Could he have been Paul's murderer? A falling out over a business plan that went wrong? People have been murdered for less. And Martin Naylor had always struck me as the sort of guy who'd stop at nothing to get what he wanted. And he was probably a difficult man to do business with if the way he'd treated poor Ed was anything to go by.

So, what exactly had been going on between Paul and Martin? I was sure if I could find that link, I'd be closer to finding who had killed Paul and why.

Tomorrow, I promised myself, when I went to collect Finbar for his walk, I was going to ask Suzanne a few carefully selected questions.

.....

The next morning I walked all three dogs together again. They all got along well, which was surprising because I didn't think Prescott got on with anyone or anything. But he seemed quite taken with Finbar and the feeling was obviously mutual. Rosie was only interested in litter bins and was happy to amble along behind the other two doing her own thing.

Finbar's eyes were brighter and there was a spring in his step that hadn't been there before as he ambled along beside his new friend. They made an odd couple though, with Prescott's little legs going like an overwound clockwork toy as he scurried to keep pace with Finbar.

I walked them around the lanes and, once again, as we went past the old barn Finbar pulled towards it. One day, I promised, I would follow him and see what he found so interesting there. But not today as I really wanted to get some answers from Suzanne while Martin was, hopefully, still away. I took Prescott and Rosie back first then headed back to The Old Forge with Finbar.

"Is your husband still away?" I asked as Suzanne opened the door to the utility room for me.

"Yes." Her abrupt tone suggested she didn't want to say any more on the subject, so I tried another tack. I took off the dog's lead and picked up the towel that hung above his bed.

"That must be dead lonely for you," I went on as I wiped Finbar's muddy paws. "Why not let Finbar into the house with you? He'll be company for you. And he's lonely too, stuck out here in this room all on his own."

"Do you think so?" She looked down at the dog, who gazed up at her with his sad brown eyes. "I'm afraid it hadn't occurred to me. I don't know much about dogs."

I was no walking encyclopaedia on the subject. But I knew enough to realise they don't enjoy being shut up on their own all day. I put the towel back and scratched the top of Finbar's bristly head. "They like company. In fact, I'd go so far as to say they need it. And he's such a lovely boy. A real sweetie. How old is he?"

She shrugged. "I've no idea. Like I said, he's Martin's dog. In fact, if it hadn't been for Finbar, Martin and I wouldn't have met."

As she spoke, her voice softened, and she began to look a little more relaxed. I pushed it a little further. "So, where did you two meet?"

"It's a long story," she said.

"I'm in no hurry," I assured her.

"Ok, then." She hugged her arms around her slim waist and pulled her grey cardigan tighter. "The back garden of my house in Bristol - or, rather, my grandfather's house - opened on to a park and one evening, Martin knocked on the door. He was in a terrible state. Finbar had gone missing in the park.

He'd been spooked by some children messing around with fireworks and ran off. Poor Martin had knocked on the door of every house around the park's perimeter, asking if they'd seen him. But no one had."

"But obviously the story had a happy ending?" I prompted with a nod at Finbar.

"Oh yes. Of course. For all three of us. I felt so sorry for Martin that I offered to help him look for the dog. We didn't find him that evening but a couple of days later, Martin knocked on my door and there was Finbar, safely on a lead. He'd been handed in miles away from the park and how he got there was a complete mystery. Anyway, Martin asked me out to dinner as a thank you for my help. And that was it. We've been together ever since."

She was looking at me like she expected me to say something like how lucky she was. Martin Naylor was the last person I'd want to end up with but, as Gran Latcham used to say, one man's meat is another man's coconut. And, no, I don't know what she meant by that either.

"Cool. I love a story with a happy ending," I murmured.

She appeared lost in thought and didn't seem to have heard me. I was starting to think she'd forgotten I was there when she said, "Do you know, I think you're right." Then she looked down at Finbar and said, "Come along then."

The dog looked up at her with anxious eyes as she turned back to me. "Would you mind helping me move his bed into the kitchen? It's such a big awkward thing, I doubt I could manage it on my own."

An invitation into the house was exactly what I'd been hoping for. Now, perhaps I could get some answers, particularly as Martin was not around.

Chapter Twenty-One

I helped her carry the huge dog bed into her shiny black and white kitchen. We placed it in the far corner and Finbar got in, turned around a couple of times then settled down with a long sigh of contentment.

"He looks a lot happier now," I said. "And I'm sure you'll sleep better with him in the house with you."

"Why would you think I'm not sleeping?" Her tone had sharpened again.

"With your husband being away. And next door being a holiday cottage and not occupied at the moment. It must be pretty quiet along here at night."

"You're right, of course. It is a bit on the quiet side," she admitted. "Look, I'm just about to make myself a coffee. Would you like one?"

"I'd love one, thanks. I didn't have time this morning."

I watched her making coffee with the sort of machine that looked as if it should be powering the waterwheel of Gerald Crabshaw's mill, instead of making a single cup of coffee.

I took the cup she passed me and inhaled the rich, aromatic steam. It was certainly worth all this hissing and clanking. "This smells amazing."

And it tasted even better.

"So, how did you come to settle on Much Winchmoor of all places?" I asked as I took another sip of what was probably the best coffee I'd ever tasted. "I seem to have spent my entire life trying to get away from it."

She smiled. "I love it here. It's the sort of place I always dreamed of living in. Somewhere to put down roots and make a real family home. I want to give my children the sort of childhood I never had. You see, my parents died in a car crash when I was ten years old."

"I'm sorry," I murmured.

"After that, I went to live with my grandfather in the house I was telling you about. He promptly sent me away to boarding school, St Philomena's, over on the other side of Dintscombe."

"That must have been tough. Losing your parents and then being sent away to school."

She cradled her coffee cup as if her hands were cold. "I wasn't very happy there. To get on at that place, you need to be either academic or sporty and I was neither. I found it difficult to make friends. And I didn't enjoy the lessons, apart from music. My mother -" her voice shook as she stumbled over the word. "My mother was very musical. She used to play the piano and I seem to have inherited her aptitude for it. I could - and still do - lose myself in music. And it makes me feel closer to her. Anyway, the music teacher at St Phil's was Mrs Fairweather, wife of the vicar here in Much Winchmoor. I understand she's since passed away."

"Mrs Fairweather? She's not dead. She ran off with the organist."

"Really?" Suzanne looked shocked. "I didn't realise. I thought when the vicar mumbled something about her no longer being with us, he meant... well, you know."

"As far as I know, she's alive and well and, according to Elsie, still 'living in sin' with her organist."

"I'm glad. I mean, of course, I'm glad she's not dead. She was very kind to me. One year, - it was when I was in the fifth form - she organised a concert in the church here. They were raising money for a new roof or something and I, along with several other girls from the school played and sang. I fell in love with Much Winchmoor that weekend."

This woman, I couldn't help thinking, didn't have a particularly good track record when it came to the people - and places - she fell in love with.

"Anyway," she was saying. "When Martin and I were looking to move out of Bristol and settle in the country, I remembered this village and to my delight, discovered that this place was on the market. It was fate, wasn't it?"

172

All the time she was reminiscing I could feel her gradually relaxing, the tension which had been so obvious when Finbar and I had first come back was slipping from her face. In the far corner of the room, the dog began to snore. We looked across at each other and laughed.

"He sounds right at home," I said. "So, is that why you were so keen to start a choir in the village? Keeping up Mrs Fairweather's tradition? About the concert, I mean, of course. Not running off with the organist."

She gave a soft laugh and looked years younger as she did so. "That's hardly likely, is it, seeing as Mrs Clarke is close on seventy-five and happily married to the churchwarden. But yes, I'd like to carry on Mrs Fairweather's tradition. She held those concerts for several years, I understand. So when I heard about the fundraising effort to raise money for the children's play area, I realised I could help. It would give the choir something to work towards and would benefit the village at the same time. After all," she gave a coy smile. "Martin and I don't have children yet, but we hope to. Just as soon as Martin's workload eases off a bit."

"I think your idea of a concert sounds great." I said and wondered if I should warn her to keep Gino away from the Elvis songs. But then, I figured, if it was for a concert in the church, maybe she'd get away with it. Not all of Elvis's songs were suitable for singing in a church.

"Perhaps, if I've still got a job with the paper, I'll be able to give the concert a bit of a plug," I went on. "I've already been roped in with this play area thing."

"Do you have children, then?" she asked.

"No, thank goodness," I said quickly, as I remembered the way Zack's shrill cries had pierced my eardrums the other day. "It's just that my friend, Jules Fuller, is one of the organisers. And she's one very determined lady."

At the mention of Jules' name, Suzanne's face darkened. It was as if the sun had just gone in. Her mouth tightened and her silvery eyes became like flint.

"Did you say Fuller?" Her voice was cold. "Would that be that any relation to Ed Fuller?"

I could have bitten my tongue. There I was trying to get her all relaxed and chatty and I had to go and mention the guy who'd tried to skittle her husband down, along with a plate of spaghetti bolognese. Would I never learn to think before I speak?

I looked around the kitchen for a way of changing the subject and steering us back to the relaxed friendly mood of a few moments ago when I spotted something I recognised. It was the same book I'd found in the file Dilys had filched from Paul McAllister's desk.

"*The History of Somerset's Hidden Villages*" I picked it up, trying to act all casual like. "You interested in local history, then?"

"A little. I was surprised when I read it to learn how very old Much Winchmoor is."

I nodded. "It certainly is. And, of course, one of the oldest places in the village is Winchmoor Manor. It's on the outskirts of the village, set back quite a long way from the road so you don't really know it's there. It's empty at the moment and has been for the last couple of years. Have you ever seen inside it?"

Her panicky eyes reminded me of the sheep that Will and I had winkled out of the hedge the day before. "Me? Been inside Winchmoor Manor. No. Of course I haven't. I'm not interested in it at all. It's not -" she reached across, snatched the book from my hand and tossed it into a drawer. "And now, if you don't mind- "

She got no further. Because at the same time as she opened the drawer, the kitchen filled with the sound of angry Irish curses.

"Pick up the flipping' phone, you eejit."

She looked down at the phone, her pale eyes wide with terror. Her hands were shaking.

"That's not your phone, Suzanne, is it?" I said gently.

She shook her head.

"It's Martin's?"

She nodded. She snatched it up, rejected the call and stuffed it back in the drawer.

"Where is he, Suzanne?" I asked, and waited for her to tell me to mind my own damn business.

But she didn't. Instead, she slumped back into her chair and buried her face in her hands, her shoulders shaking. As she did so, Finbar crept out of his basket, edged towards her and laid his big hairy head in her lap.

"I - I don't know where he is," she whispered, while she absently stroked the dog's bristly fur. "And I'm out of my mind with worry. I've been trying to find him. Going to all the places where he might be, but no one's seen him. He - he said he'd only be away a couple of nights. But when I realised he hadn't taken his phone - " She lifted her face, which was streaked with tears. "Martin never goes anywhere without it."

"He probably just forgot it," I said, more for reassurance than because I actually believed it. "I'm always doing that."

She shook her head. "It's not just that," she whispered. She took the phone out of the drawer and held it between her long slender fingers. "He's been getting threats. Ever since... well, ever since poor Mr McAllister was - since he was murdered."

"What sort of threats?"

"At first they were just various people after money. Martin had - I mean, he has this job going in Bristol which has hit a few snags, so I've had to field quite a few angry calls from unhappy subcontractors who haven't been paid. They calmed down when I said to send me the bills and that I would settle them and those sorts of calls stopped. But then, a few days ago, the real threats started."

"How do you mean, real threats?"

She handed me the phone. "See for yourself. They're all from the same man. Ed Fuller."

"Ed? You're kidding."

Her voice hardened. "Do I look like I'm joking? I heard they had a fight in the pub the other night and -"

"I wouldn't say it was a fight," I murmured as I scrolled through the messages. And stopped dead. Unable to believe what I was reading.

The threats were indeed from Ed. And there were loads of them, each one angrier and more threatening than the last.

"This can't be true," I said. "Ed would never do something like this. There must be some mistake."

"I don't think so." Her voice shook. "I was told that Ed hit Martin in the pub the other night. Knocked him to the ground. That it was only because there were people in the bar to hold him back that he didn't beat Martin to a pulp."

"That's not what happened. Ask anyone who was in the bar that evening. They'll tell you."

"They did," she said. "They said Ed Fuller was like a madman. I'm going to take this to the police. I kept putting it off because -" she looked uncomfortable. "Because I thought at first my husband had - what is it they say? 'Done a runner?' That he'd got in a mess, financially (and that's nothing but the truth if the bills I've settled in the last week or so are any indication) and had run away rather than face it."

"Leaving you to face it instead?"

She shrugged. "Something like that. I didn't report him missing because that would make me look pathetic. A woman whose husband only married her for her money and even then couldn't hold on to him."

"I'm sure that's not true," I murmured. Not that I believed what I was saying but I wanted to say something to make her feel better. But I could have saved my breath.

"But now I don't think that," she said. "I don't think Martin has run away. Since these texts started coming -" she took a long, shuddering breath and held on to Finbar as if he was a lifebelt and she was just about to jump off the Titanic. "You see, I think - in fact, I've got this terrible feeling that something really bad has happened to my husband."

I was beginning to get that feeling too. In fact, it all made sense. The flash car in the garage, the fancy phone he never went anywhere without. What was it that Paul and Martin had been mixed up in, so that now one was dead and the other? Well, who knew what had happened to him? It wasn't looking good.

The only thing I did know was that Ed had nothing to do with it. Only I don't think Suzanne would have believed me.

"Look," I began. "Before you contact the police -"

Before I could get any further, my phone rang. I glanced at the caller and saw it was Mum. She never phones me during the day. Unless it's pretty important.

"Mum? Is something wrong?"

"Oh Katie. Yes. There most certainly is," she sounded distracted. "I've tried to get hold of your dad but he's not answering his phone as usual. Where are you?"

"I'm at Suzanne Naylor's. I've just taken Finbar back and -"

"Then come home as quickly as possible. I think I could do with ... with some moral support or something."

"What's wrong?" I asked her again. "Mum, you're worrying me."

"The police are here." Her voice rose on a swell of indignation. "A whole van load of them. You know Ed laid the patio for us yesterday?"

"Of course."

"The police arrived about half an hour ago. And they're digging it up again. And when I tried to stop them, this officious little man said I could be arrested for obstruction if I didn't step away and let them get on with their job."

"Did you ask them what they're hoping to find?" I asked.

"They wouldn't say. But whatever it is, they think Ed put it there." She broke off and swore. My mother never ever swears. But she did then. She came out with words I never knew she knew.

"Mum? What's wrong?"

"I'll tell you what's wrong," she said. "Not only are there a couple of big clumsy policeman digging up my lovely sun terrace and scattering all those Busy Lizzies I've spent all morning planting, but the Press have arrived as well. Get yourself home right now, Katie."

Chapter Twenty-Two

It was like the circus had come to town and parked up in our road. There were cars littered everywhere, including a large white police van blocking most of the pavement. A knot of people had collected outside our next-door neighbour's gate, which had sent her yappy little dog into a barking frenzy.

But there was nothing for them to see as a big white tent now covered what had been, if only for the briefest of times, Mum's cherished sun terrace.

As I opened our front gate, Liam was coming down the path from the back garden. He was scowling.

"Liam?" I was almost scared to ask. "Have they found... anything?"

"Who knows? They won't tell me anything. Just said there will be a statement issued later and basically told me to clear off. Which I'd rather not do. We're ahead of the dailies at the moment. I'd like to keep it that way."

"But how did you get here so quickly? Mum called me just now and said they'd only just arrived."

He looked across at the knot of people across the road. "Thank the Lord for nosy neighbours. What would we do without them? Someone who wanted to remain anonymous phoned the paper and said something was going on down here that we might be interested in. So here I am."

"Why you?" I thought how Mike North, his predecessor, only ever left his desk to go home. "Don't you have reporters to scurry around to do your bidding?"

"Cutbacks, Kat, cutbacks," he said. "Besides, I like to get out and about. I'm a hands-on man, as you'll find out." He gave me a wicked grin and his bright blue eyes sparkled. "Figuratively speaking, that is. So, would you happen to know what is it they're digging up? They wouldn't tell me. The

178

vegetable patch, maybe?"

"I wish it was. It's Mum's new patio. It was only laid yesterday." I didn't want to tell him that Ed had laid it. At least, not yet. "Do you know what they're looking for?"

"The patio, eh? That's a cliché if ever I heard one. Maybe that's the wrong question, Kat." There was a frisson of excitement in his voice. "Maybe it's *who* are they looking for? You've heard the expression burying bad news? In our case, it could well be good news. For The Chronicle, that is."

I shook my head. "Jeez, Liam, you're all heart, aren't you?"

He shrugged. "Bad news sells newspapers. And we all know what's going to happen if we can't get the circulation numbers up, don't we? Mitch wasn't making an idle threat about selling the site for housing."

"No, I didn't think he was."

"So," he said. "Have you seen Ed Fuller lately?"

I drew a sharp breath and looked towards the white tent. "You don't think -" I forced myself to think the unthinkable. "You don't reckon that's Ed under there, do you?"

"Shouldn't think so. Not if you say the patio was laid yesterday. Because I interviewed Ed about an hour ago and he -"

"You did? But I told you there was nothing to be got from speaking to Ed."

"So you did," he said quietly. "But I like to make up my own mind about these things."

"What did he say?"

He shrugged. "He wasn't very forthcoming, but I had a strong feeling he was lying when he said he was tucked up in bed beside his wife when Paul McAllister was killed. Says he had the hangover from hell and doesn't remember very much."

"Ed had nothing to do with Paul McAllister's death," I said, while trying not to think of the threatening texts he'd sent to Martin. They were completely out of character.

Or were they?

Ed had always had a bit of a short fuse, that was for sure, and he'd been quite handy with his fists in his younger days. But that had been on the rugby pitch. And Ed had given up

179

rugby after picking up an injury that kept him off work for six weeks, not good when you're self-employed.

But then there was the way he'd gone for me when I told him about giving the wallet back. That had been a side of Ed I'd never seen before. Nor ever wanted to see again.

I shivered. "So who do you think is under there? Oh my god," My heart gave an uncomfortable lurch. "You do realise Martin Naylor is missing, don't you?"

That got his attention. "You're kidding."

"I wish I was. I think he and Paul were involved in something dodgy and they'd had a falling out about it. But now -"

"How long has he been missing?"

"A few days, I think. I've just come from his house and his wife's worried sick. She's going to report it to the police." I didn't tell him how he'd not taken his phone - or about the threatening messages on it. "I've been digging around and I think Paul and Martin were involved in some deal to do with Winchmoor Manor."

Liam looked surprised. "What? That big house just outside the village?"

"According to one of my sources, they could have been looking to buy it. Or at least put together some sort of consortium to do so. Only now, one of them is dead and the other one is..." I paused and tried not to look at the white tent in our back garden. Wherever Martin Naylor might be, I fervently wished he wasn't going to be found under my mum's sun terrace. Or under anybody else's, come to that. "Who knows where he is?"

Liam stood up straighter. His eyes shone. "And you think he might be -?" He, too, looked towards the white tent.

"Like I said, he's been missing for several days."

"And this might have something to do with Winchmoor Manor?"

"Yes. There has to be a third person, or maybe more, involved in that particular project because, from what I gather, neither Paul nor Martin were in a position to fund that sort of million plus purchase."

"And you know this because...?"

"I have my sources," I said, trying not to sound smug. "And, as you know, a good journalist never reveals her sources. I thought maybe it might pay us to do a bit of digging around. There was a lot of shady goings on around Winchmoor Manor last year. It'll be in the paper's archives. If, that is, you're interested."

He gave me a long, straight look than smiled. "I might just do that," he said. "And now you're here, I'll head back to the office. You'll give me a call as soon as there are any developments, won't you?"

As if on cue, my phone rang. It was Dilys. I waved goodbye to Liam and went into the house to take the call.

"Oh, hi, Katie," she sounded like she'd just run up a flight of stairs. "I'd better be quick in case you know who comes back. But I thought you'd be interested to know that I've just had a rather strange phone call."

"You have?" I walked into the kitchen where my mother had stationed herself in front of the window, gazing out at the back garden, although the only thing she could see was the white tent, whose walls were quivering as a result of goodness knows what activity going on inside.

"Oh Katie, will you just look at it," she wailed. "My lovely sun terrace. As for my poor Busy Lizzies, they'll never recover."

I signalled to her that I was on the phone and that I'd be back in a minute and headed for the stairs.

"Hang on a moment," I said to Dilys. "It's a bit of a madhouse around here right now. I'm just going upstairs. The signal might go any moment -"

And of course, it did. When I rang her back from my bedroom, I crossed to the window and looked out on to the back garden where there was absolutely nothing to see, apart from the quivering tent.

"Sorry, Dilys. The signal died but it's ok now. You were saying something about a strange phone call?"

"Yes," her voice still sounded a bit breathless. "This man, who works in our Bristol office, has just called. Luckily, I was

181

here to answer it. He asked to speak to Paul. He said he should have got back to him on Friday but that his wife had gone into early labour and that had pushed everything else out of his mind and he's only just got around to it. And that, in all the upset and excitement of the baby's early arrival, he'd lost Paul's mobile number which was why he was phoning the office. He obviously didn't know Paul had died and I didn't tell him. I just said he wasn't here, and could I take a message? Do you think that was terrible of me?"

"Of course not. That was very sensible. So, what was the message?"

"He said to tell Paul that the man he was asking about was called Greg Mason and that he's a property developer based in Bristol. He said he didn't have a contact number for him yet but that he'd find out and get back. The poor man said he hadn't slept properly since Friday and his head was still all over the place."

"That makes sense," I said. "Because when Paul was in the pub on Friday night, he left early, saying he had to get back as he was expecting a call. This could well have been the call. Thank you, Dilys, that's brilliant. I've got a feeling you've just given me the name of the third person involved in the Winchmoor Manor deal."

"Yes, I've had a look at that, too," Dilys said. "The Manor is still on our books, which is why I was surprised it wasn't being marketed. But it could be that it's on hold because of legal issues."

"Does the name Greg Mason mean anything to you?" I asked.

"No. I'm sorry. But I can ask around, if you like."

I thanked her, made a note of the name and then went down to try and stop my mother finally losing it and telling the police to get the hell out of her sun terrace and take their quivering tent with them.

But I needn't have worried. She'd calmed down by the time I got back to the kitchen, as she'd had a visit from 'that nice Ben Watkins'.

"Is he still out the back?" I asked, thinking that maybe he'd give me a quote. That would be one up on Liam.

But she shook her head. "I offered him a cup of tea and an energy bar - he looked as if he could do with it - but he said he was in a hurry."

"I'll bet he was," I murmured, thinking that Ben wasn't a detective for nothing. He obviously remembered Mum's cooking of old. "So what did he say?"

"He said that, when they'd finished, they would put the garden back and it would be even better than it was before. And they'd replace all the Busy Lizzies and he personally would come round and plant them."

"He did? That seemed an odd thing to do."

But Mum smiled. "I think he was just being kind."

"So, if he was that kind, did he happen to say what they were looking for?"

She shook her head. "He asked me if I'd been around when Ed was laying the patio and what time Ed had got here. I explained that no one was around when Ed arrived as I was visiting my mother and you'd gone out to lunch with Will. But that we both got back before he finished. He wrote it down and off he went." She bit her lip and looked anxious. "What are they looking for? Do you have any idea? Honestly, the way everyone's carrying on, it's like they're expecting to find a body buried under there."

"Of course they're not," I said with a confidence I was far from feeling.

"I hope not. I mean, I realise this is going to sound horribly selfish. But my business is in enough trouble at the moment, without anything like that giving people even more excuse to stay away."

I glanced out of the window, where the small crowd were still hanging around. "Shouldn't think so. You'll probably get a flurry of bookings now, all anxious to get the inside story."

"Well, they won't be getting it from me," she snapped. "Even if I knew what was going on, which I don't. For pity's sake, don't they have anything better to do than standing around, gawping at nothing. For two pins, I'd go out there and tell them to mind their own damn business."

"Best not, though, eh?" I advised her.

Before she could answer, my phone rang again. This time, it was Gino, sounding all upset and Italian.

"Katie, Katie, we have the big problem here," he said. "My poor Norina. She is in the agony. And has to go to dentist. He say to come in right now. Can you come here and help out? We have a party of eight booked in for lunch. We'll pay you extra."

The 'pay you extra' was music to my cash strapped ears. I promised him I'd be there straight away, and he rang off, assuring me of his - and Norina's - undying gratitude. His, I believed. Norina's? Not so much. She didn't do gratitude, undying or otherwise.

Mum promised she'd phone me if or when there was any change in the police activity in the back garden, so I hurried off to the pub.

Gino came bustling out of the kitchen as he heard me arrive. He looked touchingly pleased to see me and I thought for a moment he was going to hug me. I sincerely hoped that Norina was safely off the premises if he did.

"I'm so grateful for you to step in like this, Katie, *bach*," he said. "I will make for you a special lunch as a thank you. Anything you like, off the menu. I cook it for you. The *Spaghetti alla Vongole* is very good today."

"How about a burger with all the trimmings?" I asked.

Gino shook his head and pulled a sad face. "You have no good taste buds, Katie."

"So I've been told," I laughed. "I'll go and lay up in the dining room, shall I?" I went behind the bar and checked along the shelves. "And it looks like the mixers need topping up. I'll do that as well."

"You're a good girl, Katie." His little round face was serious. "This I tell Norina every time. Katie is a good girl. And so, I am going to tell you. Just don't tell Norina I tell you, ok? You promise?"

"I promise," I said, although I had no idea what I was promising about.

He dropped his voice, even though there was only one other

person in the bar, and he was right down the other end, totally engrossed in his newspaper.

"Is not true," Gino said.

"What's not true?"

"What Norina say. She's only seventeen."

If Norina was going around saying she was only seventeen, that was her choice. Although she was forty if she was a day so I couldn't see anyone believing her.

"Well, if that's what Norina wants people to believe -" I said, trying to pick my words carefully.

He looked at me as if I was the one losing it, not Norina.

"It's not Norina who's only seventeen. Is Rhianna. Her sister's girl."

"Rhianna's only seventeen?"

"Is what I said. So, you see, she can't work. Not in the bar. Because of license."

Of course she couldn't. You have to be eighteen to work behind a bar. And Norina would have known that. She'd obviously been using the threat of Rhianna to keep me in line.

"So, you can stop worrying now," Gino beamed. "Only don't tell Norina you know. Else I'll be the one doing the worrying."

"Thank you, Gino," I said then picked up a couple of menus off the bar and went across to give them to a couple who'd just come in.

It was surprisingly busy for a lunchtime service and I wondered if word had got around about the police activity down the other end of the village. As well as the party of eight, Gerald and Fiona Crabshaw came in and settled for Gino's special *Spaghetti alla Vongole*.

They ate their meal in silence, and I was clearing their plates away when another couple came in. One of them was Will's dad. The brassy-haired woman with him, I assumed from Will's less than flattering description, had to be Tina.

"Hello, John," I said. "Are you here to eat? Only I think the special's just finished. But grab a couple of menus off the bar and I'll be right with you."

"Thanks, Katie. I'll do that."

185

"We don't see you in here very often during the day," I said a few minutes later after I'd finished sorting out the Crabshaws' bill. Tina had perched on one of the bar stools and was studying the menu with a frown. John was looking uncomfortable.

"You don't see me in here at all since I gave up drinking," he said. "But Tina fancied a drink and there was nothing in the house. So I said why not stop in here?"

"So what will it be?" I asked.

"I'll have a large vodka and coke, please," Tina said quickly. "I need it. After all that unpleasantness."

She looked meaningfully at John, who looked even more uncomfortable.

"Will can be a bit of a straight talker, when the mood takes him," he muttered, "As Katie here knows right enough. She and Will have been friends since school days."

She ignored me. "There's straight talking and then there's downright rudeness, John. And your son was downright rude." She sniffed. "I'm not used to that sort of confrontational behaviour. It upsets me."

"I'm sure he didn't mean it, love," John said.

Knowing Will the way I did, I was pretty sure he did mean it. I poured the drink and passed it to her. As she took it, the sleeve of her floaty top fell back, and I saw a tattoo on her arm. At the same time, I heard Elsie's voice, inside my head.

"And she has this tattoo, a snake, curling all the way up her arm. It gave Olive such a turn when she saw it, I thought she was having a fit of historics."

"You're Crystal, aren't you?" I said.

She smiled and flicked back her brassy blonde mane. "That's right, dear."

"Crystal?" John looked puzzled. "You told me your name was Tina."

She gave me one of those aren't-men-stupid looks. "And so it is. Tina is short of Christina. And Crystal is my business name. Lots of people in the beauty business have two names. Crystal Hair and Beauty. It has a ring of quality to it, wouldn't you say? Talking of which, sweetie," she let her gaze travel slowly over my hair which, that morning was a combination of my favourite purple and blue stripes. "You look as if you could do with my help. Your skin's looking pretty ropey, too. All those open pores." She gave a little shudder. "Would you like one of my cards?"

"Thank you." I made a huge effort to keep my voice level and not indulge in a spot of confrontational behaviour myself. At least not until I was ready to. "So where is your salon? In Dintscombe?"

"I don't have premises at the moment, although I am actively seeking. But, for the moment, while I'm building up my clientele, I will come to you. And the sooner the better, by the look of it. I do nails as well. Yours look in dire need. Are you sure you're getting enough Vitamin D in your diet?" She reached into the huge patchwork bag on her shoulder and took out a pink notebook with a unicorn marked out in silver glitter on the cover. "Would you like me to book you in?"

"I'll tell you what I would like, Crystal/Tina or whatever you choose to call yourself," I said as I let the grip on my anger slip. "I'd like to know why you are hell bent on putting my mother out of business. What has she ever done to you?"

Chapter Twenty-Three

She stepped back as if I'd slapped her. "Excuse me?" She looked towards John, obviously expecting him to intervene. But he stood, looking from one of us to the other, like a spectator on Centre Court.

"My mother. Cheryl. You've been systematically working your way through her client list for the last few weeks."

"You're Cheryl's daughter?"

"I am."

"Well, dear, you're not a very good advert for her, are you? As for poaching her customers, it's not my fault she can't hang on to them. All's fair in love and hairdressing, as they say." She gave a little giggle. "It's a cut-throat world out there, you know."

Cut-throat? Oh, I wish she hadn't used that expression because, just for a moment, it threw me straight back to Paul McAllister and I almost lost my train of thought. Almost, but not entirely.

"Why have you been telling her customers she's giving up hairdressing?" I asked. "Or is telling lies all fair in love and hairdressing as well?"

There was a sudden silence. John looked first at me, then at Tina/Crystal. She had two red spots high on her cheeks that were not makeup.

"I'm not staying here to be harangued by a barmaid," she said as she tossed back the rest of her drink and banged her empty glass down on the counter. "What is it about this village? No wonder you all keep murdering each other. I've never encountered so much rudeness in all my life."

As she stormed out, John followed, his face like thunder.

Great. Now I'd upset him as well. But at least I now knew who'd been trying to wreck Mum's business. What I didn't know was why.

I was finishing up in the dining room when my phone rang. It was Mum.

"Can you get back here quickly," she said. "Only it looks like the Police are packing up and leaving."

***

Gino was quite happy for me to rush off. Apart from one thing.

"But I was doing your burger," he said. "Can you not wait while it finishes? I'll do you extra fries. And sweet chilli sauce. Your favourite."

My stomach rumbled at the very thought of it. "Sorry, Gino, I've got to dash. Some other time, eh?"

I couldn't help worrying what Liam would say if I got home and they'd all gone. They certainly weren't there very long. And the fact that Mum said they were packing up the tent suggested they hadn't found whatever - or whoever - they'd been looking for.

I was in luck. The first person I saw when I got back to our road was Ben Watkins. He was walking towards his car and gave me a big smile as I hurried towards him.

"Katie -"

"Kat."

"Sorry, Kat. I wondered why I hadn't seen you. You've missed all the excitement. That's not like you."

"So, what were you looking for?" I asked as I took my notebook out of my bag and flipped it open. I clicked my pen.

"I take it I'm talking to Kat Latcham, reporter?" he said.

"Is that ok?"

"Sure. The sergeant said I could 'deal with the bloody press' were his actual words."

"He's a charmer, your boss. So, what were you looking for? And did you find it?"

He shook his head. "It was always a long shot. But we have to follow these things up. And make sure we follow the correct procedures. We're always grateful when the public give us information. And we take it very seriously."

"You say you have to follow 'these things'. What things exactly? What did you think you were going to find?"

"We had this tip off that we might want to check out this newly laid patio -"

"Sun terrace," I corrected him. "Mum insists on calling it a sun terrace."

"The caller said patio," he said.

"And I take it, from the fact that your tent's now been dismantled and that it's all being put back, including, I hope, Mum's precious Busy Lizzies, that you found nothing?"

"We found a Mickey Mouse watch that your mother said you'd lost years ago. But apart from that, no. Nothing. But we have to follow these things up, you know. Even when we're pretty sure it's a wild goose chase."

"Where did this tip off come from?" I asked.

"It was anonymous."

"Another one?"

"What do you mean by that?"

"Liam also had an anonymous tip off to the newspaper about the police activity. We assumed it was one of the nosy neighbours. But maybe it wasn't. Maybe it was the same person who tipped you off about the patio? What do you think?"

He gave me a long, serious look. "I hope you're not going around playing detective again, Kati- Kat," he corrected himself just in time. "I don't have to remind you that a man's been murdered."

"And another -" I was about to say that another man was missing. But I stopped myself. If Suzanne, for whatever reason, had decided against reporting it, that was up to her. For now, at least. "And another day has gone by," was the best I could come up with. "Are you any closer to finding the killer?" I asked, giving my pen an extra couple of clicks.

"A statement will be issued in due course," he said in that tone of voice that told me the interview, such as it was, was at an end. "I'll see you around," he said and walked towards his car.

But as he reached it, he turned back. "I meant what I said, Kat. Keep out of it. It's not a game of Cluedo, you know."

Then, before I could come up with a suitable retort, he got in his car and drove off.

***

I hadn't been back in the house a couple of minutes and was waiting for Mum to draw breath so I could tell her about Crystal/Tina. But she was in full flow, going on about her precious Busy Lizzies and how they'd probably never recover from the trauma of being dug up and replanted. She only stopped when the doorbell rang.

She looked startled. "I hope that's not them come back to start on the vegetable patch. Your dad would go mad."

But it wasn't the police. It was John Manning. And without Crystal, I was relieved to see.

"Is your mum in, Katie?" he said.

"Yes, come along in," I held open the door for him and wondered if he'd come to have a go at what Crystal no doubt called my disgraceful behaviour. "She's in the kitchen. I'll leave you to it. I've got some work to do."

But as I turned towards the stairs, he called me back.

"No. Don't go. I want you to hear this too."

My heart sank. So, this really was about me being rude about Crystal/Tina. And I hadn't even had chance to give Mum my side of the story first.

"John, this is a surprise," Mum looked delighted to see him. "We don't often see you out and about during the week. Would you like a cup of tea? And I've got some freshly baked energy bars, if you'd like one."

"I'm good, thanks. The thing is, I've come to talk to you, Cheryl." His voice was low, his face dark.

"My goodness, that sounds serious," she said.

"I'm afraid it is," he said. "You've been done a terrible wrong and it's all my fault."

"Whatever are you talking about, John?" Mum asked. "And for goodness sake, sit down. You're making me nervous, looming over me like that. Are you sure you don't want a cup of tea? You look as if you could do with one. I'll just put the kettle on and -"

"No. Please Cheryl. Just listen." He sat down at the kitchen table, opposite Mum, then looked across at me. "And please, Katie, don't interrupt. Let me tell it my way, ok?"

I nodded.

"You know how much I miss Sally, don't you?" he went on.

"Of course," Mum's face clouded. "God knows, I miss her, too. I can only imagine how much worse it is for you."

"One of many things I miss is her cooking. Do you remember that apple cake she used to bake? And the treacle tarts? And -" He broke off and pushed his hands through his hair in a way that reminded me of Will. "Sorry, I'm rambling. It's because I'm nervous."

"What about?" Mum asked gently. "John, we've known each other for years. There's nothing for you to feel nervous about."

"I'm trying to tell you about this woman I met. Her name is Tina and she works in this cafe in Glastonbury. I went in there one day when I had some time to kill and had a slice of her apple cake and although it wasn't quite up to Sally's mark, it wasn't far short. So I got in the habit of going in there, regular like, just to taste the apple cake. After a while she began taking her break when I came in and would sit down with me and we'd chat."

"That sounds good, John. Sally would be pleased that you're -" Mum paused. "Making new friends."

John flushed. "That's just it. I don't think Sally would be very pleased with what happened next. It turns out Tina used to live around here and, she told me, went to school with Sally. Claimed to be one of her best mates."

"And that's a problem?"

"Well," he drew a deep breath. "Yes. Tina and me ... well, we've just had a little clearing of the air -" he looked across at me and his face reddened. "And it seems she wasn't quite straight with me. About who she was. "

"So, who was she?"

"Does the name Christina mean anything to you?"

Mum gave a sharp intake of breath. "Christina? Yes, of course it does. It was the name of the girl Terry was going out with - practically engaged to, in fact - when Terry and I first met. I was going out with someone else at the time too. But we met, and that was it. Terry broke it off with Christina and I broke it off with James." She gave a short laugh. "My mother never forgave me. Or Terry, come to that."

"Neither, I imagine, did Christina," I said. "Or rather, Tina. Or Crystal. Or whatever she chooses to call herself."

Mum looked from one to the other of us. "And you're saying that you are seeing Christina?"

"Not anymore I'm not," John said fiercely. "Not after what she did to you. And it was all my fault."

"For heaven's sake," Mum exclaimed. "Will you stop saying it's your fault and tell me what you're on about? Katie, you seem to know so much about it. What's going on?"

"I know that Crystal/Tina/Christina is the one who has been trying to wreck your business, Mum. That's right, John, isn't it?"

John nodded.

"But how is that your fault?" I asked.

John clasped his large hands together tightly, his fingers intertwined and looked back at Mum. "I was so proud of you and all you've achieved here with your salon that I really talked it up. I had no idea she was Terry's ex. I said how you'd built up this really great business over the years. And, so she's just told me, it sent her wild with jealousy, thinking of the life that you had, that should have been hers. She'd had a miserable time in Liverpool, married to a real no-hoper. A couple of months ago she just packed up and left him and came back here to make a new life for herself."

"But how did she get hold of Mum's clients?" I asked.

"Well," he took a deep breath. "This is the bit that really was my fault. I told her how you keep all your clients' details in a little book because you don't trust computers."

"How on earth do you know that?" Mum asked.

"Because I remember when Sally was thinking of getting a

computer for the farm shop. And you told her how you didn't trust them and kept all your records in this little blue book. And, I suspect, you still do?"

"Well, yes, I do. Katie's always going on at me to get my records computerised. But it's the security aspect that bothers me. All this cyber-crime you hear about. Anyone could steal them."

I could have pointed out to Mum that someone, somehow, had stolen her non-computerised customer records but I didn't want to interrupt John now he'd finally got started.

"Tina came into your salon a few weeks back," he said. "Didn't say who she was, of course. She said she saw you keep going back to this little book down by the side of the till and she remembered what I'd told her about your little blue book. So when you were busy with 'some old dear' (her words, not mine) and went off in the kitchen to make her a cup of tea, she got hold of the book and, as cool as you like, took photos of as many pages as she could. She ended up with about twenty names and phone numbers by the time you came back. She slipped the book back. And you never even noticed. She actually sounded quite proud of it."

"And after that," I said, "She worked her way through the names she had, telling them that you were giving up hairdressing and had sold her the client list."

"I told Tina that I wanted nothing more to do with her after hearing that," John went on. "And she just laughed in my face and said she'd got what she wanted out of me - a way to get at you. Said I was boring and that she'd had enough of life in the back of beyond and that she was heading back to Liverpool."

There was a long silence. I held my breath and waited for Mum to explode. But it didn't happen.

"I'm sorry things didn't work out, John," she said gently. "But you needn't worry about my clients. They'll be back, I'm sure. Katie and I are planning on bringing out a leaflet about the beauty salon soon. It'll be a good opportunity to get in touch with everyone and put things straight."

John looked visibly relieved. "It's good of you to take it like that, Cheryl. I still feel bad about it though."

"Nonsense. I don't want to hear any more about it. So, now we've cleared the air, how about that cup of tea?"

"That'll be grand, Cheryl. And I'll have one of those energy bars, if the offer still stands. I didn't get chance to have any lunch. And I can sure do with some energy."

I tried to signal him, if he cared for the state of his teeth, to give them a miss but at that moment my phone pinged with a text.

It was from Ed.

"Need help. Urgent. Come 2 barn. NOW. Hurry !!!!!"

***

When I got to the barn there was no sign of Ed, but one of the big double doors was slightly ajar. I pushed it open fully and stopped dead in my track.

There was no sign of Ed in the barn. Instead, there was a small green car. I'm not really into cars, they all look the same to me. But I was sure it was Suzanne's little hatchback. The one that Martin was supposed to have driven away in.

So what was it doing here? And how long had it been here? It couldn't have been here on Friday night because that was when Ed slept here. He'd have noticed it, wouldn't he?

And where was Ed?

"Ed?" I called as I approached the car. "Where are you? Look, if you're mucking around and are planning on jumping out on me, I'd better warn you, I'm not in the mood for your nonsense right now. OK?"

No reply.

"Ed?" I tried again. This time there was a clatter above my head. I looked up quickly, but it was only a pigeon. Now I was beginning to get a bit freaked out. "Where the hell are you, Ed?"

I moved in closer and approached the car. I tried the door and, to my surprise it was unlocked. On the back seat was a jacket. An expensive looking leather jacket, very much like the one Martin Naylor was wearing the last time I saw him.

I went to pick it up then pulled my hand back in horror. The coat was covered in bloodstains.

As I straightened up, there was a sudden movement behind me, and the place was plunged into darkness as the door slammed shut. The next moment there was a loud bang. I knew exactly what it was.

Someone had put the heavy wooden bar across the door handles. Meaning I was locked in.

"Ed Fuller! If this is your idea of a joke, it's a bloody stupid one," I shouted as I thumped on the doors. "Let me out this minute."

There was no reply. Only the sound of footsteps. Running away from the barn.

I grabbed the door and shook it, but knew it was hopeless. Those old barn doors would withstand a battering ram.

I took my phone out. But there was no point using it to call anyone. I'd spent many hours in this barn and knew full well that the old stone walls would block any signal.

But the other thing I knew was how to get out of there. I'd done it often enough. When we were younger Will and I used the rough stone wall as a makeshift climbing wall, and I reckoned I still knew every hand and toe hold on the way to the small window that was about halfway up the end wall.

Using the light from my phone, I made my way towards it, trying not to look at the car and its grisly contents. I found the first handhold, tucked my phone back in my pocket and began, slowly and carefully to climb.

I was surprised how it all came back to me, how one hold led to the next and there was only one scary moment when I put my hand on a stone and felt it move. I froze and inched my way towards the next, which thankfully stayed in place.

I reached the window and heaved myself on to the narrow window ledge. It was a bit narrower than I remembered. Either that, or I'd got a tad wider in the intervening years. I used my sleeve to wipe the cobwebs and years of accumulated grime off the window and peered out.

The window overlooked the lane that led back towards the village. And there, running along the lane, was a man. And, even from this distance, I could see Ed's distinctive hat, the purple and green pom-pom bobbing up and down as he ran.

I pushed at the window. For a moment, I thought my climb had been in vain and that it wasn't going to open. I didn't fancy having to break the glass in order to get out so gave it an extra hard shove.

To my relief, it finally gave way and I was able to squeeze out, praying as I did so that the old drainpipe was still attached to the wall.

Thankfully, my luck held (or my prayers were answered) and I was able to slither down. As soon as my feet hit the ground, I started running.

While I'd been working away at opening the window, I'd been figuring it all out. And I now knew exactly where he'd be heading. And why.

***

By the time I reached The Old Forge, my breath was coming in ragged gasps and I could hardly speak. The door to the garage was open and Finbar stood in the doorway, wagging his tail at the sight of me.

I hurried inside but I was too late.

Suzanne Naylor stood over the body, a garden spade in her hand. There was blood on the garage floor. The same blood that was on the purple and green pom-pom that Kylie had so painstakingly crafted for her daddy's Father's Day present.

Chapter Twenty-Four

Suzanne whirled round as I stepped into the garage, the spade gripped between her hands like a cricket bat.

"I - I think I've killed him," she stammered. "But he - he was... he was trying to steal Martin's car."

I knelt down beside the figure on the ground. To my immense relief I saw his head move. I gently removed the woolly hat and saw that the blood came, not from a head wound, thank goodness, but from a nosebleed. It looked as if he'd hit the ground face first and his nose had taken the brunt of it.

"He's not dead," I told her then turned my attention back to the 'body'. "Can you sit up, or do you need some help, Martin?"

"Martin?" Suzanne let out a shriek. "Oh my god, Martin! But I thought - I thought... when I saw that ridiculous hat I thought it was that awful Ed Fuller come to steal the car. I thought he'd -"

As Martin began to move, I fished in my bag and took out a packet of tissues. I handed him the packet.

"Don't try to sit up yet," I said.

"What the hell-?" He held a wad of tissues to his nose, struggled to a sitting position and glared at Suzanne who was still holding the spade. "What the hell did you do that for? You stupid -"

"Oh, my darling, I didn't know it was you. But why were you dressed like that? The scruffy old jacket. And the hat. You looked just like -"

"He looked just like Ed Fuller, which was exactly what he'd intended. Isn't that right, Mr Naylor? Or, is it Mr Mason? Mr Greg Mason?"

"Don't be ridiculous," Suzanne snapped. "I should know my

own husband." The spade fell to the floor with a clatter as she knelt down beside him and put her arm around his shoulder. "I'm so very sorry, darling. Do you need an ambulance?"

He took the tissues away from his nose and glared at her. "Of course I don't need a bloody ambulance. If you must know, the bobble took the brunt of it. You just took me by surprise, that's all. Knocked the wind clean out of me for the moment."

"Are you still bleeding?" she asked anxiously.

"No. It's stopped now. Help me up and then we'll sort this nonsense out."

"Yes, yes, darling. Of course."

Suzanne helped him to his feet. As he straightened up, he shrugged off her arm which was under his elbow. He put his hand in his pocket and took out a gun which he pointed at her.

"Let's everybody stay very still, shall we?" He spoke quietly, the way I've heard Will talk to his young heifers when they get spooked. And let's face it, I can't speak for Suzanne, but I was seriously spooked at the thought of being less than two feet away from a man holding a gun.

More to the point, a man who, from the steely look in his eyes, wouldn't hesitate to use it.

"You're too clever for your own good," he growled as he pointed the gun in my direction. I stepped back and banged my elbow hard on the garage wall. "How did you know I was Greg Mason?"

"I didn't." I pressed myself as far into the wall as I could, all my attention focussed on the gun. "I knew Greg Mason was the other man involved in the purchase of Winchmoor Manor, but I didn't know it was you. I just threw that in to see what reaction I got."

"You're Greg Mason?" Suzanne's eyes were wide with shock. "What's going on? You told me the deal was all settled and that as soon the £500k I put in to match Mr Mason's £500k was in the bank it would go ahead. I don't understand."

"Paul McAllister was trying to warn you about all the problems involved in buying a building that was Grade 2 listed, didn't he?" I said. "But that seems a bit extreme to

199

murder someone just because he was trying to explain the planning laws to you."

"That wasn't the reason," he snapped. "The stupid man thought he was doing me a favour and protecting my investment. Something about the deal felt 'a bit off' was how he put it, so he'd asked his colleague in their Bristol office to do some checking up on Greg Mason. But I couldn't let that happen, could I? That would have brought everything I've worked for all these months crashing around my ears."

Suzanne was still looking bewildered. "So are we going to buy Winchmoor Manor or not? I'm not sure I understand what -"

"I never had any intention of buying the bloody Manor," he snarled as he swung the gun in her direction. "I'm a property developer, for pity's sake. I know only too well the nightmare of dealing with listed buildings. I didn't need Paul McAllister to remind me."

"Then what is it about?" she asked. "Please, Martin, stop waving that gun around and tell me."

"It's your own fault. Keeping me so damn short of money all the time. Having to go cap in hand to your grandfather's bloody solicitor every time I wanted anything."

"But he never refused you. And it's not fair to say it was my fault. That was my grandfather, being over-cautious as always. Frightened someone would marry me for my money." She paused and lifted her chin. "Which, of course, is exactly what you did, didn't you?"

"Not exactly," he said with a smile that never reached his eyes.

I could see the hope flood into her face. "You mean, you married me for love?"

"I mean, sweetheart, we aren't exactly married." His voice was harsh, his eyes cold and cruel. "There are rules against getting married using a false name so I'm afraid we were never legally married."

Poor Suzanne still looked totally bewildered, as if her brain was struggling to catch up. "But the wedding and everything. You're saying it was all a sham? But why?"

"It was what you wanted, remember? I'd have been happy enough to have lived together - for a while at least. But oh no, that wasn't good enough for you, was it? It was a wedding ring. Or nothing. So I went along with it."

"For a while? You mean, you never had any intention of staying with me?"

He gave a sneering laugh. "Of course I didn't. I had my escape route planned from day one. I was going to put it into place the minute the money was safely transferred to my account."

Her brain had caught up at last. "I'll put a stop on it -" she began but broke off when he levelled the gun at her.

"First rule of survival, sweetheart. Never argue with or upset the guy holding the gun."

Suzanne looked as if she was about to faint. I grabbed her and held her hand tight.

"So, let me see if I've got this right," I said, trying to draw Martin's attention while she recovered. "You and Paul McAllister plotted to convince Suzanne that you were buying Winchmoor Manor and that you needed half a million pounds to do so. What was Paul's cut of that going to be?"

"Not so clever as you thought you were, are you?" he sneered. "Of course he wasn't in on the deal. He didn't have the backbone for that sort of thing."

I was relieved to hear that. I'd liked Paul McAllister and didn't have him figured as Martin Naylor's partner in crime. "So how did he fit in then?"

"For a small fee, he took Winchmoor Manor off the market when it came into his office so nobody else would start sniffing around it. That was all. But, of course, once he'd agreed to do that, I had him. Any trouble from him and that was his job gone. I had a similar nice little arrangement with a woman in one of the Bristol estate agents, too." He turned back to Suzanne. "And that, my sweet, is how you and I met. She told me how you'd just inherited a big fat property portfolio from your very rich and recently deceased grandfather, and I 'engineered' a meeting."

"Engineered a meeting?" Suzanne echoed. "You mean,

Finbar was never lost?"

"I mean, I never owned a dog. Remember the day I knocked on your door to say I'd found him and to thank you for your help? Well, it wasn't a total lie. Because I had just found him. At Bristol Dogs Home. He wasn't my dog at all. But some women can never resist a sob story involving a dog, can they? It worked a treat."

"Oh, poor Finbar," Suzanne's eyes swam with tears as she looked down at the dog. "That's so cruel."

"What's cruel about giving a stray dog a home?" he asked. "But his job's done now."

As he spoke, Finbar gave a low rumbling growl and moved closer to Suzanne. Her hand snaked down and touched his bristly coat.

"Don't worry, boy," she said to him. "You're going nowhere."

"That's what you think." Martin glanced at his watch. "Time's getting on and I've got a bit of tidying up to do here. That includes you two and, of course, the dog. That horrible Ed Fuller, who's been threatening you and has already killed two people, goes berserk and kills the pair of you. The dog gets it too, of course."

"Hang on." I was getting pretty desperate now. Anything to keep him talking. "How do you mean, two people? You killed Paul and framed Ed for it. But who else is Ed supposed to have killed?"

He grinned. "Haven't you worked it out yet, Miss Marple? It's Martin Naylor, of course."

"You're going to fake your own death and blame Ed?" Then I remembered the car and the bloodstained jacket. "That's why you left the bloodstained leather jacket in Suzanne's car, isn't it? But whose blood was on it?"

I felt sick at the thought that it might be Ed's blood and wondered how Jules and the kids would cope without him.

He stared at me for a second. Then he snapped. "That was not bloodstains. That was bolognese sauce. From the pub. That idiot Fuller ruined a perfectly good jacket. I said he'd pay for it and I've made damn sure he will."

202

"You set him up," I said.

"Stitched him up like a kipper." He gave a self-satisfied smirk, like he was expecting a round of applause.

"It was you sent those texts, wasn't it?" I said, still desperately playing for time even though I knew there was no chance of the cavalry arriving. "Somehow you got hold of Ed's phone and used it to send threatening texts to your phone for Suzanne to find. And then, just now, you sent me one, asking me to go to the barn."

"How the hell did you manage to get out?" He growled

I didn't answer. I wanted to encourage him to keep talking. "And I suppose it was you who sent the anonymous tip off to the police suggesting they dig up my mother's garden?"

He laughed. I saw Suzanne flinch as he did so. "That was such a laugh. I saw Fuller had been working there and thought it would create a nice little diversion. As for the texts, they fooled you both, didn't they?" The gun swung round in my direction again. "And, just so you remember that I'm the one who gets to ask the questions, not you, I'll ask you again. How did you get out of the barn?"

"I climbed out the window. And I saw you running away. I knew it wasn't Ed, from the way you were running. Ed's played rugby for years and he runs like a charging bull. You were running like - "I gave Suzanne an apologetic shrug. "Like a girl. That's how I knew it was you. And that you'd be coming here. But why implicate Ed? Was it just because he took a swing at you that night at the pub?"

Martin's face darkened and for a moment I was afraid I'd gone too far.

"Nobody does that and gets away with it," he said. "I could have killed him there and then. But not in front of a bar full of witnesses. Besides, I had a rather more urgent problem on my mind that evening. What to do about Paul McAllister after he told me he was getting his friend to investigate Greg Mason. After he left, I was sitting there, going through a range of possibilities in my mind when his fool of a neighbour came in, and I saw that ridiculous story in the rag you call a newspaper. And it all fell into place. "*Heads roll again in murder village*" was what it said, I believe. And it gave me this brilliant idea. At first I was going to make it look like an accident, fix a tripwire across the path, then remove it."

"But that was hardly guaranteed to kill him," I said.

"True. But the whack on the head with a fence post would have done," he said calmly. "I'd have made sure of that. So after I left the pub, I went round to Paul's and sussed it out. I could see immediately what they'd said about the dangerous post and found the perfect spot for the trip-wire. He'd told me earlier how he planned to get in an extra early bike ride the next morning as he was going somewhere later. I decided to come back in the morning before it got light, fix the trip-wire and wait. Then while he was on the ground, finish him off with the fence post. But, as it turned out, I didn't need to hit him at all. Because he landed on that iron post and .... " He made a horrible squishing sound and drew his hand across his throat. "Job done."

Suzanne gasped, turned a horrible grey colour and looked as if she was about to throw up.

"And Ed?" I asked. "Where did he come into this?"

He grinned. "That was pure genius on my part. Plus, I have to admit, a bit of luck. Ok, back to Friday night. I'd just finished checking the place out and was on my way home when I saw Fuller staggering off down the lane, drunk as a skunk. So I followed him with the intention of giving him a thorough beating. At first I couldn't make out where the hell he was going. But then he turned into this old barn. I waited for a while then went inside. He'd passed out cold. There on the floor beside him was that stupid hat he always wears, a set of keys and his phone. That was the moment I realised there was a better way of getting back at him than beating him to a pulp. I took the hat, keys and phone and the drunken fool didn't stir."

"His keys?" I frowned. "But he told me he'd lost them earlier in the week."

Only, of course, he hadn't lost them then, had he? I didn't think his story about going to Paul's house to give him a quote rang true. Knowing Ed, he just said that to shut me up. It was far more likely he'd had his keys with him on Friday night but had been too drunk to find them.

Martin shrugged. "Well, if he had, he'd found them again, for they were there on the floor beside him."

"Poor Ed. He was looking for his phone everywhere. And his hat. His daughter made that for him, you know."

"My heart bleeds," he said coldly. "It came in very handy. I went back home, got the trip-wire and my 'escape pack' together and, as soon as it started to get light, headed off. Like I said, it went better than I could have hoped. Paul was dead and it was, after all, an accident."

"No, it wasn't. You put the trip-wire there."

He shrugged. "Well, apart from that. I also left Fuller's keys by the tripwire when I fixed it. I told Suzanne I was going away on business and would take her car, as it would be less likely to get stolen in the station car park. I was sorry to part with the Ferrari but it's a tad too distinctive for my needs at the moment."

"But why did you send those texts to your phone?" Suzanne asked.

"I wanted you to report me missing, you stupid woman. To think I was yet another victim of Fuller's murderous rage."

"But I thought you were lying low because of all the people chasing you for money," Suzanne said. "I've paid out an awful lot of money on your behalf this last week. Talking of which, your wallet was handed in. You must have dropped it in the pub."

He swore. "Of course I didn't. Fuller was supposed to have taken it. I thought he wouldn't be able to resist spending the money. Then, when everyone was convinced Martin Naylor was dead, that would be another nail in his coffin. I can't believe he handed it in."

"He didn't," I said. "I did. I figured Ed was in enough trouble without that additional complication."

"You're an interfering little baggage, aren't you?" he said, his voice full of menace.

"I've been called worse," I said, surprised to hear how steady my voice sounded. "But if you were so clever and had it all worked out so well, what went wrong? Sounds to me like your plan wasn't such a great one, after all. Why have you risked everything to come back here?"

He shrugged. "A slight miscalculation on my part. I need some proof of identity (my real identity, that is) to be able to transfer the money from my business account, which was where Suzanne paid it in, to the account in my real name. Only in the excitement of everything, I forgot it. There's a hidden safe in my car and that's where I kept my real passport. So I had to come back for it. I parked Suzanne's car in the barn and have been hanging out there for a couple of days, waiting for my chance to come back and get it."

"You stayed in the barn?" I asked.

"That's what I said. Bloody uncomfortable it was, too, trying to sleep in that poxy little car."

"So that's why Finbar kept pulling towards the barn," I said and the dog flicked his ears at the sound of his name. "You must have been in there and he caught your scent. I should have let him go and followed him."

"I wish you had," he said. "I'd have shot the pair of you, there and then. Much more convenient than here."

"Where people will hear you," I said.

"You reckon? Look at this place, during the day. All the holiday cottages are empty and of the houses that are lived in, everyone's at work. There's no one around to hear. And if they did, they'd probably think it's that idiot yokel Abe Compton shooting rabbits."

"Of course they won't," I said. "A shotgun sounds quite different to - whatever that is."

"Just shut up!" He waved the gun under my nose. "This is one case you won't be around to solve, little Miss Marple."

I needed to calm him down and get him back to his story. At least then he was relaxed and, with any luck, might let his guard (and that big scary gun) slip.

"So what made you come back in broad daylight?" I asked. "You were taking a hell of a risk."

"You reckon? I tried coming back at night to get it, but that damn dog made a fuss, so I had to abort it." He turned back to Suzanne. "Then I remembered you have your precious choir practice this afternoon, something you never ever miss so I thought it would be safe to go back then. Only -"

"Only I hadn't gone to choir practice today because it's been cancelled. Half the choir is down with a tummy bug," Suzanne said. "I was in the kitchen, having a coffee when Finbar started barking. I let him out and he came straight here - and that was when I found you. And hit you. Only now, I wish I'd hit you a bit harder."

His eyes hardened. "You shouldn't have said that, my dear wife. Story time over." He pointed to the far corner of the garage. "Over there. Both of you."

"You're not going to kill us in cold blood, are you?" Suzanne said, her voice trembling.

"I'm afraid so. It wasn't part of my original plan. But if I'd known how easy it is to kill someone and get away with it, I'd have married you legally. Then I'd have inherited your estate. That was a miscalculation on my part."

"But why go to all that trouble of setting up a false identity?" I asked, still trying to distract him. Still trying to buy us time. Still hoping for a miracle.

"Because Greg Mason has a bit of a record," he said. "If it came out, which, knowing that nosy solicitor of hers, it would well have done, there was always the risk Suzanne would call the wedding off."

"But I wouldn't - " Suzanne began, but he cut across her.

"Besides which, I'm already married. Nikki's waiting for me in Spain. Now she's a proper woman, not a wishy-washy excuse of one. Believe me, I've earned every damn penny of that half a million. And nothing, or no one is going to come between me and it."

Suzanne gave a cry of pain. "I knew you only married me for my money. But that was ok. That was why I kept paying out. I thought once we settled down and had a family -"

"That was never going to happen, sweetheart. I'm not a family sort of man," he said.

"You utter bastard! You strung me along, promised we'd start a family as soon as the Winchmoor Manor deal went through when all the time -"

Before I could stop her, she snatched up the spade and made a lunge at him. As she did so there was a deep throated snarl and Finbar leapt at him, knocking the gun clean out of his hand. Martin staggered back, fell and Finbar pinned him to the floor.

Which was where he stayed while Suzanne called the police. And I called Liam and told him to bring his camera.

Only when the police arrived did the dog step back and allow the policeman to haul Martin to his feet.

"You might want to listen to this," I said as I handed them my phone. "I recorded it all. Just in case he tries to talk himself out of it."

Chapter Twenty-Five

Four months later.

Martin Naylor (or Greg Mason, to give him his real name) goes on trial next week for the murder of Paul McAllister. He's also being charged with various accounts of fraud, although Suzanne is not pressing charges. The £500k he'd been trying to transfer to his personal account was still in their so called 'joint account' but as it was in an illegal name, the account is frozen while the legal stuff is all sorted out.

But Suzanne has a very clever - and expensive - family lawyer, so it will probably all be sorted out in the end.

Liam and I are now officially BFFs - that's Best Friends Forever, according to Kylie who knows these things. This is on account of him being on the spot to capture all the drama of Martin's arrest, thanks to my timely phone call to him.

At first glance, Martin appeared to go quietly and was led out of the garage and along the narrow path that led to the front gate. He wasn't handcuffed or anything, because he looked like a man who'd completely run out of steam and had accepted his fate.

But all that changed when the little procession made up of policeman, Martin, policeman reached the end of the path. Martin gave the policeman in front of him a mighty shove and landed him in the middle of the laurel hedge, from where it took some considerable time to extricate him. His peaked cap was never the same.

While the unfortunate constable was floundering around in the bushes, Martin made a dash for the road and he could well have succeeded in getting away if it hadn't been for Finbar.

There was a mighty whoosh of long legs and bristly grey fur as the dog hurled himself along the path and took off up the road after Martin. He brought him crashing down in a flying tackle that would have earned him a place in the England rugby team. Finbar was the hero of the hour and has been put forward for an award.

Liam managed to get a cracking shot of Finbar in mid leap which made all the papers, TV and went viral on social media. We also beat the nationals to the story, so Mitch was delighted. And the paper's circulation soared as a result. The pub's takings also soared and Norina played the 'murder capital of the south west' card for all she was worth and has been talking about putting on murder mystery evenings in the pub.

I think it's a really bad idea and I won't go if it happens. I've had more than enough of murders, thank you very much and from now on will be more than happy to spend my time being bored to death listening to parish councillors droning on about missing streetlights and potholes in the roads. Believe me, when you've been staring at a psychotic maniac who's waving a gun at you, you realise there are worse things in life than being bored.

But, on the plus side, Martin's arrest has earned me more money than I've seen in a very long time, enough to pay Mum back for the loan on my scooter and a bit more besides. And all three of my portfolio jobs - the paper, the pub shifts and *Paws for Walks* - are safe. For now. Suzanne's even promised to keep paying me to walk Finbar, seeing as he and Prescott have become such good friends.

Mum's new Salon and Spa opens next week and everything is looking quite brilliant. Her appointments book is full (and her little blue book is now kept safely under lock and key) and Sandra's already grumbling about having to work extra hours so Mum's looking to employ an apprentice. (As long as she isn't looking at me).

Suzanne has finally given in to Liam's pleas and has

agreed that, as soon as the trial is over, he can write the story of "How I lived with a cold-blooded killer" or words to that effect. She says it will be healing and cathartic for her - but I think it's more to do with the fact that she blushes like a fourteen-year-old every time Liam looks at her and has got a bit of a thing about him.

She also paid Ed the money Martin owed him for the work he did. So Jules is talking to him again and they're planning a trip to Disneyland in Paris sometime soon. Suzanne offered to replace his hat. But he wanted the original one back, even though it had Martin's blood on it. But, Jules assured me, it washed up like new.

Now here's the best bit of news I've heard for a long time. It makes me smile every time I think of it.

Dilys has moved in to Paul McAllister's cottage. He left it to her in his will. Can you believe that? His horrible stepson and ex-wife were furious and tried to contest the will, but Paul had, it appeared, been of sound mind when he wrote the following words:

"To my ex-wife, who had almost every last penny from me, I leave one penny so that she can complete her collection. And to my dear friend and loyal colleague, Dilys Northcott I leave Mill Cottage, Mill Lane, Much Winchmoor in the knowledge that she will love and care for it and will restore my father's garden to its former glory."

The change in her is truly astonishing. Gone is the little woman in the long skirts and droopy cardigans who used to creep about, apologising for the space she's taking up. Gone, too, the weird orange hair style. Now, there's a spring in her step and a sparkle in her eyes and she is (with a bit of encouragement from me) applying for the job of manager in the Dintscombe Estate Agents office.

Of course, someone who isn't thrilled about Dilys' change of fortune is Gerald Crabshaw, who will now never realise his ambition to own Mill Cottage.

And, to add to his woes, (and you must know by now how I relish adding to Gerald's woes) it's emerged that it wasn't Paul McAllister who damaged his precious peacock after all. It was Gerald's wife, Fiona.

Dilys and Fiona have become quite friendly since Dilys moved in to Mill Cottage and Fiona confessed her one evening when they were sharing a glass of wine or two in Dilys' cosy sitting room that, in fact, she was the one who decapitated Gerald's precious peacock.

"We'd had a blazing row," she told Dilys. "Because I found out he'd destroyed something very precious to me. A book given to me by a very dear friend who's no longer with us and who I miss every day. He threw it on the bonfire, can you believe it? He said it was an accident. But I knew it wasn't. I could have killed him."

She didn't, obviously. Otherwise that would be another story. Another murder in the murder capital of the south west. Instead, she took a pair of garden shears and vandalised one of his favourite things, his precious peacock.

***

So, it's Saturday afternoon. A cold November day. I've just finished my lunchtime shift at the pub and am on my way home when I see a gaggle of people standing around the village pond.

The first person I see is Elsie. She's never forgiven me for knowing more about Martin Naylor and his goings on than her. Now, she turns around as I approach, a great big grin on her pointy little face.

This worries me. Elsie only grins when something really bad is going to happen.

And it does. Because there is Will, standing in the pond, in the shallow bit, where the brackish, weed strewn water comes up to his knees. His bare knees.

They're bare because he's wearing nothing but a pair of navy-blue boxer shorts. And, in his teeth, he holds a red

212

rose.

"She's here!" Olive cries.

"Off you go then, lad," Elsie shouts.

"Will, no! Don't -" I shout but I'm too late.

"Katie-Kat. I love you. Will you marry me?" It doesn't come out quite that clearly, owing to him having a rose clenched between his teeth. Which maybe explains why he makes my name sound like a chocolate bar.

"For pity's sake," I yell at him. "Get out of there, you idiot. You'll catch your death."

He takes the rose out of his mouth and holds it towards me. "Not until you give me an answer," he says. "Will you marry me, Katie-Kat?"

Behind me, I hear Elsie mutter, "I wouldn't kick him out of bed. Not with a body like that."

He has long straight legs, a trim torso, well-toned arms. And the sweetest smile you could ever see. Even with a rose between his teeth.

And, do you know what, Elsie? Neither would I.

THE END

Read *Murder Served Cold* and *Rough and Deadly*, *the first and second in the series.*

Fantastic Books
Great Authors

darkstroke is
an imprint of
Crooked Cat Books

- Gripping Thrillers
- Cosy Mysteries
- Romantic Chick-Lit
- Fascinating Historicals
- Exciting Fantasy
- Young Adult and Children's
  Adventures
- Non-Fiction

Discover us online
www.darkstroke.com

Find us on instagram:
www.instagram.com/darkstrokebooks

Printed in Great Britain
by Amazon